RUTHLESS VALLEY

Center Point
Large Print

Also by Wayne D. Dundee and available from Center Point Large Print:

Dismal River
Rainrock Reckoning
The Forever Mountain
The Coldest Trail
The Gun Wolves
Massacre Canyon
Wildcat Hills
Devil's Tower
Rio Fuego
Ride to the Bullet

RUTHLESS VALLEY

A Lone McGantry Western

WAYNE D. DUNDEE

CENTER POINT LARGE PRINT
THORNDIKE, MAINE

This Center Point Large Print edition
is published in the year 2025 by arrangement with
Wolfpack Publishing.

Copyright © 2024 Wayne D. Dundee.

All rights reserved.

This book is a work of fiction. Any references
to historical events, real people or real places
are used fictitiously. Other names, characters,
places and events are products of the author's
imagination, and any resemblance to actual events,
places or persons, living or dead, is
entirely coincidental.

The text of this Large Print edition is unabridged.
In other aspects, this book may vary
from the original edition.
Printed in the United States of America
on permanent paper sourced using
environmentally responsible foresting methods.
Set in 16-point Times New Roman type.

ISBN: 979-8-89164-606-3

The Library of Congress has cataloged this record
under Library of Congress Control Number: 2025934460

PART ONE

Chapter One

"Remember," Sue Leonard was saying, "how I told you he'd take her back in a heartbeat if she returned, even at the risk of making a fool of himself all over again?"

Lone McGantry nodded in response to the question. Then he said, "I also recall something bein' said about big sister blackenin' both of her eyes if she ever showed back up."

Sue's mouth twisted ruefully. "Boy, don't I wish I would have followed through on that. Or done whatever it took to stop her from once more sinking her claws into him."

"I take it James's wanderin' wife . . . what's her name again?"

"Rosemary!" Sue spat out the word like it was a bad taste in her mouth. Then she added, "The faithless little witch!"

"So your brother gave Rosemary another chance against your judgment and advice, and it didn't work out any better than before."

"It worked out worse. Far worse." The expression on Sue's pretty face turned very grave. "That's why I wired you and asked you to meet me here. Thank God you came. You're the only one I could think of who might be able to help keep things from turning worse still."

Here was the Ignacious Hotel in downtown Cheyenne, Wyoming, not among the city's most elite hostelries, yet still in quite a respectable range. It was the middle of a blustery fall afternoon yet the windswept street outside the tall glass windows of the spacious front lobby where Lone and Sue sat in discussion was busy with wagons and buggies rolling in either direction, men on horseback weaving in and out among them. On the boardwalks, foot traffic passed hurriedly to and fro, men with collars flipped up over the backs of their necks and hats jammed down tight on their heads, women wrapped snug in shawls and headscarves. Lone had been among the latter throng only a few minutes earlier, traversing on foot from a livery stable close by the train station where he'd boarded his big gray stallion Ironsides after the two of them had arrived on the westbound out of Ogallala, Nebraska.

Though recently voted the state capitol and touted by its promoters as "the Magic City of the Plains," Cheyenne still remained rustic enough so that the sight of cowboys or long riders of various ilk were not an uncommon sight on its streets. Even at that, however, Lone McGantry was of a size and rugged appearance to draw more than a few lingering gazes as he strode along with his saddlebags and possibles pack hoisted on one shoulder. Standing a whisker short of six-three, wide-shouldered and thick-chested under a weathered, squarish face set with clear blue eyes and a prominent nose that showed signs of having been broken more than once, he was plainly someone not to be trifled with. Reinforcing this impression was the Colt .44 holstered on his right hip, openly displayed under his "dressiest" corduroy jacket worn in concert with his newest, crispest white shirt, least faded Levi's, and freshly polished boots.

The train had been the quickest way to reach Cheyenne, but since Sue's telegram hadn't given any details to indicate what might be in store after arriving there, Lone had loaded up Ironsides and brought him along just in case.

I NEED YOUR HELP. STOP. URGENT. STOP. MEET ME AT THE IGNACIOUS HOTEL IN CHEYENNE. STOP. AM COUNTING ON YOU.

That was the extent of the message that reached Lone via the rudimentary, rarely used telegram station set up in a back room of Gottlieb's general store in the tiny settlement of Sarben near Lone's modest horse ranching operation in the Nebraska Sandhills. But it was enough to bring him with all haste.

Sue Leonard was a special lady who had made a special mark in Lone's life. They had met several months prior, in the early spring, while Lone was aiding a man called Red Smith, a former outlaw fighting to shed his dark past and strike out on a new and decent path; standing in his way had been Pike Grogan, the ruthless leader of the owl-hoot gang Smith was once part of. After Lone found himself also crossways of Grogan, he joined forces with Smith and together they rode to confront and conclude matters with the outlaw boss right in the backyard of his North Dakota stronghold. They'd succeeded in bringing things to a bloody end, but not without encountering complications and needing to spill other blood along the way.

One of the complications had involved Sue, who for a time was actually taken by them as a hostage. She'd become an ally before it was all over, however, and in the process she and Lone had developed strong feelings for one another. But, in the final analysis, Lone couldn't see it going any farther. Sue, a widow of some prominence in her hometown, the sister of a doctor—him a former Indian scout and drifter nowadays aiming to settle down on a piece of land with a handful of hayburners and a sod hut he called a horse ranch . . . no, the chasm between those worlds seemed too wide and too deep. Plus, the tragic loss of Lone's beloved Velda remained too recent, still too raw of a wound on his emotions for him to feel ready to get involved with another woman.

For all of these reasons, Lone had ridden away from Sue; though with a sincere and now seemingly prophetic parting statement: *"But if the time ever comes you need me, just say the word and I'll be there."*

So the time evidently had come, the word had been sent, and now here he was.

The sight of Sue coming down from her room and entering the lobby after the desk clerk sent notification of Lone's arrival, stirred the former scout's heart more than he was prepared for. She looked even lovelier than he remembered. Middle twenties, tall and slender with high, proud breasts pushing out from the confines of a simple white blouse; pleated maroon skirt flowing from a trim waist. Her mane of auburn hair was pulled back behind her ears, held that far with a ribbon matching the color of her skirt, then the rest left tumbling loose down over the back of her neck and shoulders. When she rushed forward with a welcoming embrace and his arms wrapped around her, a part of Lone's brain was instantly knifed—though not for the first time— by the question of whether or not his pride and stubbornness had been too quick in deciding the chasm between their worlds could not be bridged.

For the moment, however, that question was pushed aside by Sue immediately starting into the explanation of why she had sent for him. As soon as their embrace ended, she'd taken him by the hand and led the way to a cushioned bench over in a corner of the wide lobby close to the front window but away from the front desk. There were only two or three other guests milling on the opposite side of the lobby so they were able to converse privately.

"You remember my brother James," Sue had begun. "Well, I fear he has gotten himself into the worst kind of trouble and danger. And it's all because of that no-good cheating wife of his!"

Once they'd sorted through a few more quick incidentals about the return of James's errant wife and his apparent unwise choice to give her another chance, Lone got around to asking, "So is James also here in Cheyenne? Is this where he's got himself in trouble and danger?"

Sue shook her head. "I don't know *where* James is! That's only part of the cause for my desperation. I only know that he came here and that there was serious trouble involving the man who accompanied him when he started out from back home." For both Sue and James, "back home" was a small South Dakota town called Coraville. Continuing, Sue said, "You likely remember the man I'm talking about, the one who came with James—it was Chico Racone, the Twin V wrangler who rode with the posse that chased after you and Smith back when."

Lone scowled. "Yeah, I remember. He was supposed to be some kind of tracker for 'em, right?"

"And that's also why he was accompanying my brother on this occasion. When Rosemary took off on him again, this time James made the foolhardy decision to follow her and try to win her back. He hired Chico as a tracker to help him run her down."

"And the trail led to Cheyenne?"

"So it seems." Sue's expression became anguished. "We only know that here is where Chico ended up getting killed . . . and James is the prime suspect for the crime."

Lone grimaced.

"Papers found in Chico's pockets tied back to Coraville," Sue went on, "so the Cheyenne authorities notified Marshal Kurtz back home. They also included a description and mention of James's name as someone who'd been spotted fleeing the scene of the killing. When the marshal conveyed this troubling news to me, needless to say, that was enough to bring me here seeking to find out more about what happened and naturally what had become of James."

"How did the law here in Cheyenne so quickly connect James, by name, to Chico?" Lone wanted to know.

"From Marshal Kurtz, for one thing. He had little choice but to wire back and confirm that link," Sue answered. "Also, James had booked a room for the two of them here at the Ignacious, and that they'd been going all around town together—up to and including the night Chico was killed. That came a short time after they got into a heated argument in a rather seedy saloon called the Dust Cutter."

"An argument *between* James and Chico?"

"That's right. According to witnesses, James stormed out—no one is quite sure where he went—before it came to blows." Sue paused, frowning. "Then, about a half hour later, Chico also left the Dust Cutter. Two shots were heard out in the street. When other customers came pouring out, they found Chico lying mortally wounded and James was spotted fleeing down an alley. That's the last anyone has seen of him."

"So there's no other suspect besides James? No other disturbance in that saloon that might've involved Chico?"

"No. Nothing else." Sue wagged her head in dismay. "Up to that night, every indication is that James and Chico had no hint of trouble as they went about trying to find some trace of Rosemary or Drake."

"Wait a minute. Who's Drake?" Lone wanted to know.

Sue appeared suddenly a bit flustered. "Good Lord. I'm hopping all over the place, aren't I? I can't very well expect you to help get to the bottom of this mess if I don't settle down and present everything that's happened so far in a more orderly fashion."

Lone smiled tolerantly. "Yeah, I reckon that'd help."

"Very well. Let's start over someplace where we can have more complete privacy," Sue stated. "I suggest we retire to my room. In addition to my babbling, I fear I haven't been very considerate. You must be weary from your long trip and probably haven't had lunch yet. I'll have some food and drinks sent up and we can finish our discussion there."

"I wouldn't mind clearin' out of this lobby," Lone admitted. "For one thing, the front desk clerk and that hombre standin' over there jawin' with him have both been slippin' me the stink eye every chance they get when they think I ain't noticin'. Was we was to stick around much longer and they kept it up, I might have to go see what their damn problem is."

Sue arched a brow disdainfully. "I don't think their problem is with you. That stiff-necked little sparrow of a clerk—his name is Hemmings, for what it's worth—has been looking down his nose at me ever since he found out I'm the sister to a former guest who had the bad taste to make himself a murder suspect. Like he thinks I'm some kind of shady accessory or something. And the goon talking to him is Muldoon. He's supposed to be in charge of hotel security, but I see him as more of a glorified bouncer in case any guests get too rowdy."

Now that Sue had mentioned it, Lone did see a sparrow-like resemblance to the narrow-shouldered, flighty acting clerk. And tree stump-shaped Muldoon, with a flattened nose and a pair of cauliflowered ears that marked him as having likely spent some time prize fighting, looked practically born to become a bouncer.

"So I guess me bein' in your company," said Lone, his smile turning into a crooked grin, "marks me as a shady character in their eyes too."

Sue smiled. "Does it bother you, consorting with a dubious sort like me?"

"Yeah. Because I really care what a couple of knot heads like them think," Lone said dryly. Then, turning more serious, he added, "But with them already havin' their hackles up where you're concerned, are you sure it's a good idea for me to—"

"Go up to my room with me?" Sue finished for him, her tone turning defiant and somewhat annoyed. "I think it's a perfectly *fine* idea for all the reasons already stated. So, unless you have a problem with it, those two morons can gawk over it until their eyes pop out of their heads for all I care! We're two adults and I have that room paid for in advance, so who I choose to have as a caller there is nobody else's damn business!"

Her voice rose steadily in volume toward the completion of this statement, drawing sharp looks from the pair at the front desk as a result.

But when Lone twisted around and glared back at them, they quickly found somewhere else to shift their eyes.

Sue stood up. "Grab your gear and come on. My room's on the second floor. I'll get a room service menu from Hemmings and have him send someone up in a little while to take an order after you've had the chance to look it over and make your selections."

"Sounds good. Just so it ain't that ugly-assed Muldoon who delivers the grub," Lone remarked. "That might spoil my appetite."

Making a brief detour to the front desk, Sue picked up a menu and put in her request for someone to be sent up in a little while for follow-up. She was assured by the sparrow behind the counter—though with a pinched-mouth, disapproving air—that the matter would be taken care of. That done, Sue led Lone on to the broad, thickly carpeted open stairway that led to the hotel's second floor.

They'd only gotten about a quarter of the way up, however, before a harsh, demanding voice called from the base of the steps, "Hold it right there. That's damned far enough!"

Lone came to a halt with one foot raised to the next highest step. He twisted at the waist, turning to see who had called out. He expected it to be Muldoon, the so-called security man, and though it seemed unlikely an interruption by him would

17

warrant gunplay, the former scout's hand dropped automatically to the Colt on his hip. When he saw who *was* standing at the bottom of the stairway, it not only came as a surprise but made reaching for the Colt less unreasonable after all.

Sue also stopped and turned at the command. She displayed equal surprise at the speaker's identity and was quick to express her reaction in words. "Johnny! What in the world are you doing here?"

Chapter Two

Scowling up at them was Johnny Case, ex-deputy marshal from Sue's hometown in South Dakota. He was a tall, lanky number, in his late twenties and, though he appeared somewhat more haggard than Lone recalled, was still clean cut and even featured to a degree, most would consider handsome. Attire-wise, he was dressed much like Lone—Levi's, short-waisted jacket, six-gun riding on one hip.

In response to Sue's question, Johnny said, "What I'm doing here is lookin' out for you. Like I've been doing ever since you took off on this stubborn, foolish chase after your brother and that runaway wife of his. I was worried what might happen to you." He paused for a moment, just long enough to sneer and add a surlier tone to his next words. "What I didn't expect was that I'd have to worry about what you'd do to yourself—getting mixed up yet again with the likes of *him!*" This last came with a thumb jerk toward Lone.

Sue's eyes were blazing by the time Johnny was finished. "You mean you've been *following me?* By what right? Who do you think you are?"

"Somebody who cares about you, that's who!" Johnny snapped back. "More than you care about yourself or certainly your reputation, by the look of it. The way you're fixing to take this saddle tramp up to your room without any regard for—"

Lone had heard enough. "Mister," he grated, cutting the ex-deputy short, "you'd best be real careful what next comes out of that hole under your nose, else I might have to plug it with my fist."

"To hell with you! I ain't afraid of you," Johnny replied defiantly. "You should have been locked behind bars a long time ago. And if you try anything here in a civilized city like you've gotten away with out in the wild country, that's exactly where you'll by-God end up!"

Lone turned fully around and started down the steps.

"Here now! Let's quiet this disturbance. What's the trouble here?" Muldoon, the security man, came lumbering hurriedly up beside Johnny and then edged partially in front of him as if to block Lone's descent.

Lone halted once again, saying nothing but eyeing Muldoon's balled fists with a cold stare. Sue was suddenly at his shoulder, and she had plenty to say.

"This man," she exclaimed, pointing at Johnny, "has apparently been *stalking me* here in this establishment you are supposed to be watching over. Is that the kind of security you provide for all of your guests? And now, on top of admittedly following me, he is attempting to interfere with me proceeding up to my room!"

"Proceeding up to her room," Johnny echoed, "with a man who is clearly not her husband. I thought this was a respectable establishment. I'll re-state her question—what kind of security do you provide for decent-minded guests? Is the kind of improper behavior being displayed by these two something you regularly allow?"

Muldoon was clearly flustered by this bombardment of questions. He was used to handling problems with his fists, not being asked to judge behavior or explain policy. Seeing this, the sparrow of a clerk came skittering over, his mouth puckered into an alarmed, perfectly shaped "O" and his hands flailing about like he was swatting away mosquitoes.

"People, people," Hemmings wailed. "You're making a scene. Please calm down and let us settle this like rational adults."

"Rational adults don't stick their noses into the personal business of other adults," Sue snapped.

"They do if they care about another adult who is making a fool of herself," Johnny was quick to counter.

"Maybe," Lone snarled in response to that, "a certain so-called adult oughta take the advice he's already been given and start carin' about himself first—before that nose he's stickin' where it don't belong gets flattened."

The scowl that had never left Muldoon's face bunched even tighter. "If you're talkin' rough stuff, mister, then that means goin' through me first."

Lone nodded. "That can be arranged. Plain to see that beak of yours has already been flattened plenty. Too bad it ain't taught you not to butt in."

"Please! Please!" Hemmings' wail was even more desperate. "This is getting out of hand. Everyone must calm down!"

For a frozen moment, the scene teetered on escalating further. Until Sue suddenly turned back around and began ascending the steps once again, declaring, "This is ridiculous. Come on, Lone, we have more important ways to spend our time than with these fools." Over her shoulder, she crisply added, "Hemmings, I still expect someone to be sent up to take our room service order. And Johnny, if you continue pestering me, I swear I will file a complaint with the local law. Go back home and mind your own business!"

Two hours later, the room service lunch having been delivered and long since consumed, Lone and Sue continued to talk in the privacy of her comfortably appointed room. Outside the window, the shadows of late afternoon were lengthening and growing dimmer. Lone sat astraddle a simple wooden chair provided to serve the washstand, his thick arms folded across the top of its laddered back rest, facing Sue who was occupying an upholstered reading chair tucked into one corner.

In the course of this private time, a calmer, more thoroughly detailed account of all that had transpired to the point of her sending the wire to Lone had been presented by Sue. It basically amounted to filling in the gaps between several of the things she'd first mentioned in a more excited and disjointed manner back in the lobby.

The whole thing, as had been made plain enough from the first, hinged on the reappearance and then repeat flight of Rosemary, the wayward wife of Sue's brother, Dr. James Risen. Back when Lone had initially encountered Sue and her brother, Rosemary had already run off on James the first time and had been gone for more than a year. This had sent James into a downward spiral of despair that resulted in him reaching for alcohol as a means to cope, nearly ruining his medical practice. The only thing that kept him from crashing all the way to the bottom was Sue, steadfastly at his side, repeatedly sobering him up and aiding in—at times practically taking over—his treatment of patients.

The course of events that caused Lone and his companion Smith to sweep through Coraville and end up with a posse unjustly sicced on them was when they felt forced to take Sue as a temporary hostage in order to hold the posse somewhat at bay. This abduction of his sister was enough to shake James out of his self-pity and booze dependency and compel him to join the posse when it resumed its chase. Said chase lasted for several days before the outlaw boss Pike Grogan was dispatched, Sue was released, and the posse—unsanctioned to begin with—had cause to give up further pursuit of Lone and Smith. The experience as far as James was concerned sobered him and hardened him into a different man by the time he returned to Coraville. He had his sister by his side once again, as an assistant not an enabler and mother hen this time, and he resumed his practice with a fierce determination and a head cleared of torment over his errant wife.

And so it had gone, smoothly and with steadily rebuilding trust throughout the community, for several months. Through the balance of the summer and into the start of fall.

Until Rosemary came back. She looked worn and somewhat shabby (an appearance purposely designed to help play on James's sympathy, in Sue's opinion), and was oh so contrite and apologetic. Begging for another chance. She was met by a cold rebuttal from the newly hardened James—at first. But it didn't hold up for long. Physically small and "terminally cute" (another assessment by Sue), Rosemary displayed a mastery at being irresistibly pitiable while pleading for forgiveness. ("I kept reminding myself what a manipulative little rip she was," Sue related, "but damned if her act didn't even tug at my cold heart a little.") After only a couple days of this, James caved and agreed to give their marriage a second chance.

Their relationship seemed better than ever. Wonderful. James seemed happier than anyone could ever remember. This lasted for all of a week . . .

And then Earl Drake showed up in Coraville. He was a dashingly handsome rogue, middle thirties, tall and trim, swarthy complexion with a precisely trimmed pencil mustache and wavy coal black hair, dressed in tailored, expensive threads and custom-made boots. He began immediately making inquiries where to find Rosemary and made no bones about having had a former relationship with her that he was bent on resuming. Upon being informed she was a married woman, he merely laughed sarcastically and proclaimed that was of no consequence to him.

When he arrived at the Risen house, where James also had his doctor's office at the front, Sue, in her role as receptionist/nurse, answered his knock on the door. As soon as the caller smugly asked to see Rosemary, Sue knew it was not a good sign.

Prompted further as to what his business was,

Drake answered, "Though I think it impolite of you to pry, I don't have time to waste. Simply tell her Earl Drake is here and I have come to take her back where she belongs."

Naturally, this didn't go over at all well with Sue. When she ordered Drake to leave the premises, he refused. A loud argument broke out that drew James from his office and Rosemary from elsewhere in the house. This quickly built into a bigger, louder argument. Rosemary demanded Blake leave her alone, insisting she was all through with him. When Drake wouldn't listen and still refused to leave, James tried to force him to do so and the two got into a fistfight in the front yard. James was badly outmatched and soon beaten to the ground. Drake left at that point, laughing haughtily, and telling Rosemary she hadn't seen the last of him.

James promptly filed charges with Fred Kurtz, the town marshal, and Drake was arrested for trespassing and assault. He accepted apprehension without resistance, spent the night in jail, calmly paid his fines in the morning and was released. From there, after taking a leisurely breakfast at the town's best restaurant, he returned to the Risen house and began strolling up and down beside the street out front. When Sue came out and demanded to know what he was doing, Drake answered with a sly smile, "Just out enjoying the fresh air, dear lady. Though

I admittedly am in hope Rosemary will come out in due time. She must, sooner or later. And truth be told—though I'm sure it pains your brother to hear—I assure you she *wants* to. I know her better than she knows herself. She's had her tiff, put on her little show, she will now soon enough come to her senses."

A fresh appeal to Marshal Kurtz did little good. He spoke with Drake, warned him to stay in line, but when it came right down to it—as the lawman patiently explained to Sue, James, and Rosemary—there wasn't much he could do about a man just walking alongside a public street.

And so it had gone for two more days. Never interfering with the flow of patients who showed up for doctor visits, never confronting either James or Sue on occasions either of them left the house, Drake quietly spent each forenoon and afternoon strolling back and forth on one side or other of the street out front. He was never seen in the vicinity after dark, but more than once, it seemed like his presence could be *felt* somewhere out there, watching. Rosemary, who lived practically like a prisoner inside the house, refusing to go out for any reason, grew more and more unnerved. She wouldn't go into any details about what her relationship had been with the man other than to say it had been a terrible mistake on her part, and she wanted nothing more to do with him.

And then, on the evening of the third day, a shootout at a local saloon—half a dozen cowboys who rode for opposing brands exploding into an argument over a card game—demanded the attention of Dr. Risen at the scene. Four of the men were left with life-threatening wounds. The seriousness of the situation warranted Sue accompanying James in her role as his nurse. This meant leaving Rosemary alone at the house, which was cause for concern. But she assured James and Sue she would be all right, promising to lock all the doors as soon as they left and not open up for anyone until they returned.

"The scene at the saloon was indeed a bloody mess," Sue related. "Two of the men were shot up so bad we were unable to save them. Two others were so critically injured they'll be disabled for the rest of their lives, but at least we managed to pull them through. It took over two hours to do what we could, and all during that time, the marshal and his deputies had their hands full trying to keep more trouble from breaking out between other riders for the warring brands. James begged for somebody to go check on Rosemary but none of the deputies could be spared. Finally, one of the bartenders went to have a look and came back reporting everything looked okay as far as he could tell."

Reading the gloom that had settled on Sue's face as she reached this point in her telling, Lone said, "But it wasn't, was it? Not by the time you and James got back."

Her head moved slowly back and forth. "Rosemary was missing. Vanished with barely a trace to show she'd ever returned. No sign of a break-in or any kind of struggle. The carpet bag she had arrived with, her clothes and personal things—all gone . . . as well as her horse from the stable behind the house where James keeps his buggy horse along with a couple of saddle mounts."

"So Rosemary had her own horse?" Lone queried.

Sue smiled bitterly. "From before, when they were first married. Her and James used to go riding and enjoy the sunsets together. Her horse was a sturdy little roan filly named Precious. James kept it after Rosemary ran off the first time—saving it for when he believed the no-good tramp would return. Little did he know he'd be providing her the means to take off on him again."

"Is there any chance," Lone said, scowling in thought, "Rosemary might've took off this time to try and escape that Drake hombre more than just runnin' out James?"

"It was considered. It's certainly what James was ready to believe—at the start." The bitter twist that remained in Sue's smile was not a flattering look. "But then some other pieces started falling into place. Like the fact that Earl Drake arrived on the stage, but on the second day he was in Coraville he purchased a horse for himself, including a saddle and all other necessary gear. He also purchased a sackful of trail supplies that he kept along with his newly purchased mount and gear at the livery where he'd bought the animal and was continuing to board it."

"Sounds like a fella plannin' to head out on the trail before long."

"Exactly."

"But only one horse don't exactly show he was plannin' on havin' company," Lone pointed out.

"Unless he somehow knew about Rosemary having her own horse," countered Sue. "At any rate, on the night of the bloody saloon shootout, two other incidents are confirmed as having happened. Rosemary disappeared, and Earl Drake took his mount and gear from the livery and was seen riding away in the company of a dark-haired young girl on a roan horse. You remember nosy old Driscoll, the Coraville liveryman, right? He's the one who spotted them. He won't swear the girl was Rosemary, but he's positive about Drake. And he also swears there was no sign the girl was being forced or threatened in any way."

Lone hiked his brows. "Don't leave much room for doubt, does it?"

"Not in the eyes of anybody but James," Sue replied with a sigh. "He refused to believe that Rosemary wasn't somehow made to go against her will—if not by physical force, then by some other threat. Convinced of that, he was bound and determined to go after her, to *save* her, and nothing anybody could say was able to deter him in the least. He took money out of his savings, hired Chico away from the Twin V, and off they went on the trail of Rosemary and Drake. James promised me he would keep in touch, wire me regularly to let me know their progress. But I never heard a word . . . until Marshal Kurtz was notified about Chico's murder. That was four days after they rode out. I took a stage for here the next morning and on the way decided I would wire you for help as soon as I arrived."

"What about Johnny Case? Seems clear he must have followed right on your heels. I'm surprised he let you head out alone to begin with," said Lone.

Sue's brows pinched tightly together. "That stubborn, romantic fool. He just can't accept I will never be interested in him as more than just a friend. And whether he knows it or not, he's coming close to ruining even that much. Yes, he begged me not to come here alone. He insisted that he should accompany me, for protection and to help in my search for James. For a moment, I actually considered agreeing—for the reasons he stated. But, in the end, I knew what more he would have on his mind, and I couldn't afford that kind of distraction on top of everything else.

So I turned him down very bluntly, thinking that would put an end to it." She gave an angry shake of her head. "I never dreamed he would follow along anyway and, worse, resort to *spying* on me!"

Trying to sound more confident than he actually felt, Lone said, "Well, let's hope his long-standin' dislike for me coupled with the fact I've now shown up at your request will be enough to discourage him into turnin' around and goin' back home."

"We can hope," Sue replied. "But, like I said, he's stubborn and, in his way, can be dangerous. He'd never do anything to harm me, though that doesn't mean he wouldn't try to make trouble for you if he got the chance. I think it is best for us to keep that in mind."

Lone clenched his jaw. "In that case, what's best for him is to keep in mind he was warned."

Chapter Three

When Lone went to book a room for himself at the Ignacious, he was told by the sparrow at the front desk (in a totally unconvincing display of regret) that the establishment was full up and no rooms were available. Lone was certain that was a petty damned lie but, considering his earlier confrontation with Muldoon and Johnny Case, on top of his association with the already unfavorably looked upon Sue, it didn't really come as a surprise. At any rate, he didn't feel like making an issue of it, so he walked two blocks down the street and took a room instead at a perfectly suitable place called the Traveler's Rest. There was no need to advise Sue of this change inasmuch as they had arranged not to meet again until early the next morning for breakfast at a nearby restaurant she'd given him directions to.

Something else he hadn't bothered advising Sue of was the fact that, no matter where he booked a room, he had no intention of immediately settling in for the night. This in spite of feigning weariness from his trip and telling her that was his plan. He was somewhat weary, that was true enough, but Sue's tale about her brother and the trouble he was in had sent Lone's mind spinning too busily for him to be ready to try and rest right away. He had some things he wanted to check out, the sooner the better, and they involved going to places where Sue tagging along—which she'd be bound to want to do—wouldn't be a good idea.

It was full dark by the time Lone left the Traveler's Rest after getting some directions from the desk clerk, a hearty, friendly, florid-faced Irishman named O'Feeney who was about as opposite from birdlike Hemmings as you could get. When Lone asked him how to find the Dust Cutter Saloon, O'Feeney had chuckled knowingly before saying, "Aye, so it's a den of rompin', stompin' rascals ye be lookin' to fall in with, eh? For most of me guests, I'd likely advise against makin' such a choice. But you, ye be plenty strappin' enough to look able to handle yourself okay." Then, with a twinkle in his eye, he added, "Though ye gotta promise to share with me the tellin' if ye get into a good noggin-knocker while yer there, right? And if ye come back all bloodied up, try not to stain the bed sheets too bad, hear? It's me wife does the laundry for this place, and I have to listen to the old girl complain something mournful over havin' to scrub out bloodstains."

A grinning Lone had promised the old scalawag to do his best on both counts, then had started out on the twelve-block hike to where he'd been told he would find the Dust Cutter. The night was chill, though the gusting wind had mostly died away. The vicinity of the Traveler's Rest and the Ignacious was far less busy than it had been that afternoon. As Lone drew nearer to his destination, turning down a side street called Edge, the boardwalks turned emptier still. In some spots, there simply wasn't any, empty or otherwise. The street lamps became notably fewer and farther apart, and traffic on the wider, dustier street consisted only of men on horseback passing intermittently to and fro. The buildings lining Edge Street included a number of boarded-up, failed businesses and those remaining trended decidedly toward loud, brightly lighted saloons, smoky pool halls, flop houses, and a smattering of cheap hash and bean joints; all sending the message that this part of town had seen better days yet was still where cowboys and other low-pay working men came for their entertainment.

When the Dust Cutter hove into sight up in the next block, there was nothing about it that gave it any particular distinction. Except for what had recently happened there and in the street out front. This was a rough part of town to be sure, but not so rough that a fatal shooting was looked on as insignificant. The latter was what Lone hoped to tap into, while it was still reasonably fresh on everybody's minds. He had an idea for how he might be able to stir the memory in some of those minds and perhaps turn up a useful nugget or two that other investigators so far hadn't been able to. It was hardly a secret that folks like those found in areas such as this kept tighter lips around lawmen than they did otherwise.

As far as James Risen himself, Lone's direct experience with the man last summer had been pretty limited and had mostly been at a time when James was at his booze-sodden worst. The impression he left on Lone wasn't very favorable; but, then again, there was little doubt James saw him in a similar light. Things had evened out a bit by the conclusion of dealing with Pike Grogan, and in the brief amount of time he spent around James at that point Lone *did* notice a change in the doc after he'd sobered up and hardened some from his time on the trail with the Coraville posse. In addition, Lone had seen other good men knocked sadly off course after tangling with the wrong woman. So there was a certain amount of empathy in the former scout for any unfortunate who went through something like that. Whether or not James deserved any further understanding for this latest display of bullheadedness by believing in and chasing after the woman who'd already forsaken him once, that remained to be seen. But his safety and trying to keep him from getting deeper in trouble—for Sue's sake, if for no other reason—was the thing at hand. And no matter what else and in spite of his limited past experience with the man, Lone's gut told him that James Risen flat wasn't the type to kill and flee the act without strong justification.

Yet for all that, the role Lone planned to play once inside the Dust Cutter wasn't as somebody harboring any kind of lenient feelings toward Risen. Rather, he aimed to come across as just the opposite.

As he approached a nameless cross street that separated the block he was traversing from the one he was aiming for just ahead, Lone noted a pair of empty, dismal-looking buildings facing each other on diagonal corners of the upcoming intersection. The dreariness of these structures and the defeated businesses they represented seemed to give this end of Edge Street—which looked like it would be petering out entirely not too far beyond the Dust Cutter—an added sense of despair that had been building all along. And made it, Lone couldn't help thinking, a mighty lousy place to die.

Ironically, less than a minute after this thought crossed his mind, the gloomy intersection damn near became the place where he met his own fate.

He'd been well aware of the lone horseman clopping slowly up the street behind him. But, since other riders had been passing sporadically back and forth ever since he'd turned onto Edge, he paid this one no particular attention. A number of saddled nags were already tied to hitch rails in front of the different establishments, including the one Lone was headed for. In fact, he reckoned this hombre coming along might very well be on his way there too. Glancing over his shoulder, Lone saw that this individual sat slouched in his saddle, chin resting on chest, in a way that indicated he was either very exhausted or—if the Cutter was indeed his destination—then the fare there would hardly be the first he'd guzzled in the past few hours. Lone's mouth twisted wryly at the thought of the kind of bust-head hangover this fool would be waking with in the morning. In his younger, wilder days, the former scout had suffered more than a few of those himself and didn't miss 'em one damn bit.

As Lone started across the nameless intersecting street, the horseman coming up Edge had drawn nearly even with him off to his left. And then, unseen by Lone, the man in the saddle suddenly straightened up out of his slouch. All in one motion he clapped his heels against the horse's ribs and jerked the reins sharply to his right, propelling the animal at that angle and causing it to slam a muscular shoulder hard into the unsuspecting Lone. Blindsided, caught off balance, the powerful bump sent Lone staggering and then toppling to the dirt. As he fell, he heard the rider shout, "Now! Hurry up and get him while he's down!"

Two men came rushing out of the deep shadows alongside the abandoned corner building. They swarmed Lone viciously, leading first with kicks and stomps and then going to work with their fists. No, not merely fists—rather fists gripping short, heavy, leather-sheathed clubs. Blows rained down relentlessly on Lone's back, shoulders, and arms. They didn't hold back from trying for his head too, but he instinctively protected that for the most part by turtling down and wrapping it in his thick arms. Attempting to scramble free, trying to fight back at that point would have only exposed him to more serious, more debilitating strikes. As it was, for the moment, he was able to endure the blows continuing to hammer him, even though they sent white-hot jolts of pain all through his body.

The attackers grunted loudly with every swing of their clubs. When they thought they had him sufficiently subdued but still wanted to do deeper damage, they ceased with the clubs and reached with clawing hands to pull Lone out of the fetal position he'd curled into, tugging to jerk his arms down in order to get at his face and head.

That was where they made their mistake.

With the two men hovering close over him now, their clubbing momentarily halted, Lone uncoiled out of his fetal tuck with the guttural snarl of a cornered beast. Pushing himself through and past the score and more of pain points knifing into him, Lone first lashed out with his feet and drove his boot heels into the ankles of one of his attackers. His pins knocked out from under him, the polecat fell to the ground with a painful yelp.

That left the second attacker leaning directly over Lone, close enough so that Lone could see the gleam of his narrowed eyes even in the dim illumination. But that meant he was also jammed too close for Lone to make a grab for his gun or get any force behind a punch. So, instead, Lone thrust both of his hands up through the tight space between their bodies, fingers curled like claws, and clamped on the bastard's murky, anger-twisted face, trying to twist it off his neck. Feeling one thumb sink into an eye socket, he dug at it savagely. The man jerked back with an agonized scream, pulling away so forcefully he lost his balance and he too toppled to the ground.

"The sonofabitch tore out my eye! Kill him—gun him down!"

"No shooting!" the horseman quickly countered.

Lone scrambled frantically, awkwardly, trying to regain his footing. The muscles in his legs and especially his arms throbbed with pain from the pounding they'd received. The man who'd taken the kick to his ankles came surging back. He threw himself onto Lone and wrestled him back down. They rolled on the ground, drilling knees, fists, and elbows into each other. The varmint with the damaged eye seemed to be out of it, at least for the short term. He lay sprawled off to one side, wailing and cursing and holding one hand cupped to his injury.

Lone tried to take advantage of having just one assailant to deal with. But that was no easy task. He was battered and stiff-muscled from being beaten, and the hombre he was tangling with was no lightweight. What was more, he clearly knew a thing or three about infighting. He kept wasting effort, though, trying to use his club when there was really no room to put any power behind it. The same was true, unfortunately, for Lone once again not being able to land a solid punch.

So they had to settle for continuing to pummel one another as they rolled and thrashed in the dirt. Lone could hear his opponent begin loudly gasping for air. Trouble was, Lone was starting to do the same. Finally, the former scout got enough of an opening to allow him the chance to draw back his head and then slam it forward, hard and fast, crashing his forehead against the other man's nose and mouth. He heard cartilage pop and teeth crunch, felt hot blood squirt down over his face. That created an even wider opening that freed Lone to throw a somewhat cramped right hook to Smashed Nose's temple. He followed it instantly with a second, more powerful blow.

That broke the log jam. The two men rolled apart from each other. Gasping, dripping sweat and secondhand blood, Lone came to a stop on his belly. Immediately he started pushing up, meaning to climb back to his feet.

He made it as far as his hands and knees before the horseman launched from his saddle and came crashing down on him. The impact of the man's full body weight hammered Lone flat. Air exploded out of him. When he tried desperately to suck some back in, he inhaled choking mouthfuls of swirling dust. Starbursts and pinwheels spun wildly in his vision, and he knew he was on the verge of blacking out. He fought not to let that happen, realizing that only a few seconds of unconsciousness would leave him totally at the mercy of these bushwhacking bastards.

Shaking his head furiously, like a wet dog dispelling water, Lone planted his palms flat on the ground and shoved up with all his strength, trying to dislodge the horseman still locked onto his back. He could feel the man slipping and grasping desperately to maintain his hold. That gave Lone incentive to shove and buck even harder . . . until the heavy, leather-encased club came down on the back of his head and flattened him all over again.

Lone's face dropped heavily to the ground. More choking dust. Starbursts flashing brighter in the midst of a thick black fog that was closing in fast and tight, as if it were swallowing him. Lone cursed inwardly. This time, he didn't think he was going to be able to fight off losing consciousness.

The man still astraddle his back shouted frantic orders. "Cleve! Mojave! Get up off your asses and help me with this big bastard—bring those goddamn ropes so we can hogtie him and drag him out of here!"

Clinging to the barest slice of awareness, Lone sensed the other two moving sluggishly closer. It gave him a faint surge of satisfaction to hear their groans of pain—pain from the damage inflicted by him—as they did so. His arms were jerked roughly up behind his back. A loop of a coarse rope encircled his wrist. But then, all at once, something changed. First, it was just a feeling, like a sudden shift of the wind. Then came the sound of hard, fast footfalls growing louder and nearer as other feet began scuffling in a much choppier, seemingly uncertain manner. Muffled curses turned into yelps of surprise and pain truncated by a flurry of meaty thuds unmistakably signaling hard blows landing on flesh and bone. The sound of one such strike came from directly above Lone, and the weight of the man on his back suddenly lifted and went hurtling away.

"Beat it, you cowardly bastards! Scat! Run like the yellow dogs you are!"

The voice issuing these orders sounded vaguely familiar. But although the man's identity wasn't clear, what was plain and most welcome—even through the fog of Lone's stunned condition—was that this newcomer was successfully breaking up the attack by the three bushwhackers. Amid fading curses of pain and despair, Lone could hear them withdrawing and fleeing off into the deeper shadows of the nameless cross street.

All of this had a reviving effect on Lone. He rolled onto his side and pushed up on one elbow, looking around to see who his savior was. His eyes fell on a tall, lanky figure who stood with his back turned, gazing down the cross street after the retreating trio. The man stood with feet planted wide and in one hand he was gripping a broken-off, four-foot length of two-by-four. There were dark stains near one end of the piece of lumber, colorless in the current poor illumination, but their wet, shiny appearance left little doubt they were smears of fresh blood.

At the sound of Lone stirring, the tall man pivoted around. He stepped into sufficient lighting for his identity to be revealed and, when it was, Lone's surprise nearly knocked him off the elbow he was propped on.

The hombre who'd just saved his bacon was none other than Johnny Case!

Chapter Four

"You so quick to make friends wherever you go?" Johnny asked sarcastically. At the same time, he was leaning down and extending a hand to help Lone back to his feet.

Lone took the offered assistance without comment. He was too busy gritting his teeth in order to keep from groaning out loud. Once standing, he replied, "Sometimes it takes folks a while to warm up to me."

Johnny chuffed. "Hate to see if this bunch was out to make it any hotter for you."

"Yeah. There's that," Lone agreed.

Johnny tossed away the length of two-by-four, then faced Lone squarely. "Well, we might as well get it over with. You gonna raise hell about me following you?"

Lone regarded him with a scowl but again wasn't in a hurry to respond. When he did, he said, "Before we get to that, I reckon I owe you a 'much obliged' for the way you waded in to help me. You and your two-by-four. Lot of men would've stopped to consider those three weren't likely to welcome a party crasher to the hoedown they was throwin'."

"Wasn't something I stopped to think about. I'd've done the same was they gang-stompin' an alley cat."

Lone inclined his head slightly. "I believe you would."

"Far as the two-by-four," Johnny said, "that sort of just happened. When I got close enough to see what was going on, they were clumped around you too tight for trying to use my six-gun. But I spotted that chunk of wood leanin' against the corner of the building and, well, you might say it spoke to me. So I snatched it up and went to work with it like swatting away pesky bugs."

"Happens I can vouch for them bugs packin' some mean stingers, I won't argue that. Again, I'm grateful you and your swatter showed up."

"What were they after, anyway. Out to rob you?"

Lone scowled again. "We never got around to discussin' what was stuck in their craw. But I don't think lookin' to rob me was it. In the first place, robbery of anybody walkin' in this part of town would likely make for slim pickin's, 'specially split three ways. Plus, they had a mighty elaborate ambush set up for a simple robbery of one person . . . no, I think plain beatin' the tar out of me might've been their main goal. Oh yeah, and I recall one of 'em sayin' something about hogtyin' me and draggin' me off."

Johnny looked baffled. "Damn strange business, that's all I can say."

"You're tellin' me."

"How about this," said Johnny. "There's a

watering trough and a pump back down the street just a little ways. Sloshing some cool, fresh water on those stings and bruises might feel good. Might help clear your head some more, too."

"Don't sound like a half bad idea. Also be a chance to clean off some of this dust and grime from rollin' in the dirt with those jaspers. Go ahead, lead this creaky ol' hoss to that water, son."

Only a couple minutes later they were at the trough. Lone had removed his jacket and was bent at the waist, leaning low with his head stuck under the spout of the hand pump mounted at one end. Johnny was working the pump handle, bringing up surges of cold water that gushed over the back of Lone's head and neck. After he'd taken on a good dousing, Lone straightened up and tossed his head, throwing a rooster tail of water. Then he untied his neckerchief, wrung it out, and used it to mop at his face. The brisk night air sent a slight shiver through him.

"Feel any better?" Johnny asked.

"Gettin' there." Lone tied the bandanna back around his neck and used his jacket to dry his face and hair some before shrugging into it once more. After raking fingers through his hair a couple times and then donning his hat, he announced, "There. Now I feel like only *half* a buffalo herd ran over me. 'Spect a cup of coffee and a couple shots of whiskey would thin the herd even more."

"As you can see, there ain't no shortage of whiskey to be found all up and down this street. Comes to coffee, there's a place right over yonder"—Johnny pointed to a small, unobtrusive little restaurant diagonally across the street—"where they've got plenty of that. I ate supper there last night, as a matter of fact. It's run by an old German couple who stay open late to serve the saloon crowd. They dish out German potato salad, sauerkraut tart enough to pucker your lips tighter'n a virgin's kiss, sausage spicy enough to singe a Mexican's nose hair, and coffee stout enough to turn a .44 slug shot straight into it."

"You make it sound like you oughta be on the payroll advertisin' for 'em," Lone grunted. "But you also make it sound like just the medicine I need. Let's go give it a try. While we're there, we can get around to you explainin' why the hell you was tailin' me."

There weren't very many other customers in the little eatery when Lone and Johnny entered, but the place was filled to the brim with delicious aromas. More than enough to remind Lone that the room service lunch he'd shared with Sue was sitting mighty light in his stomach. So he gave in to temptation and ordered a plate of potato salad and sausage to go with the coffee—which proved to be everything it was promised to be. Johnny opted for coffee only.

The German couple who ran the place remembered Johnny from his previous visit and, despite their rather dour demeanor, seemed pleased to have him back. When Johnny mentioned how Lone had encountered a robbery attempt out on the street, the pair clucked consolingly and bemoaned how the neighborhood was changing for the worse. In response to a none-too-subtle hint that something to ease the aches and bruises from the attack would be most welcome, a bottle of schnapps was brought forth and placed on the table. Johnny expressed his appreciation and added a generous splash of the liquor to his coffee as well as Lone's. Although the former scout had never tried schnapps before, he found it not only palatable to his taste but also reasonably soothing to his aches.

With the plate of food additionally provided and turning out to be every bit as good as it smelled, Lone found himself grudgingly admitting to the ex-deputy, "You're makin' it steadily harder for me to be agitated over that tailin' business."

Johnny grinned ruefully. "There's a switch. Usually folks like me okay at the start but then grow *more* agitated with me."

"I didn't say I was ready to give up on it."

"Okay, let's lay it on the table. You and me don't like each other and never have since we got off on the wrong foot over that shootout on Twin V range outside of Coraville. I didn't cut you a lick of slack in believing your side of things and, let's face it, you didn't help much with some of the follow-up actions you took. For what it's worth, I've since come around to buyin' that you and the fella you called Smith *didn't* have any part in that shootout."

" 'Bout time."

"Though much of rest of what happened—Smith turning out to be Wild Red Avril and all and being left to slide the way he did after Pike Grogan got taken out . . . that still ain't ever sat right with me." Johnny took a drink of his coffee. "But the long and short of it is, the decision makers on that weren't swayed any more by you than by me. So the main reason I stayed not liking you came down mostly to petty jealousy on account of Sue taking such an obvious shine to you. For reasons I was damned if I could understand."

"That makes something we have in common," Lone remarked.

"After you went back to Nebraska," Johnny continued, "I figured she would eventually come to her senses again and I might be able to get back in her good graces. Unfortunately, I can't say that's been going as good as I hoped. But then her brother's runaway wife came back only to take off once more, and next thing you know, everything's caught up in a whole new mess. James hires Chico Racone to help him go chase down his tramp of a wife, Chico ends up dead, and Sue heads out to try and chase down James."

"Causin' you to decide to chase after Sue, even though she turned down your offer to help."

"I couldn't just stand by and do nothing, no matter what she said. You can understand that, can't you? Chico's killing made it pretty clear there was something risky and dangerous about whatever the hell was going on. No way I could hang back and leave Sue charge off strictly on her own."

"No, I suppose not," Lone allowed with a frown.

"In my place, tell me you'd have done any different."

"Maybe not. But I guarantee I wouldn't've been stumble-footed enough to let her *know* I was foggin' her, especially after she told me to lay off."

"It wasn't how it looked from the way I 'fronted you two at the hotel," Johnny insisted. "I hadn't been skulking her every move, the way she took it. Sure, I followed her here to Cheyenne. And, yeah, I was keeping an eye on her. To make sure she stayed safe. But I was also doing some checking around to try and help get a line on what became of James. That's how I ended up here for supper last night—*after* I paid a visit to the place I figure you're headed for."

"And where's that?"

"The Dust Cutter Saloon, where else? The

place where James and Chico reportedly got in an argument, and then Chico ended up gunned out in the street. With James now being on the run as the main suspect."

Lone regarded him. "You believe there's any chance he actually did it?"

"No." Johnny's answer was quick and firm. "Me and James never saw eye to eye. I thought he was a weakling and a fool for the way he let his wife twist him around. Then, after she left him the first time and he took to drinking, I liked him even less for the way he treated Sue and took advantage of her babying him. When he chased after his wife this second time, I thought him even more a fool. But at my lowest opinion of him, I'd never count James for a yellow back-shooter."

"You find out anything worthwhile at the Dust Cutter?"

Johnny squirmed uncomfortably in his seat. "No. I handled it all wrong. Tried to play it like I was still a lawman from Coraville—you know, same place as James and Chico. I thought that'd carry some weight, but it worked just the opposite. Everybody in the place clammed up and I came away with shit. The only thing it earned me was a knock on my hotel room door first thing this morning from a local deputy, a hardcase named Remson, advising me against falsely claiming to be an officer of the law and warning me to keep my nose out of business real lawmen were already handling."

"Sounds like you're buildin' a habit of havin' folks tell you where not to stick your nose," Lone pointed out.

"Been my day for it, that's for sure," Johnny said sourly. "First Remson, then you and Sue."

"Yet here you are again, on my tail. Something I reckon it's time we got to addressin'."

The ex-deputy scowled. "Look, me causing a ruckus the way I did at the hotel—that was flat overstepping my bounds, okay? Stupid jealousy again, seeing you show up out of nowhere and head with Sue to her room . . . I handled that worse than I did barging into the Dust Cutter. I talk about James making a fool out of himself over his wife, I don't come across a whole lot better when it comes to Sue. I been mooning over her for years and never getting any smarter on how I go about it. Way I acted back home even cost me my deputy's job."

"So what's that got to do with tailin' me tonight?" Lone wanted to know.

"Don't you see? I wanted to find out if you was here to truly help try and find James . . . or if you was just looking to try and take advantage of Sue in this troubled, vulnerable state she's in."

Lone let some air hiss slowly out through his teeth. "You jackass. Right when I'm on the brink of thinkin' maybe you ain't so bad after all, you say something like that and make me once more want to belt you in the mouth."

Johnny's expression didn't change. "Before you do, you might be interested in hearing that I think you're on the level about wanting to help. And whether you belt me or not, you ain't gonna stop me from still caring about and looking out for Sue."

Chapter Five

Passing through the batwings and then the inner latch door closed against the chill night air, Lone found himself in the noisy, smoky, moderately crowded interior of the Dust Cutter. Just another saloon not very different from a couple hundred others he'd set foot in over the years. Rectangular room with a long bar off to the right, tables arranged in no particular pattern down the middle, a pool table crowded over in one corner, and a small performance stage located off-center against the back wall. Nothing was happening on the stage this night and, by the look of the faded, frayed curtains hanging behind and to the sides, Lone couldn't tell if it was a relic from the past or if still saw intermittent activity. Tonight, in the meantime, a bit of entertainment was being provided by a whip lean Mexican gent in a fancy vest who was strolling around strumming a guitar.

Lone bellied up to an empty space at the bar and ordered a beer. The schnapps he'd taken in his coffee earlier was still working in him, so he held off on any whiskey, at least for the time being. The bartender who served him, like the stage at the end of the room, appeared to be something of a relic himself. Stick thin and bony-shouldered, pale as death with sunken cheeks and tired eyes. Wisps of snowy hair drifting atop his head were the only part of him whiter than his skin, the latter showing color just in a few liver spots here and there and where bluish veins stood out on the backs of his big-knuckled hands. Despite his cadaverous look, however, the old fellow moved about with surprising briskness and spoke in a strong, resonating voice.

Lone sampled the beer, found it to be crisp and cold and good. Planting a hip against the bar and leaning one elbow down on top of it, he turned to make a closer scan of his fellow customers as he leisurely enjoyed more of his beer. Before him spread a mixed bag of working-class men, predominantly cowboys from outlying ranches interspersed with teamsters, freight handlers, and a few rail yard laborers in sooty bib overalls. A couple low stakes card games were in progress. Otherwise, except for two other solitary drinkers like Lone holding up the bar a ways farther down, it was small groups huddled together over shots and beers, jawboning and swapping jokes.

There didn't appear to be any real hardcases in the bunch and the level of chatter was fairly tame, nothing too raucous except for an occasional outburst of bawdy laughter. Often as not these displays seemed to include one of the three barmaids mingling among the tables. Each of the gals was a bit past her prime—thick-waisted and heavy-breasted, faces hardened from listening to too much boastful talk, too much inhaled smoke, and too many watered-down drinks—but their spangly dresses still showed enough bare shoulder and deep cleavage to make them plenty appealing to the clientele. There was a blonde, a redhead, and a brunette; and, if Lone was any judge, only the latter was not aided by hair dye. What he wasn't able to judge for sure was whether the gals were just drink hustlers or if they were also available, for a price, to participate in some private backroom activity. Not that it factored either way as far as his plans for the night. His encounter out on the street and his talk with Johnny Case—who he'd parted ways with upon leaving the German restaurant—hadn't altered said plans to any particular degree.

His mug drained, Lone turned back around for a refill and the pale relic was promptly there to draw a fresh round. Apparently two drinks—and the fact nobody else was clamoring for service at the moment—was enough to warrant some conversation from the old fellow.

"Don't recollect seeing you hereabouts before," he said in his deep, rich voice. "And you're the kind of fella a fella would remember. Stranger in town?"

"Guess you could say so," Lone answered. "Been through here a time or two in the past. Not for quite a spell though."

"Towns a-growin' and changin'."

"So I noticed."

"Not to my dad-blasted likin', though, I'll tell ya." The oldster took an angry swipe across the bartop with his washcloth, as if trying to sweep away what wasn't to his liking. "Lucky so far it ain't affected our part of town. But it's just a matter of time, I figger, before the 'Magic City of the Plains' crowd starts stickin' their noses in around here and lookin' to try and spruce us up too. Reckon my bones'll be in the ground before then, which is just as well. Was I still up on my pins when they showed with their high-minded 'Civic Pride' notions, I'd put 'em on the run with a double dose of buckshot up their fancy asses!"

The barkeep was getting himself worked up to the point of stirring a hint of color into his cheeks. Lone grinned. "You better calm down, old timer, 'fore you blow a gasket. How about I buy you a drink to settle you some?"

That earned him a grin in return, a wide, toothless one. "By God, you're the kind of customer we need more of around here!" A glass and a bottle of redeye thumped onto the bartop, and the glass was quickly filled to the brim by a steady hand. Raising the glass in a toast, the oldster said, "Don't like to drink with folks I ain't been introduced to. My name's Homer."

Lone gestured in kind with his beer mug. "Call me McGantry."

"Here's mud in yer eye."

"Back at ya."

Homer's glass got emptied in one long gulp followed by an exclamation of, "Ah, mother's milk!"

Lone took a drink of his beer. "You own this place, Homer?"

"That's what all the paperwork says." Homer topped off his glass again. "Way I figger it, though, me and the joint sorta own each other. Every nickel I have goes into keepin' her afloat, and every nickel I get comes from havin' her in operation. With the wife and kids all gone to the Hereafter, the Dust Cutter's the onliest kin I got. When I kick, all my so-called friends—the suds swallowers and whiskey guzzlers you see scattered about the room—will likely empty the kegs and shelves of whatever stock I leave behind and then find some new joint to become regulars in. The old girl will set empty and boarded up until the civic pride vultures come along to tear her down and put up something they find to be more . . . what's the word? . . . 'ecstatically pleasin' to the eye.' "

"I think you might mean 'aesthetically' more pleasin'." Lone suggested.

"Who gives a shit. It's all hogwash. No matter what they put up instead, to my eye—was I around to see it, that is—it'd never be as pleasin' as this pile of weather-beat old planks held together with spit and bob wire." Homer threw down his second glass of redeye.

Lone cocked a brow. "Kind of a grim outlook, wouldn't you say?"

"In case you ain't noticed, son, life has a way of bein' damned grim at times." Homer wrapped his hand around the bottle again but, instead of pouring any more from it, slid it back and put it away down behind the bar. When he straightened up, he eyed Lone with tighter scrutiny than before. Then he said, "Comes down to it, though, I'd say you've likely had yourself a brush or two with the grim side of things. In fact, I might go so far as to say you look like somebody who's got some grim business on his mind right now."

"I didn't come in here lookin' for trouble, if that's what you mean." A corner of Lone's mouth quirked up. "But you're right in thinkin' I got some grim business on my mind. Some grim business that already took place here—just a few nights back."

Homer looked suspicious, but also curious. "Go ahead. Cut to it."

"I'm talkin' about the ambush killin' of a man named Racone. Chico Racone."

"Took place in the street outside, not in here."

"But, unless I've been told wrong, it's generally suspected that an argument which *did* take place inside here is what was most likely behind the shootin'. You disagree with that?"

Before Homer could reply, one of the hombres leaning on the bar farther down thumped down an empty beer mug and called, "Hey, Homer. Need a refill down this way."

Homer made a waving-off motion with one hand. "Hold yer horses a minute. Can't you see I'm palaverin' here?" But then the businessman in him reconsidered the delay to a paying customer. This caused him to call out to the redheaded barmaid who was working a nearby table, leaning close over the shoulders of two of its occupants, showing lots of cleavage to keep their thirst worked up. "Hey, Minnie gal. Take a break from the tables and come over to work the stick for a spell while I do me some visitin'."

"Sure thing, Home," Minnie replied willingly. When she straightened up to go do as bid, the men at the table grumbled with disappointment. Minnie put them at ease with a saucy smile and a promise, "Don't worry, fellas. I won't be gone long, and when I come back, I'll be just as soft and cuddly as ever."

Once Minnie had made her way around behind the bar and was drawing a fresh brew for the hombre in need of one, Homer turned his attention back to Lone. Planting his bony elbows on the bartop between them, he pushed his scowling face close and said, "Now then. You some kind of lawman or bounty hunter?"

"Neither," Lone assured him. "All I am is

a fella interested in seein' that the skunk who gunned Chico don't get away with it."

"There's men who *are* lawmen already workin' on that."

"Uh-huh. The West is full of lawmen workin' on cases of men who got gunned down or back shot or what have you. Trouble is, a hell of a lot of varmints who've done those kind of things remain runnin' loose."

"Why the particular interest in what happened to Chico? You a friend of his?"

Lone drank some of his beer. "More like I *ain't* a friend of that Risen polecat who cut him down."

Homer pooched his lips. "Still makes it sound personal."

"Reckon you could say that," Lone allowed. "That's what I figure might make the difference in me takin' an interest over the marshal and his men who're already workin' on it. Not meanin' in any way to short-change them or how they do their job. But that's the thing that could give me the edge. It bein' personal to me means I can concentrate on it alone. To them it's just a job— and only part of their bigger job of keepin' the overall peace and worryin' about a passel of other trouble."

"The deputy assigned to the case is named Brady. He's a mite young, but a hard worker and by all reports, honest as the day is long. Still, it's like you say—the marshal only has three full-time deputies so they're stretched awful dang thin comes to coverin' this whole bustin'-out-at-the-seams town."

"This Brady sounds like somebody worth talkin' to, unless he freezes me out if he thinks I'm pokin' in where I don't belong."

"He might," Homer said. "But, like I said, he tends to be reasonable and honest. More apt he'd be willin' to talk with you . . . providin' your plan for Risen, if you catch up with him, amounts to more than just haulin' off and doin' to him what you suspicion he did to Chico."

"Was he to force my hand, I'd do what I had to," Lone told him. "But I ain't settin' out to be judge, jury, and executioner. All I want is him caught and held to account."

Homer gave him another close eyeballing. Then he announced, "I believe you. I also believe I damn well wouldn't want to be in the shoes of any hombre you set out to do some score-settlin' with."

Lone drained his beer. Before pushing it across the bar for a refill, he asked, "That mean, for starters, you're willin' to talk to me too? Fill me in on what happened in here that night between Chico and Risen that appears to've somehow led to the shooting outside?"

"You slick-talkin' rascal! You snookered me into that, didn't you?" growled Homer. Then, after refilling Lone's mug, he reached under the bar and brought out his bottle of redeye again, saying, "Palaverin', especially answerin' questions, is thirsty work. Let's git to it."

Chapter Four

Over the next half hour, Lone got a good idea of what had gone on during the time James and Chico spent in the Dust Cutter prior to the shooting out in the street. Much of this information he got from the saloon owner himself, helped by some added input provided by a couple of regulars who'd been on hand that night, called over by Homer to tell what they'd seen and heard. But the most thorough details came from none other than Minnie, the red-haired barmaid/sometimes bartender who'd been seated at a table with James and Chico for a big share of the time they were present.

The main reason for the pair showing up at the Dust Cutter, it was revealed, was the hope of finding a man named Dale Faeger there. Faeger owned and operated one of Cheyenne's smaller livery stables and was indeed a regular patron of Homer's establishment, as James and Chico had been told. Their interest in wanting to talk with him had to do with some horses they'd spotted being boarded at his place, in particular a certain roan filly (the mention of which Lone immediately recognized as likely the one belonging to Rosemary). Specifically, they admitted, they were seeking the person the roan belonged to; and, though they didn't say it in so many words, they gave the impression there might be some question of ownership regarding the animal.

Unfortunately, only Faeger's hired man had been present at the stable when they spotted the roan. Since he wasn't on duty when the horse came in, he couldn't provide any information on who left her off. For that reason, he directed them to Faeger and suggested they might find him at the Dust Cutter. Arriving there, they found that their man wasn't present but were advised he likely would be showing up before long. So they'd taken seats at a table, ordered some drinks, and waited.

That's where Minnie had come in. Chico took a shine to her right away when she served them their drinks. He offered to buy her one if she'd join them and so, because things were kind of slow just then, she went ahead and sat with them for a while.

"Chico was real loose and friendly and talkative," she related. "But the younger fella, James, he was all antsy and impatient right from the get-go. He didn't talk overly much, just kept watching the door and asking me every time anybody came in if it was Faeger. When it wasn't, he just got moodier and more impatient. And it seemed to annoy him that Chico was relaxed and having fun talking with me. He didn't like it much, neither, that Chico was throwing down drinks pretty steady. When James said to him he oughta slow down, Chico told him he could handle his liquor and to mind his own business."

"Is that what led to the argument between them?" Lone asked her.

Minnie shook her head. "No. Not right then, anyway. More than anything, it was the impatience building up in James. The more time passed without Faeger showing up, the more irritable he got. Finally, after about a half hour or so, he pounded his fist down on the table and said, 'Goddamn it, this is getting us nowhere!'

"Then he demanded to know if anybody knew where Faeger lived, said him and Chico would go to his home if they had to. When nobody had an answer for him on that, James told Chico they should go back to the stable and get the information from the hired man there." Minnie paused, her brow puckering more deeply before. "I could see by his expression that Chico didn't like the sound of that at all. So that's when I told James how Faeger didn't do *all* of his drinking here at the Cutter, that I knew he sometimes stopped at the Brown Bottle just up the street."

"Damn traitor," grumbled Homer.

Minnie continued. "Well James liked the sound of that. He was keen to try it right away, said they'd wasted too much time here already. Trouble was, Chico still wasn't much inclined to leave. Among other things, he seemed bound and determined me and him was gonna . . . well, you know. Even though I kept trying to get it through his head I ain't that kind of gal." She actually blushed, almost as bright a red as her hair. "Anyway, James got really pissed about Chico refusing to go with him. Called him a drunk and a bum and worse. Chico warned him he'd better watch his mouth, said something about James being nothing but a whine-ass and no wonder his wife run out on him."

"Yeah," grunted Homer. "I heard that part halfway across the room. Everybody in the joint did—those two were goin' at it pretty loud by then."

Lone said, "I take it that's when James went stormin' out?"

Minnie's head bobbed. "Off to check out the Brown Bottle, is what we all figured. Later on, the folks there confirmed as much. Went asking for Faeger, same as here. Only, also same as here, found out Faeger wasn't there neither. So he sat around for a while, waiting some more. In the meantime, Chico hung back here. He was getting a little drunker and a little handsier, until I had to put him in his place real firm. I don't mind some pawing, that's to be expected. But enough is enough, you know? When he finally got it through his head he'd got as far as he was gonna get with me, he grumbled how he might as well go waste time with James. That's when he got up and left."

"And then it wasn't but a couple minutes later," Homer cut in, "that his time-wastin' days was over permanent-like. He was barely out the door when we heard the shots. Two of 'em, close together. Some of us crowded to the doorway, sorta cautious at first, and there was Chico layin' in the street with a bullet smack through his pump. And hot-footin' it into the mouth of an alley catty-cornered across the way was the other fella. No doubt it was him, by that fancy wine-colored jacket he was wearin'."

"Poor Chico," said Minnie, with sadness in her voice and showing on her face. "I feel lousy that the last words he ever heard anybody say was me being so blunt and stand-offish to him."

Homer patted her shoulder with a gnarled paw. "There now, gal, I told you before you got no call to be hard on yourself. Reckon that jasper didn't deserve what he got out in the street, but what you said to him he pushed for 'til you had no choice."

"What Homer's sayin' is right," added Lone. He was reasonably satisfied with what he'd learned in his time here and didn't like seeing Minnie feel so remorseful after what she'd shared. There was still a couple more things he wanted to probe, but Millie didn't need to be part of it. The best thing for her, Lone judged, would be to get back to serving and flirting again with the other customers.

Right about the time he was thinking this, it turned out that somebody else was having the same notion. Namely, one of the three cow-pokes—a blue-jawed, bleary-eyed number—who was occupying the table where Minnie had been lingering before Homer called her over for some duty behind the bar. In the time since she'd been away, Blue Jaw apparently had grown impatient for her return. His impatience, it was also apparent, had been stoked by guzzling more than his share from the near-empty bottle of popskull on the tabletop before him.

"Hey, Homer!" he suddenly shouted in a loud voice. "How much time and how many goddamn people does it take to serve one goddamn saddle tramp?"

Homer shot a quick glare in the man's direction. "As long and as many as I want! That answer your question? You don't like the way I run things here, Bafford, there are plenty of other joints you can do your swillin' in. But while you're in mine, keep it down and keep your lousy attitude in check, you hear?"

"Or what?" Bafford challenged. "You gonna throw me out, you old bag of bones?"

"You push too hard, bucko," came the growled response. "I got a sawed-off Greener behind this bar that'll fix it so you go out in *pieces*."

"Homer! Clay!" wailed Minnie. "Stop it . . . don't be ridiculous."

Bafford cut his narrowed, bleary eyes to her. "You wanna talk ridiculous? How about the price on this watered-down drink I bought you? The one you went off and left barely touched. I don't like being played for a sucker like that!"

Minnie looked uncertain but also clearly wanted to try and calm things down. "Okay, okay," she said. "I told you I'd be back, didn't I? And I will. I'll come back and sit with you and finish my drink, but only if you promise to behave yourself and quit being rude."

"I ain't the rude one. It's that goddamn stranger," Bafford insisted, suddenly thrusting a finger at Lone, "who barged in and caused you to get called away. Now your drink is piss warm and spoiled. Ain't gonna be no enjoyment in that for nobody. I say the stranger owes you a fresh drink, which you're gonna set your ass back down here and have at this table . . . and he also owes a round to me and my pals for hogging your company away from us."

The surrounding room had grown mostly quiet by now, eyes shifting back and forth between Bafford and Lone, watching to see how the big, square-faced stranger would react to the words tossed his way.

But before Lone could say anything, Homer spoke again, exclaiming, "Bullshit! I warned you, Bafford. You had your chance to get back in line, but now your mouth has done—"

Lone made a quick hand gesture, cutting him short. Then, slowly, he turned his face and planted a flat gaze on Bafford. The two other cowpokes seated at the table with him appeared somewhat uncomfortable yet nevertheless crowded toward siding with their pard.

"Seems like," Lone drawled, "you make a halfway reasonable point about me takin' up so much of the young lady's time it allowed her drink to go bad. That was thoughtless of me. For that reason, I got no problem buyin' her a fresh one. Where and with who she chooses to drink it is up to her."

Now all eyes swung back to Bafford. Since he was the one who'd set this confrontation in motion and the booze in his gut was continuing to fuel his belligerence, there was no room for him to ease up now. "You not hear so good or something?" he sneered. "I'll say it once more, a little slower and plainer . . . the girl is damn sure gonna have that drink at this table. And *you* are gonna set up a round for me and my pals to have with her. Got it clear this time?"

Lone turned full around now and regarded Bafford for a long beat, saying nothing. The aches and bruises from the earlier pounding he'd received suddenly felt deep and sore again, no longer soothed by the schnapps or the beer. The last thing he was in the mood for was absorbing any new ones from this blue-jawed jackass. Exhaling a ragged breath, he said over his shoulder, "Homer, set that bottle of redeye back on the bar and pour me a shot. Just one."

While the old man did as requested, Lone kept his eyes locked on Bafford. Once the glass was filled, he picked it up and quickly drained it. The fiery liquid burned down through his chest and into his gut. He clapped the glass back onto the bar top and said, "Again."

This time when the glass was full, Lone didn't touch it. He took his eyes off Bafford just long enough to rake them over the other two cowpokes at his table. "You fellas have been smart enough to keep your yaps shut so far," he told them. "Just keep playin' it smart by stayin' out of this." Then his gaze cut back to Bafford. "You. I'll say this slow and plain so you understand it clear. Here's a shot on the bar. A round I'm payin' for. You want it . . . come take it."

The silence in the barroom took on an edge, a heightened tension.

The sneer on Bafford's face faltered. His mouth pulled into a tight, thin line. Minnie, still behind the bar, moved a few steps back away from Lone.

Bafford pushed his chair back and slowly stood up. He didn't say anything. Nobody did. He took a step toward Lone and the full glass on the bar-top. The spurs on Bafford's boots chimed with clarity in the stillness. His gaze and Lone's were locked, unwavering, as he came forward.

Homer stood motionless, watching, a corner of his mouth raised in a strange, anticipatory smile.

Bafford reached the bar, stopped about four feet from Lone. The full glass of redeye stood on the polished wood between them. Bafford gave it a quick glance, then his eyes lifted back to Lone. Neither man spoke. Slowly, Bafford reached out and took the glass of redeye. He raised it partway to his mouth and paused for a moment. Then he tossed it down quick and lowered the glass. Eyes still locked with Lone's, he placed the empty glass gently back on the bar. But he didn't let go of it right away. Until, suddenly, he jerked his hand away—balling it into a fist as he did so— and swung it up and across in what was meant to be a clubbing backhanded blow to the side of Lone's face.

But the former scout was poised, ready for just such a move. His right arm shot out, blocking the intended strike in mid swing. Then, leaning in and using his greater strength, he forced Bafford's arm back and down, slamming it, just above the wrist, hard against the edge of the bar. There came the thud of impact, cracking of bone, and Bafford's howl of pain, all rolled into one.

Continuing in motion, Lone pivoted and whipped his left elbow around, smashing it to Bafford's ear, driving his face down onto the bar top. Next, reaching with both hands, Lone grabbed a double handful of hair and jerked the cowboy's head a foot up off the polished surface before hammering it back down again. When he let go, Bafford hung draped over the edge of the bar for a moment, blood streaming from his mashed nose, then slid slowly off and dropped to the floor.

Just that fast, it was over.

Or it would have been if, less than a minute later, a heavy-jowled, big-bellied slob with a deputy's star on his shirt and a long-barreled Remington in his fist hadn't come barging in through the front door. He bulled forward, a mean scowl taking in Bafford sprawled on the floor and Lone standing over him. Then, without hesitation or warning, he raised the Remy and rapped its heavy barrel across the crown of Lone's skull.

Chapter Five

The thinly blanketed jail cell cot Lone lay on wasn't a hell of a lot softer or warmer than the floor of a high-country cave he remembered once holing up in to wait out a late winter blizzard. But then, the way his head was pounding and his whole body ached at the moment, he likely wouldn't have found much comfort even if nestled on a featherbed. The only solace he found was in reflecting how he'd seen to it—with an assist from Johnny Case and his two-by-four—that most of those responsible for the way he felt were somewhere out there suffering miseries akin to his. All but one; the fat deputy who'd bent a gun barrel over his head. Lone harbored a special kind of ache over having been unable to get any return licks in on that fat bastard. Not yet.

The recollection of how he'd ended up here in this cell only came from brief snatches of semi-clarity between longer stretches of unconsciousness following the blow to the head. He recalled being loaded onto the bed of a small wagon or cart . . . being carried roughly down a flight of stone steps . . . and then the realization he was behind bars. (In a cell block, he would eventually learn, located at the rear of the marshal's office which was in turn located in the basement of the city/county courthouse building.)

Apparently he had slept or been unconscious through most of the night. He only knew it must be morning now because a short time ago a plump, gray-haired, almost friendly-seeming Negro jailer had woke him to see he felt up to having some breakfast. Lone had declined any food but said some coffee sure sounded good. The jailer said he'd fetch some, but so far hadn't returned with any.

Morning. Breakfast.

Jesus, he was supposed to be meeting Sue for breakfast this morning. What would she think when he didn't show up? What would she think about him being in jail? How would she even know he was *in* jail?

Damn.

Lone wondered what time it was. He'd been relieved of his pocket watch along with his wallet and belt and all other personal items except his shirt and pants. He sat up on the cot and swung his feet over the edge. They'd left him his socks too, but the coldness of the floor quickly seeped through them.

When the jailer returned, Lone would find out what time it was. He'd also ask about seeing a judge or making bail or whatever the procedure was for getting out of here. There was enough money in his wallet to pay any reasonable fine . . . or at least there *had* been. It wasn't unheard of for men landing in the hoosegow of a town where they were strangers to find themselves being mysteriously minus some or all of the dinero they'd had on them prior to their arrest. And it wasn't hard for Lone to picture the badge-wearing slob who'd cold-cocked him for no reason as being the sort who would be "innocently" baffled by how such a lousy break could happen.

Lone thought back to something Homer the barkeep had said about the deputy assigned to Chico's murder being a young, honest fellow named Brady. Fatso, from the brief glimpse Lone had got as the Remington barrel came streaking toward his head, hadn't looked particularly young. And his unprovoked action sure as hell didn't seem what you'd call proper or honest. So if he turned out to be Brady, then Homer's people-judging skills left a lot to be desired.

The sound of a heavy door opening and clanging shut, followed by hollowly echoing footsteps and voices drew Lone's full attention. He realized that, up until then, he hadn't heard any other movement or talk within the cell block, leaving the impression he must be its only occupant. Since it sounded like the jailer was returning with company of some sort, Lone wondered if it was another prisoner.

When the jailer came in sight, he was indeed not alone. But none of the three people accompanying him were new prisoners. One was a tall, square-jawed young man wearing a stern expression and a deputy's badge. Lone had never seen him before. The other two were quite familiar and, even if one of them was Johnny Case, mighty welcome sights to Lone at that moment—especially Sue Leonard, in spite of her finding him in these circumstances.

Lone moved up to the wall of vertical bars and wrapped his fists around a pair of them. On the other side, Sue stepped up and put her hands over his. She smiled crookedly. "I can't leave you alone for a minute, can I?"

"You're the one who brought me to Cheyenne . . . I'm your responsibility," Lone told her.

"That's a part of the deal I clearly should have thought through more carefully."

The stern looking young deputy spoke, addressing Lone. "My name's Marv Brady. Miss Leonard has posted your bail. You'll be released in a few minutes, but first I want to have a few words with you about what happened last night. Specifically, I'd like some details on the brawl that landed you here and what your business was in the Dust Cutter prior to that."

"I got plenty I want to say about last night," Lone replied. "For starters, the fracas you call a brawl wasn't hardly—"

Brady cut him off. "We'll talk privately, you and I. Here in the cell, while you're reclaiming your things and having your coffee. Miss Leonard and Mr. Case can wait in a more comfortable holding area. We'll join them there shortly and finish up the paperwork." He turned to the jailer who was holding a lumpy cloth sack in one hand and a mug of steaming coffee in the other. "Frank, go ahead and unlock the cell, give McGantry his belongings and his coffee. Then show Miss Leonard and Mr. Case to the holding area, please."

"Sure thing, Deputy Marv."

A handful of minutes later, Lone was re-outfitted in the gear he'd been relieved of, from boots to hat, and was once again seated on the edge of the cell cot, holding a cup of strong black coffee between his palms. The cloth sack in which jailer Frank had been keeping his collected belongings lay on the cot beside him. Nothing had been missing. Lone's gun belt, holstered Colt, and sheathed Bowie knife remained in the sack. Deputy Brady had explained that policy didn't allow any weapons to be worn by non-law officers inside the lock-up area. Made sense.

Brady sat facing Lone, perched on a backless wooden stool he'd pulled in from somewhere. He had just built and lit a cigarette and was now talking through a cloud of exhaled smoke. "Drunk and Disorderly. Disturbing the Peace. Assaulting an officer of the law . . . those are the charges on record for why you ended up here. What's your side?"

"And those would be charges filed by the, uh, other deputy I had the pleasure of meetin' last night. That it?"

"That's right," said Brady. "Deputy Arn Remson."

"So where is Remson now?"

"He worked the late duty last night. I expect he's home sleeping about now. You still haven't told me your side of what happened."

Lone's eyes narrowed. He briefly considered mentioning the three ambushers who'd jumped him but decided against it. Better to keep this focused on the incident inside the Cutter, not bog it down with anything more. "Okay," he said. "The short version is what you laid out is a pack of lies. You want me to break it down, it goes like this: For starters, I'd had a few drinks, but I was a long way from bein' drunk. Second thing, the dust-up between me and that proddy cowboy who *was* drunk sure didn't come close to anything I'd call a brawl. And finally, me assaultin' that so-called law officer who came bargin' in is the biggest lie of all. I barely turned my head to look at the . . . er, at him, before he hauled off and clubbed me over the head."

"Was he taking action to break up the fight?"

"Was no fight to break up. It was all over. The cowboy was on the floor, and I was just standin' there. And no, I wasn't fixin' to put the boots to him or nothing like that."

"Can you produce witnesses to any of this?" Brady wanted to know.

"There was a whole barroom full of folks lookin' on." Lone frowned. "But bein' a stranger hereabouts, I don't know any of 'em by name or—yeah, on second thought, I do. There was Homer, the barkeep and owner. And Minnie, one of the gals who work for him. It was them I was talkin' with when that proddy damn cowboy started . . . say, what about him? Did he get arrested on any of those charges?"

Brady expelled a cloud of smoke and looked somewhat troubled. "I didn't see anything about that on the report. Jailer Frank informed me, however, that another participant in what's listed as a brawl had to spend the night in the care of a local doctor due to the injuries he suffered. Maybe Remson held off bringing charges against him until he was cleared by the doc, I don't know. There's a lot I don't know since I only got in a little while ago, barely in time for your friends to show up and start clamoring to see you, demanding to know what it would take to get you out."

"No offense, but where's the full marshal? Shouldn't he be on hand to handle some of that?"

"Marshal's out of town to attend a funeral. Left

ahead of first light. I'm the day man in charge until he gets back," Brady explained.

"Homer at the Dust Cutter says you're an honest, hard worker on a crew of lawmen spread too thin to cover everything expected of you," Lone told him.

Brady grunted. "Never knew old Homer to have much good to say about anybody."

"He also mentioned you were headin' up the investigation into Chico Racone's gun down and the hunt for the main suspect, James Risen."

"I was wondering if you'd get around to that." Brady's mouth formed a thin smile. "Wasn't hard to put it together once Miss Leonard showed up wanting to spring you. You're here to help her in her belief that her brother, Risen, is innocent. Correct? That's what you were doing at the Dust Cutter last night in the first place—trying to get the lowdown on when Risen and Chico were in there arguing only a little while before Chico got gunned."

"That's about the size of it," Lone admitted. "Naturally, Sue wants to believe her brother is innocent. I lean the same way, though maybe not as strong. Mainly, I agreed to help her try and run him down before he gets himself in deeper, maybe even ends up toes down himself."

"Why would an innocent man, a formerly respected doctor, be at risk for anything like that?"

Lone cocked a brow. "Come on. If you've talked to Sue, if you're workin' to sort out this shooting and all, then you must know about what brought her brother and Chico here to Cheyenne. How they were chasin' after Risen's runaway wife and the hombre she took off with—a shifty, likely dangerous character named Drake. If Drake *is* the kind of dangerous varmint some think and he takes a strong enough dislike to Risen houndin' him and the girl . . . well, there's the worry for what the doc might run up against."

"Do you think there's a chance it was this Drake—Earl Drake, I believe is his full name—who gunned Chico?"

"I got no call to say on that one way or the other." Lone shrugged. "I never met the man. I just know, from the impression he made on Sue, he sounds like the kind of snake who *could* have. More so than something a body would expect out of James Risen, I'll say that much."

"Did you find out anything worthwhile in your time at the Dust Cutter?" inquired Brady.

"Got interrupted before I was done with all my askin'."

"But what if you *had* learned anything pertinent?"

Lone grunted. "First I would've had to figure out what the hell 'pertinent' means." Then, after taking a drink of his coffee, he said, "Look, Brady, I ain't meanin' to horn in on your business.

84

I ain't no damn detective or anybody out to solve Chico Racone's killin'. That's up to you and the rest of your crew. And if you run down James Risen and you figure he's your man, then you gotta do your job. I understand that and I believe Sue does too. But in the meantime, if Risen is on the run and still chasin' after his no-account wife, then my skills as a former Indian scout and tracker might have a chance of catchin' up, like I said before, ahead of the damn fool makin' things worse for himself. That's why Sue sent for me and how, as a friend, I'm willin' to try and help."

Brady took a final drag off his cigarette, dropped it on the floor and crushed it under a boot heel. He eyed Lone closely for a beat before saying, "I'm going to go ahead and release you on bail. It'll be up to a judge to set a final fine, which you'll be expected to appear for. So I'll make the bail high enough to cover it, in case you're not. That'll still get me my ass reamed by the judge and the marshal, though it won't be the first time. And Arn Remson is sure to be piss-burned when he hears I tampered with one of his arrests, but *that* I care about not one whit."

Lone eyed him in return. "So why stick your neck out for me, even just a little bit?"

The deputy shrugged. "Lots of reasons. None of which would necessarily make sense to anybody but me. Mostly, I trust my judgment when it comes to reading people. I think you and Miss

Leonard are leveling with me about not wanting to see Risen get away with murder but rather you're only out to try and keep her brother from getting deeper in trouble. As far as Earl Drake, he's no stranger to me. He's passed through here before. He used to be an operative for a private detective agency out of Denver; I forget the exact name. Last heard, he branched out on his own.

"Indications were that the Denver outfit he worked for wasn't above taking on some pretty shady clients and Drake himself was reported to be especially unscrupulous in the way he went about things. Pushing the boundaries of the law to the limit, maybe sometimes beyond. I never trusted him, thought him dirty of a couple shenanigans right here in my backyard but could never prove it. He's damn sure sleazy if not, as you suspect, downright dangerous. If Risen is barkin' on his heels, yeah, he needs to be careful."

"You figure any of the three are still in Cheyenne?" Lone asked.

"No, I don't. Not Drake or the wife, for sure. That's another reason I got for turnin' you loose. What makes me think those two are long gone starts with having learned that Drake and a dark-haired young woman fitting the description of Mrs. Risen arrived in town a short time back and boarded their horses at a local livery run by a man named Faeger. Said they wanted their horses put up for a day or two. If you found out anything at all during your time at the Dust Cutter, you must have heard that Risen and Chico went there looking for Faeger."

Lone nodded. "That's right. They spotted the two horses at his stable and recognized one of them as belonging to Mrs. Risen. Expect they were hopin' Faeger could tell 'em something about who left the horses off."

"Only they never caught up with him, and Chico ended up getting gunned. Then, early on the morning following the shooting, Drake came 'round, rousted Faeger, and made a deal to sell the horses to him, saying him and the young lady had a sudden change of plans and no longer needed the animals. A little later that same morning, two stages left Cheyenne—one bound for Denver, one for Laramie. The passengers on each, unfortunately, included a man and a young woman who also fit descriptions that could have been Drake and Mrs. Risen, though neither pair used those names."

"Damn," Lone muttered. "So if one pair was who we're thinkin'—and it sure fits as bein' likely—then there's no way of knowin' which way they went. And something else that fits is the timin' of them changin' their plans and takin' off so quick on the heels of the shooting. Goes back to your question about Drake maybe havin' a hand in gunning Chico, wouldn't you say?"

"Hard not to wonder about it," Brady admitted. "But a bigger wonder, because he was spotted at the scene and made himself the prime suspect by taking flight, goes back to Risen. He and Chico were boarding their horses, their mounts as well as a pack animal, at a different livery. Risen's horse and the packhorse went missing in the middle of the night of the shooting. Nobody's seen hide nor hair of the doc since."

Lone rubbed his jaw. "So since we know he was there when Chico got shot—either by him or somebody else, maybe Drake—he panicked and lit a shuck outta town. That ain't so hard to understand. But where would he go? And, if he was still set on chasin' after his wife, would he have any way of knowin' that her and Drake lit out too?"

"Those are some real interesting questions," Brady allowed. "You and Miss Leonard are free to go wrestle with 'em all you want. As for me, if those three are all gone from town, I can't afford to fret about 'em too much more. Don't mean I don't care, I'm just being practical. Far as Drake and the wife, there's nothing I could do about them anyway, not if they were standing right here in front of me. Comes to Risen, I'll still be on the lookout for him and we'll likely send out some Wanted On Suspicion posters. But his description is about as common as dirt, so I don't expect much." The deputy rose from his stool. "Come on, let's go get the paperwork over with so you can be on your way."

Lone stood also, reaching to take with him the sack containing his weapons.

Just outside the cell door, Brady stopped and turned partially back around. "Something else," he said, his tone as flat as his gaze. "Arn Remson and me wear the same badge and work on the same crew. But our way of representing the law forks apart considerable. The marshal is a good man but, for my money, he cuts Arn too much slack for his heavy-handed ways. Goes back to loyalty for when times were a lot wilder here and Arn's method was maybe more necessary. Like I said, neither of 'em—Arn especially—are likely to be happy about me letting you make bail. I'll handle any blowback on me. But Arn wouldn't be above looking to take his anger out on you again if he got half a chance. So if you plan on sticking around town very much longer, watch out for him."

Chapter Six

Albeit later and under more strained conditions than originally intended, Lone and Sue were still able to have their breakfast together. They were joined by Johnny Case who, in spite of prior misgivings where he was concerned, had undeniably proven himself beneficial in the past fifteen or so hours. First, he had shown up to help turn back the street ambush on Lone and then he'd been the one to inform Sue of the former scout's incarceration so she could proceed to arrange bail.

Johnny's awareness of Lone's jailing stemmed from him hanging around after Lone went into the Dust Cutter, waiting to see how that turned out. The last thing he expected, though, was to see Deputy Arn Remson show up and then, a short time later, watch him drag an obviously pistol-whipped Lone off to the hoosegow. The only reason Johnny didn't try to take any action right then was due to his own previous run-in with Remson; he had a strong hunch that him stepping forth too soon in a matter once again related to a Dust Cutter incident would only give the thug deputy a reason to somehow make matters worse. So Johnny held off until morning, when he figured the marshal and some other personnel would be on hand to handle things more reasonably and professionally. He'd gone to Sue's hotel room and, once he was able to talk his way past her threats and demands for him to immediately leave, filled her in on what had happened then accompanied her to the jail.

When the three of them left the courthouse building now, they found an out-of-the way little café on a nearby side street. They threaded their way through a moderate crowd of other breakfast customers and took a table near the back. Though Lone had declined anything to eat at the jail, the cooking aromas filling the steamy, low-ceilinged room quickly changed his mind. He ordered a platter of ham and eggs, fried potatoes, biscuits, and coffee. Johnny seconded that. Sue opted for a short stack of pancakes.

When the coffee came, Johnny unobtrusively withdrew a silver flask from his vest pocket and held it up for Lone to see. "Wondering if you could stand a touch of this? Strictly for medicinal purposes, of course?"

Lone's eyebrows lifted. "Oh man, could I ever. That jail cot would've been enough to work over a body all on its own. Comin' on top of that thumpin' those ambushers laid on me, I feel like one big ache. By all means, do *not* be stingy with that flask."

Johnny handed it over, saying, "I warn you, that ain't exactly a smooth blend. It kicks like a spurred mule. But, right about now, it's likely just what you need."

"I thought I was the closest thing to a doctor around here," said Sue, watching Lone first take a swig straight from the flask and then pour some into his coffee.

Reacting to the swig he'd tossed down, Lone puckered his mouth and exclaimed, "Whooee! That is *not* for the faint of heart!" Then, addressing Sue, he said, "Now. If you have any additional potion or elixir, I would be open to hearin' about them as well."

Sue gave him a look. "I can do better than that. I've got a sure-fire cure . . . don't go sneaking out in the middle of the night in a strange town where you run the risk of getting attacked in the first place!"

"Oh. That ol' remedy." Lone took a drink of his coffee. "I've tried it in the past. Somehow it don't ever seem to work for me."

"Darn it, Lone, I'm serious," said Sue, scowling. "If Johnny hadn't shown up, you could be lying dead in some back alley right now. Or rotting away in a jail cell. And I'd have no idea what happened or where to go looking because you didn't bother to let me know your plans."

Lone smiled tolerantly. "In the first place, I am mighty beholden to Johnny and have told him so more than once. But I don't think those varmints who jumped me in the street meant to kill me or they would've simply gunned me from the shadows. As far as 'rotting away' in my jail cell, it was hardly some *calaboza* south of the border where that kind of thing maybe does happen. So, though once again I am beholden, this time to you for gettin' me out so promptly, I likely would have made it on my own before I rotted."

"That still doesn't excuse—"

Lone cut Sue's protest short, saying, "And the reason I didn't inform you I was goin' out to do some checkin' at the Dust Cutter was because, if I had, you would have insisted on wantin' to come with me. Tell me I'm wrong."

Further discussion was temporarily halted by the arrival of a pretty young waitress with their food orders and a pot of fresh coffee from which she refilled their cups and then left the remainder of the pot.

Once the waitress had withdrawn again, Johnny said, "If I can make a suggestion—How about we put last night behind us, except for what was learned out of it, and focus on what's left ahead. Namely, catching up with James and then deciding whatever needs to be done from there."

Both Lone and Sue regarded him. Johnny set his jaw and returned their looks. "Okay. When I say 'we,' I guess that depends on whether or not you want me—will *allow* me—to continue being part of this. Damn it, I think I've earned at least some consideration toward that.

"I'll be the first to admit I haven't done myself any favors the way I went about things in the past. But it was always with your best intentions in mind, Sue. Yeah, and always with an angle toward winning you over to feel about me like I do you." He heaved a sigh. "But I'm finally willing to let go of that now. Give up, accept it ain't ever gonna happen. Either way, none of it matters when it comes to this business with James. Hell, I never even liked him all that much. Only there's something damned fishy about what's going on. Seems clear to me he's getting a raw deal, maybe more ways than one. That plain sticks in my craw and I'd like to help get to the bottom of it."

When he was done, Lone said, "That was quite a speech. My breakfast damn near got cold waitin' for it to end."

For her part, Sue was now looking at Johnny in a notably different way than with the cool, borderline indifference she'd been displaying toward him all morning. "Yes," she agreed in a subdued tone. "It was quite a speech."

Lone speared a forkful of ham and eggs. "After I got my wits about me back in that jail cell, I had time to roll some things over in my mind. Things that made me think I wouldn't mind havin' another gun at my side goin' forward."

"That could be me," Johnny stated.

Lone nodded and said around a mouthful of food, "Yeah, it could."

Sue let their gazes rest on her for a beat before responding, "Whatever it takes to get my brother back safe and out of deeper trouble."

"Goddammit! What right does that namby-pamby Brady have messin' with an arrest of mine!" Arn Remson bit off the end of the fat cigar he'd stuck momentarily into his mouth, spit it halfway across the room. Shoving the stogie back between his thick lips, he reached over onto the nightstand and fumbled for a match. After thumbing the lucifer to flame, he held it to the cigar tip. Clad in only the bottom half of a pair of long johns, he sat on the edge of his bed, hairy gut bulging out and sagging down onto his thighs, and puffed out a cloud of noxious smoke.

From the bed behind him, a whiny female voice belonging to the bare shoulder and mass of copper hair poking out of the covers wailed, "Jesus God, Arnie. You gotta light up one of them stinkin' things so damn early?"

"Shut up," Remson growled over his shoulder. "Otherwise I'll throw your bony ass out the window and into the cold alley." He hesitated a minute, listening for any further lament. When there was none, he stood up and motioned to the stocky individual standing in the doorway, the man who had just delivered the news of Deputy

Brady allowing the prisoner McGantry to post bail. "Let's go in the other room, we'll talk there," Remson said.

Tate Millen, the man in the doorway, turned and did as bid. Remson shuffled after him, trailing a plume of smoke and closing the bedroom door as he exited. This put the two men in a moderate-sized main room that comprised the rest of the modest cabin where Remson lived. It was a simple layout; kitchen area at one end, parlor area at the other, dining table and cabinets in the middle. A cast iron stove in the kitchen area did double duty for cooking and for providing heat. Right now it wasn't doing either one.

"Good God," declared the lawman. "Throw a match into that stove's belly, will you, Millen? I primed it with wood and kindling before I turned in, it oughta take right off. Damn, I should have left a banked fire in it. I didn't think it was gonna turn so cold."

"I figured you'd want to know right away about McGantry," said Millen as he struck a match and dropped it onto the waiting pile of fuel. "But I can always come back so we can talk more a little later. Maybe you oughta crawl back into bed and stay warm there a while longer until it heats up out here."

"Nah. I'm up now, I might as well stay up." Remson made a face. "Besides, that skinny bitch in there don't give off much warmth nohow. She can buck up a storm like to knock the bed slats loose, but comes to body heat there plumb ain't enough meat there. You know what I mean? With winter comin' on, I think I'll take her back to Madam Mamie and trade her in for a plump replacement. That's what a fella wants durin' the cold months—a hefty mama to keep his belly nice and warm. Know what I mean?"

"If you say so." Millen shrugged. "Me, I like 'em all different sizes. Long as they got the one ingredient that's most important."

Both men chuckled.

Remson took a seat at the table. He remained quiet for a minute, puffing smoke and alternately lifting his bare feet to rub their bottoms on a long john covered opposite leg, warming them some before planting them back on the cold floor. That accomplished, he reached for the half full bottle of whiskey standing in the middle of the table. Uncorking it, he took the cigar out of his mouth long enough to raise the bottle and gulp down a big swallow. Thumping the bottle back down on the table and popping the cigar back into his mouth, he declared, "There! A fresh cigar and a jolt of good whiskey. A real man's breakfast. You know what I mean?"

Millen made no reply. He was a thick-shouldered man pushing fifty, grudgingly short of six feet tall by a full two inches though he swore it was less than one and wore boots with an elongated heel to help back up his claim. He had pale, thinning hair, carefully trimmed sideburns, and piercing blue eyes under a ledge of almost pure white brows.

Gesturing to the whiskey bottle, Remson said, "Want a hit?"

Millen shook his head. "Nope. A bit early for me." Then, grinning wryly, he added, "Though I bet both Mojave and Cleve, if they wasn't already numbed to the bone, would sure take you up on the offer."

"Those two stumble bums," Remson grunted. "How bad off are they this morning?"

"I haven't checked on 'em yet this morning. Not hard to guess, though, that they're both feeling mighty stove up."

"I don't give a shit how they *feel*. Are they up to functioning if I was to need something more out of 'em?"

Millen scowled. "How the hell am I supposed to know, Arn? That's up to them. Mojave came away with a busted nose and some loose teeth. But none of that's a first for him so, if I was to guess, I'd say he can still go. Cleve, though, he got one of his eyes damn near gouged out . . . I wouldn't expect much out of him for a while. We took him to Quincannon. He stayed the night there."

"That drunken quack," Remson spat. "The way

he shakes, he might end up pokin' out the *other* eye. Jesus!"

"At least you can count on him to have enough whiskey on hand for keeping Cleve's pain dulled down."

"Jesus!" Remson exclaimed again. Then, eyeing Millen under furled brows, he said, "How is it those other two got tore up so bad and you didn't?"

"I already told you," Millen snapped back. "I was the one who got the better of that big bastard. Had him down, knocked half loopy, when that other jasper showed up outta nowhere swinging some kind of big ass club and knocking everything out of our control. You want to see the welts on my back and the knot on the side of my head? I didn't waltz out of there exactly untouched. Even then, if those other two had been in any kind of shape to help, I still could've—"

Remson waved a hand impatiently, cutting him off. "Yeah, yeah. I heard all that last night. Who was that other meddlin' sonofabitch? You had a chance to find that out yet?"

"Name's Case. He's staying at the Ignacious, same as the Leonard woman, the sister to that doc who's on Drake's tail. According to Muldoon, Case and the sister are connected somehow—come from the same cowshit little town up in South Dakota, I guess—but they ain't really very good friends. Leastways they weren't until this morning. That's when Muldoon overheard them talking as they were leaving together, making plans to head for the jail with the aim of bailing out McGantry. After that was when he sent word so I could notify you."

Remson's flabby-lipped mouth twisted menacingly. "And a-course my old buddy Brady jumped at the chance to grant McGantry's bail. That back-stabbing weasel. I've long known the day was gonna come when I'd have to settle his hash. He keeps chafing me, it's gonna come sooner than later."

"But that don't have to be part of what we're in the middle of right now, does it?" asked Millen, looking concerned.

"I didn't say it did, did I? When the time comes, it won't be part of nobody's business but mine. Hell, I might even make it a birthday present to myself."

"Okay. Good." Millen's expression turned expectant. "But what *about* this business we're in the middle of? What's our next play?"

"Way I see it," Remson said after some thoughtful puffs on his cigar, "that's gonna depend on what the sister and McGantry—and now this Case character, too, I guess—take a notion to do. Far as we know, Drake is in the clear where they're concerned. I don't see how any of them can know where him and the girl took off to. With a little luck, maybe they'll accept that

100

the trail has petered out and they'll turn tail for home."

"But what about the brother, the doc hounding after his runaway wife? Way he's so crazed to catch up with her, don't seem like he'll likely give up no matter what. And what the sister really wants is to catch up with him, so I can't picture her giving up on that part either."

"My deal with Drake, damn it," Remson said irritably, "was to keep any follow-up hounds off his trail. The doc was his problem right from the get-go and he only made it worse by failing to kill him when he had the chance. That's on him. And I don't see the doc sticking around town with a suspected murder charge hanging over his head, so that for sure takes worryin' about him out of our hands. What that leaves us, for however long they decide to stick around Cheyenne, is to make sure the sister and her bunch don't somehow catch a whiff of where Drake headed with the girl. We do that, whatever might happen somewhere else ain't our problem."

Millen brightened up. "I like the sound of that. Hell, that means we're most of the way there. All we have to do is keep a tight watch on the sister and her crew to make sure they *don't* catch some kind of lucky whiff before they decide to give up and move on."

"That's right. But don't get too cocky." Remson glowered. "Watch 'em tight, but don't get caught doing it. Use Mojave if you have to, so you ain't spread too thin. And remember. If the stubborn bastards *do* stumble on something before they pull out . . . well, we'll have to go back to harder measures. Even if it includes the sister. That's the deal I made."

"Understood," Millen said in a grim tone. "I'll head out now and get a line on what they're up to. Where will you be?"

Remson grinned lewdly around the cigar stuck in his face. Scratching his sagging ball of a stomach, fingernails rasping through the bristly hairs, he said, "Think I'll go back in the other room for one more round of bed slat rattlin' before I return that skinny wench to Mamie for a trade in. I finish with that transaction, I'll look you up."

Chapter Seven

Freshly shaved and emerged from a long soak in a tub of hot, steaming water (recommended by Sue as a means to ease his stiffness and aches) Lone now sat astraddle a straight-backed wooden chair in his room at the Traveler's Rest hotel. He was dressed in his pants and boots but remained shirtless, arms folded across the top of the chair's backrest. Sue hovered behind him, ministering to the numerous welts and bruises that adorned his back with generous dollops of a liniment she had purchased from a local pharmacist. Johnny Case sat on the edge of the bed, looking on with his brow wrinkled sympathetically.

"Jesus God, man," Johnny muttered. "All those new markings sure had plenty of company already waiting for 'em. You got so many scars your hide looks like a map of rough country trails leading nowhere."

Lone replied wryly, "Since I don't have eyes in the back of my head—though, if I did, maybe I could have avoided gettin' some of those scars—I'll have to take your word for the accuracy of that charmin' description."

"Unfortunately," Sue said, "Johnny's description isn't exaggerated. At least not by much. Which makes me wonder—though I'm not asking for anything too detailed—if you got left so scarred up, what about those responsible?"

Facing away, so Sue couldn't see, a wolf's smile briefly touched Lone's mouth. "Let's just say that most of them who scarred me took on some scars of their own . . . only they ain't left walkin' around to show 'em off."

"Uh-huh. And right there makes for sufficient detail," Sue said.

As she continued applying the liniment, Lone marveled at how her deft touch was able to rub the concoction so deeply into even his tenderest bruises without increasing the discomfort. In fact, the application of the liniment coupled with the recommended hot bath (and also aided, less to Sue's approval, by some additional nips from Johnny's flask) actually had him feeling pretty damned decent. He announced as much as he reached for his shirt and began pulling it back on once Sue was finished with her treatment.

"It ain't quite noon yet, so we got a big chunk of the day left to keep pursuin' some of those thoughts I worried up in my jail cell," he said. "But first, I want to hear some more about that hunch you had, Johnny, the feelin' of somebody followin' you and Sue earlier."

During the time Lone spent returning to his hotel and arranging for the recommended (and now proven to be worthwhile) bath, Sue and Johnny had taken the opportunity to branch off and do a bit of checking based on some of the new information supplied by Deputy Brady. Sue had arrived in Cheyenne with a tintype she hoped might be useful in helping get a lead to her brother James. It was a photograph taken of James and Rosemary on their wedding day. Sue had folded it back to singularly display only James, the focus of her search. Finding his description already circulated all over town as a murder suspect, however, had negated any need for her to show the tintype as part of her inquiries. But now, with James taken flight minus any clue as to where— except a certainty it would somehow still be in pursuit of his errant wife—the thought occurred that getting a bead on Rosemary's destination might provide a roundabout way of catching up with James.

Since the tintype also showed an isolated vision of Rosemary on the back side of the fold, the hope was that showing this to the ticket clerk at the stage office might stir his memory more distinctly than merely the description of "a young, pretty, dark-haired girl." With any luck, maybe distinctly enough for him to recall the destination of whichever stagecoach she boarded. Unfortunately, the attempt didn't yield the hoped-for results. At least not in the short term. The ticket clerk was an old timer with barely any individual memory—except for once dishing out a ticket to "none other than Wild Bill

Hickock hisself"—of the hundreds of faces he'd seen come and go during his time on the job. He did offer a glimmer of hope, though, based on the date of the stage runs being asked about. Both the driver and the shotgun guard on the Denver-bound coach from that day were due to be coming back through again tomorrow morning. Since they tended to spend more time with and in closer proximity to their passengers, they might be able to say if they had transported the girl in the picture. Same would apply to the Laramie-bound crew from that date but they weren't due back around for two more days.

Sue and Johnny then brought this disappointing but not entirely empty result back to Lone, stopping on the way to pick up the liniment Sue had some past familiarity with. In the course of reporting their finding, Johnny mentioned the curious sensation he'd felt during much of the time they'd been out—that of someone watching, following them.

Hence, what Lone was wanting to hear more about now.

When the query was put to Johnny, he shifted somewhat uncomfortably on the edge of the bed. "Jeez, I don't know what more to say. It was a *feeling,* you know, like a current of air stirring the hairs on the back of your neck when everything else is still. It was something I first experienced during my badge-wearing days, when I sometimes got a hunch there was trouble brewing without knowing exactly why or what it might turn out to be. Sometimes it amounted to nothing. Other times—often enough so I learned not to ignore such a feeling when it came—it made me sharp, made me ready for when trouble did bust out."

"Only today," Lone said, "it wasn't necessarily a feeling of trouble in the air, but more just of havin' eyes on you. That it?"

"Yeah. Exactly. If I'd thought it held a hint of trouble or danger, I'd've said something to Sue right away and we would have hightailed it here pronto." Johnny scowled. "But it wasn't anything like that. It was just a sense of, like you said, eyes being on us. Somebody fogging us. But on the crowded streets of a strange town with nothing but the faces of strangers all around, I was damned if I could pick out who might be the source."

Sue regarded Lone. "You act as if you almost expected something like that."

"Didn't necessarily expect it," allowed Lone. "But, at the same time, it don't come as a surprise neither."

"Care to chew that a little finer?" said Johnny.

"It all fits with that notion I brewed up while I was behind bars." Lone finished buckling on his gun belt and felt whole again. The hot bath and Sue's liniment had served their intended purposes well, but the weight of his Colt and Bowie knife had its own soothing effect. "What it boils down to," the former scout continued, "is that I think Earl Drake might have salted Cheyenne with a handful of hombres left in place to make sure nobody'd be able to follow on the tail of him and Rosemary once they left here."

He let that much sink in, then went on. "Way I figure, those three who ambushed me in the street amounted to the first round of what you might call, er, discouragers. They weren't out to rob me or kill me but, like I heard one of 'em say, they figured to hogtie me and haul me off somewhere. That would have left Sue wonderin' and frettin' about what happened and, they hoped, startin' to have second thoughts about the whole business of chasin' after her brother."

"Discouraging me, in other words," said Sue, starting to follow Lone's line of thought. "Which, if I gave up, would mean also turning away from any related pursuit of Rosemary and Drake."

Lone nodded. "That'd be the main thing they're after—if my speculatin' is right."

"But, if that's the case, why *didn't* they just kill you?" asked Johnny. "That would have discouraged you permanent-like, not to mention giving Sue a pretty powerful nudge to back off."

"Only thing I can figure," said Lone, "is that they wanted to avoid another killing, especially so close to where Chico got it, for the sake of not pullin' the law deeper in. Two killings in the space of just a few days would be bound to draw a lot of attention. And more attention would add to the risk of something splashin' over that could attach to Drake. The last thing he wants."

Johnny frowned. "I guess that could explain it. But it still leaves James. Drake has got to know by now that, first and foremost, James is the one most directly committed and least likely to be discouraged from catching up with his wife."

"That's right," Lone agreed. "But he's also got to know that, with Chico out of the way, James is only one man. And a man hampered by havin' a murder charge doggin' him. I'm guessin' Drake must see it as bein' stuck with James comin' after 'em, but figurin' he can handle it if and when the time comes. Gettin' us scraped off his back trail is aimed at keepin' it narrowed to only that . . . again, if my speculatin' is right."

"Maybe there's another reason for Drake concentrating on us but not worrying so much about James."

Something in Sue's tone caused both Lone and Johnny to cut sharp gazes in her direction.

"Maybe the wicked bastard has already done something to James!"

"Don't go there, Sue. Don't do that to yourself," Johnny was quick to say.

"Johnny's right," Lone seconded. "There's every reason to believe James made good his getaway—from both the law *and* Drake. Don't mean he won't come back around and try to pick up his wife's trail again. But, for now, James is too smart not to just lay low for a while."

"When it comes to that faithless wife of his," Sue argued, "James's ability to act smart is too often sadly lacking."

Lone set his jaw. "Alright then, think of it this way: If Drake already has removed James from his tail, why wouldn't he make sure you knew? Way he'd look at it, what better way to make certain you were discouraged from continuin' on?"

"Then he doesn't know me very well, does he?" Sue's eyes blazed. "If James were to end up dead out of all this, the last thing I would ever do is abandon my commitment to seeing everyone even remotely responsible burn in Hell!"

"Which brings us back to the 'remote' varmints I figure Drake left behind to get in our way," said Lone. "If we can single out one of 'em, then we might be able to use him to make Drake's precaution backfire on him."

"How? What have you got in mind?" Johnny wanted to know.

"Just what I said. We need to figure out a way to flush out one of Drake's discouragers."

"You figure there's more than just the three who jumped you last night?"

"I think there could be, yeah." Lone scowled in

thought. "Those three were set up and ready for me, almost like they knew ahead of time I was headed for the Dust Cutter. The only person I gave any indication to about goin' there, though, was the old Irish gent, O'Feeney, who was on the desk downstairs. I asked him directions and set off straightaway. So even if he blabbed, those three would have had to scramble like hell to get in place ahead of me."

"If they're locals, it's their town and their streets," Sue pointed out. "That could explain them being familiar with some short cuts to get in front of you. As far as knowing your intentions, it *could* have been the desk clerk passing the word . . . or maybe one of the three was lurking close by in the lobby—you know, watching you the way Johnny felt somebody shadowing us a little while ago—and overheard you asking directions."

"Either way," said Johnny, "in order for them to move that fast it almost sounds like they were already primed and figuring to make some kind of move on you. If you hadn't gone out, you might have ended up with some visitors to your hotel room before the night was over."

"But why all the sudden interest in Lone?" Sue asked. "I mean, I've been in town for going on three days now, asking questions everywhere I went, yet I never ran into anybody trying to overtly chase me off. And same goes for you too, Johnny, since you were—"

111

Johnny cut her off, saying, "But nobody knew I had any connection to you, remember? Not even you. Meaning I posed no threat as somebody looking to pick up either James's or Drake's trail. Not until I put an end to all that by causing the scene on the stairway at the Ignacious. I not only exposed myself but McGantry too." Johnny paused, his expression turning sour. "Worse still, after that I was bitter enough and angry enough to spew to Muldoon, the security man, plenty of what I knew about Lone's past as a scout and a hardcase. In other words, I made him sound like exactly the kind of person Drake would want scraped off his trail."

"Johnny!" admonished Sue.

Lone cocked an eyebrow. "Good thing you came along to save my bacon on that street corner last night else I *might* decide to feel riled toward you."

"Couldn't hardly blame you if you did," Johnny responded. "And if what I just owned up to changes your mind about keeping me around . . . well, I guess I couldn't blame you for that either."

"Forget it. That ain't happenin'," Lone snapped. "You're in, and we got too much ground to cover for you to duck out now."

Johnny's mouth pressed tight. "Fine by me. I ain't going nowhere except to cover whatever ground you got in mind."

"Okay. We're gonna need to split up," Lone said. "Johnny, I want you to find O'Feeney the night clerk. He ain't on duty now so you'll have to get the information on where to find him—at home or wherever—from the day man. Don't take no for an answer, if you know what I mean. My gut says O'Feeney ain't dirty in this, but I want to make sure. Lean on him as much as you have to until you're sure he's tellin' you straight. Understand?"

"Got it."

Lone turned to Sue. "I suppose you wouldn't agree to returnin' to your hotel room and just waitin' there for a while, would you?"

"You suppose correctly. Who do you want me to go lean on?"

Lone grinned. "You would, too. Wouldn't you?"

"Try me."

"You're not going to let her go out on her own, are you?" said Johnny.

Lone cut him a sidelong glance. "You want to be the one to try and stop her?" Not waiting for an answer, he brought his eyes back to Sue and asked, "You packin' anything to protect yourself?"

Sue was wearing a wide, large-buckled leather belt cinched around her waist, flowing skirt below and snug-fitting blouse tucked in at the top. Silently, she reached to the small of her back and withdrew from behind the belt a large bore over/under two-shot derringer. She held this up for Lone and Johnny to see. "I realize this is only a close-range weapon, but both barrels carry .44 caliber loads that mean business. For good measure, I have the twin to this in my right boot."

"Okay," Lone said under lifted brows. "What I got in mind for you hopefully won't call for any lead slingin'. But it's good to know you're prepared in case something unexpected pops up."

"So what do you have in mind for me?"

"Somewhere out yonder is a fella, one of the ones who jumped me, with one eye half gouged out." Lone ignored Sue's involuntary wince and continued explaining. "While him and me was exchangin' pleasantries, his eye sorta got in the way of my thumb. I think it might've been damaged bad enough for him to need a doctor. I don't know how many sawbones there are in Cheyenne. But not so many, I don't figure, that you can't locate 'em and pay a visit to see if any have treated a patient last night or this morning with that particular misery."

"Even if one has, a patient's treatment is con-sidered private information not subject to being freely shared," Sue told him.

"See? That's why you're so right for the job," Lone said. "You know the policies and you speak the lingo. You're also pretty and you're determined. Those can be weapons almost as powerful as your two popguns. So how about this—can you work up some kind of act like bein' a tearful girlfriend or some such who just heard her man was in a terrible brawl and near lost his eye but you don't know where he was taken and all you want to do is see if he's okay? Think you could manage something like that to at least determine *if* the varmint saw a doctor? If he did and we know which doc, that might narrow down where we'll have a chance to find ol' One-Eye himself."

"Even if it means having to lean on the doctor?" Sue asked with a touch of distaste in her tone.

"How bad do you want to find your brother?" Lone countered. "I thought you were willin' to do whatever it took."

He let those words hang in the air, said no more.

Until Sue expelled a ragged sigh. "Okay. You're right. I'm not much at turning on the waterworks, but I'll come up with some kind of desperate tale and do everything I can to find out something."

"I know you will," Lone told her.

"What about you, Lone?" asked Johnny. "While Sue and I are running those checks, what are your plans?"

"I'm headed back to the Dust Cutter," Lone answered. "I got a hunch that Homer, the old relic who owns and runs the joint, knows a thing or two about practically everything that goes on in this town. For starters, I got a couple names I want to run by him. Cleve and Mojave—that's what one of my ambushers called the other two. I want to see if they mean anything to Homer."

"I tried talking to that old man right after I got to town, and he was barely willing to give me the time of day," said Sue. "What makes you think he'll cooperate any better with you? And he's such an ancient bag of bones you surely can't afford to be rough with him—he'll splinter like a handful of dry twigs."

"I didn't have any luck with that old goat either," muttered Johnny.

"You're forgettin' he already showed some cooperation when I talked with him last night. Not to mention," Lone added with a grin, "how you're also failin' to give me credit for the warm, charmin' way I have with folks in general."

"Unless their eyeball gets in the way of your thumb," Sue said dryly.

Lone ignored that. "Like I said, I'll toss out my names to Homer and see where it goes."

Grimacing, Johnny said, "Speaking of names—and much as I hate to bring this up again—there's one more that nobody has mentioned yet but one I think we for sure have to give some consideration. I'm talking about Muldoon, the Ignacious security man. It was him I shot my mouth off to after our run-in on the stairway, remember? And that's what seems to have triggered all this discouragement business. Am I wrong?"

"No, I've had the same thought," Lone conceded. "We know that Drake and Rosemary stayed at the Ignacious when they got to town. Which is why you and Sue also chose it. So Drake and Muldoon clearly crossed paths. And Deputy Brady told me how Drake has spent time here in town before, when he was workin' for that detective outfit. Brady called him sleazy and dangerous and even had suspicions about him, but nothing he could even prove."

"So Drake and Muldoon could have had past dealings."

"Uh-huh. I'm guessin' they probably did." Lone paused, his brows pinching together. "But Muldoon is positioned in a way that makes him hard to take a straight-on run at. For now anyway. But if we can flush out one of my ambushers and get him to squeal, then that could give us a lever to commence some pryin' on Muldoon next."

"This is all starting to sound far removed from finding my brother," said Sue, musing aloud. "I have to keep reminding myself that it's geared toward tracking down Drake and Rosemary and then counting on James showing up there too."

"I understand how it must seem like the long way around the barn," Lone allowed. "But I don't see anything else for us to try and grab hold of."

"I know. I don't either." Sue gazed at him

trustingly. "Let's get on with what you've outlined. I'm confident it *will* result in something we can grab hold of."

Lone heaved a sigh. "Okay. But one last thing . . . another name. Deputy Arn Remson, the so-and-so who barged in and laid me out at the Dust Cutter. Brady warned me to watch out for him on account of him likely bein' sore I made bail so quick. But I think there might be even more reason."

"What do you mean?" said Johnny.

Lone made a gesture. "Think on it. There was a gap of time, when we went to that German restaurant, between those ambushers gettin' chased off and Remson showin' up at the Cutter. Plenty of time to report that the ambush had failed and I was still on the prowl. So if I wasn't taken out of circulation by the ambush, how about gettin' it done by throwin' me in the clink for a while?"

"Good Lord!" Sue exclaimed. "If you're thinking Remson is also a part of trying to turn us away, then does Drake have this whole damn town in his pocket?"

"All I know is that Remson all of a sudden showin' up at the Cutter and clubbin' me down for no reason—then jailing me and coverin' it up with a whole stack of phony charges—is damned fishy. Brady warned me about him for reasons he saw. I got a hunch that fat slob Remson may have motives Brady don't begin to know about."

"In case nobody but me has noticed, this thing is adding up bigger and bigger," declared Johnny. "All these hombres working to hide Drake's trail and him being so all-fired determined to drag Rosemary back with him in the first place . . . ask me, that starts to seem like something more than just a fella having a hankering for a certain woman. And so many others involved speaks of somebody with money to spread around. More money than you'd figure a sleazy private detective would have. Could it be there's somebody behind the scenes who *hired* Drake to fetch back Rosemary?"

"Good Lord, Johnny!" admonished Sue. "That sounds like drivel straight out of a penny dreadful."

"I can't help it. I got one of those feelings again—about a whole heap of trouble brewing due to something we don't fully understand."

"Well something I do understand," said Lone, "is that the way to stop a thing from brewin' too strong and threatenin' to boil over, is to stomp out the fire heatin' it up. So the sooner we're able to flush out some of those discouragers Drake left behind and then put the squeeze on 'em, the better chance we got of gettin' pointed toward whatever it is he's wantin' so bad to hide. Let's get to work."

Chapter Eight

"So that was you too, eh? I'll be damned. Talk started dribblin' in a little before closing time about a ruckus down the street that left a couple fellas awful tore up. But I didn't make the tie-in to more of your work." Homer cocked his head and eyed Lone shrewdly. "How is it you didn't make no mention of gettin' bushwhacked when you first showed up here last night?"

"Because, at that point, I hadn't realized it was connected to what I came to talk about. Didn't want to muddy things by bringin' up too much at one time," Lone explained.

"Reckon that makes a certain amount of sense," allowed Homer.

It was quiet in the Dust Cutter. Though Lone had gained entrance after insistently banging on the front door, it would be another half hour before the saloon was officially open for the day's business. Homer was on hand, not surprisingly, getting things ready behind the bar. Two of his bar maids (neither of them Minnie, Lone was quick to note) were also present, laying out a spread of bread, cold-cut meats, sliced cheese, and pickled eggs to entice noontime drinkers.

When Lone bellied up to the bar he opted for a cup of coffee over anything stronger for the time being. He didn't object, however, to having a splash of good Irish whiskey added to it.

"So how is it," Homer went on to ask, "you now reckon the skunks who ambushed you had anything to do with that other business?"

"Let's just say I have my reasons for suspectin' it. That's why," Lone said, "I'd like to have another chat with one of those skunks—to see if my suspicions hold water."

Homer grunted. "From what I've seen and heard, your way of chatting with hombres don't hardly leave *them* able to hold water."

"If you mean that drunk cowboy in here last night, I did everything I could to ease him down. When he was bound and determined to push it, I wasn't in no mood to stand and trade punches with him. Not after those jackasses out in the street had already—"

"Take it easy," the old barkeep interrupted. "I ain't blamin' or sayin' you did nothing wrong. I was just makin' an observation is all. No need to be so touchy."

"If you had the knots and bruises I'm carryin' around this morning, you'd be a mite touchy too," Lone grumbled. "Not to mention the cracked skull and night spent on a torture rack they call a cot at your local jail—courtesy of that lard-assed deputy who marched in here and pistol-whipped me for no good reason."

Homer's expression soured. "Yeah. Arn Remson." His mouth twisted as if saying the name left a bad taste. Then he added, "I hope you ain't wanting to have no 'chat' with him. He's bad news, Mac. Take my advice and steer as far clear of him as you can."

Lone took a drink of his coffee, scowling as he lowered the cup. "Yeah, I already got that message. Ain't sayin' I like it, but I'll keep it in mind as best I can. No way that holds for the rest though. So how about those names I laid out for you? What can you tell me?"

Now it was Homer's turn to scowl. "What I'd *like* to tell you is that I don't know nothing about 'em . . . but I ain't got it in me to look the other way. Not this time. You might be the one who took that rap on the head from Remson, but in my own way I felt it too."

Lone found that a mighty curious statement. But he made no comment, just waited for the old man to continue.

"Up to now, you see," Homer went on, "Remson and his thugs have left this part of town mostly alone. Wasn't enough money to be made here from the shakedowns and other low schemes they're able to pull elsewhere. Plus, it's Deputy Brady who works our area on a regular basis. Him and Remson don't like each other none, and it sticks particularly tight in Remson's craw that Brady ain't intimidated by him."

"So what made Remson show up here last

night?" Lone wanted to know. "That's one more reason makes me think this whole stinkin' tangle of me gettin' ambushed and then Fatso hornin' in—and maybe even the business behind Chico gettin' gunned—might be somehow tied together."

"That's a powerful wide swipe. But I can't say it ain't possible," Homer conceded. "The part about Remson bargin' in like he did is the gob of glue that sorta makes it hang together. Can't see no other reason for him comin' around that way. The scuffle between you and Clint Bafford sure wasn't enough to draw his attention. But what you did to Cleve and Mojave—that'd be Cleve Boyer and Mojave Jones, to put full handles to 'em—might be a different matter. Especially if Remson knew ahead of time about their plan to bushwhack you."

"So who *are* Cleve and Mojave? And what's their tie to Remson?"

Homer ran a gnarled hand back over his bald crown and glanced around somewhat uneasily before saying, "The short answer is that they're a couple of lowlife scuts who scrounge around doin' the least amount of work they can to get by. And if the work that comes their way ain't exactly on the up and up, that's no never mind t' 'em 'cause it likely pays a little better than actual labor. As far as their tie to Remson, it's long been rumored—rumored, mind you, never proved—

that he uses 'em regular-like to take care of dirty dealings he don't want to directly handle himself."

"Like what?"

Homer's head wagged firmly. "Oh no. That I ain't goin' into. You want loose talk on such, there's plenty of other places you can go scrounge for it. Like I already told you, havin' Remson show up here last night and wallop you was as close as I want to come to him feelin' he has cause to come around anymore. I'm on your side, hoss, but not to the point of gettin' my own head cracked like an eggshell. I've likely said too much as it is."

"What about my third ambusher?" Lone asked. "Any idea who he might have been?"

"Man, you're really tryin' to crowd me into a corner, ain't you?"

Lone just glared expectantly at him.

"All right, damn you," Homer spat. "Most likely it would've been Tate Millen. For lack of a better description, he's sorta the brains of that sorry trio when they ain't hoppin' to some chore for Remson."

"Cleve and Mojave I figure I'll be able to spot by the damage I did to 'em," Lone said. "What does Millen look like?"

"Jesus! You want me to take you around and make formal introductions?" Homer wailed.

"Just tell me what to look for, damn it."

124

"Okay. He's short and muscular. A short man who tries to swagger big, if you get what I mean. Pale hair goin' thin, almost pure white eyebrows. The eyebrows, that's the thing about him that sorta stands out."

Lone nodded. "Good. Now I got two more names to run by you, then I'll leave you be . . . Muldoon, the security man at the Ignacious Hotel. And a fella called Drake; Earl Drake. Used to be a detective for an agency out of Denver but I'm told he may be workin' on his own these days. Either way, according to Deputy Brady, he's passed through Cheyenne quite a few times. What can you tell me about either of 'em?"

"Muldoon is easy enough to speak on," said Homer. "Up until a few years ago, he was a regular in this part of town. Did his drinkin' in the saloons, even worked as a bouncer in a couple of 'em. But after he got that job at the Ignacious—which, rumors again, some say Arn Remson had a hand in—Muldoon turned kinda uppity. Don't come around this neighborhood no more. But, from what I hear tell, he still stays in practice knockin' heads at the Ignacious if any guests get out of line."

"Why would Remson take an interest in Muldoon gettin' hired at the hotel?"

"That you'd have to ask one of them. I don't know even any rumors to offer on that part."

"And Drake?"

Homer shrugged. "Heard the name, heard how he was some kind of detective who worked cases that sometimes chafed the law. Don't know much else. Except, as you likely already know on account of your askin' about him, after Chico got gunned there was talk that Drake had something to do with the runaway wife that Chico and the doc who was her husband were chasin' after."

Lone swirled the remainder of tepid coffee left in his cup for a moment before raising it and tossing it down. Lowering the emptied cup, he said, "So where might I find Cleve and Mojave in order to have my chat with 'em?"

"You said you'd be done after askin' about those last two names," Homer protested.

"I am done askin' about *names*. This is different. Now where do Cleve and Mojave kick off their boots when they ain't usin' 'em to gang stomp their bushwhack victims?"

Suddenly, startlingly, Sue Leonard realized that the odd sensation she was experiencing was exactly the kind of thing Johnny had tried explaining about—a feeling of being *watched*. Of having eyes following her every move. Was she imagining it? Was it perhaps a false worry brought on by nerves, by being off on her own after hearing the talk of such a thing and then all the other talk of "discouragers" and the rest?

But no, Sue was hardly someone given to

fragile nerves or having her imagination stirred into false concerns. And as far as being off on her own, she had *started* this whole venture on her own. True, she had solicited the aid of Lone and had now also accepted the inclusion of Johnny, but that didn't make her totally reliant on them and suddenly fretful in their absence. Damn it, somebody *was* following her, watching her as she moved about the streets of Cheyenne. Of that she was certain. Though it was something to be concerned about and vigilant of, it made her more angry than fearful. And it sure as blazes wasn't a development that was going to make her cut short the assignment she'd been given. Accompanied by her .44 caliber friends—the derringer at the small of her back and the one in her boot— she felt quite prepared to finish checking with the town's doctors.

Sue had started at the offices of the Cheyenne Gazette newspaper. There, under the cover story of being new in town and wanting to get established with a family physician, she had been given the names and addresses of the town's three doctors. So far she had called on two of them. Although she had encountered the expected barrier of at first being denied discussion of any recent patients, her distraught wailing and pleading of just wanting to know if there was any truth to reports of injuries suffered by her estranged yet beloved husband proved convincing enough to earn her assurance that no such victim had been seen at either facility.

Somewhat to her surprise, Sue discovered that employing such histrionics—spun from the ideas initially suggested by Lone that so sharply contrasted anything in her true nature—turned out to be kind of fun. Not to discount the serious considerations behind it all, which none were more keenly aware of than Sue, but it was nevertheless an exercise that at least momentarily diverted some of the grimness.

Until she became aware that she was being followed. Then Sue's resolve turned very grim and focused. The only question was, what should she do if she were able to actually *spot* whoever it was shadowing her? Trying to take some action against him by herself, she realized, seemed unwise. On the other hand, the whole point of the checks Lone had identified for himself, Johnny, and her to make were geared toward "flushing out" one of the discouragers for the purpose of hoping to learn where Drake and Rosemary were headed. Given that, should Sue be given the chance to isolate and confront her follower, maybe it *wouldn't* be so unwise to take a risk and seize the opportunity . . .

Arn Remson had just exited Madam Mamie's bordello on Flower Street. He was coming down the front steps of the tall, pink-trimmed Victorian structure, wearing a smug smile and puffing on a fat, fresh cigar. The smile abruptly faded and the cigar drooped downward as Remson's gaze swept up the street and he saw Tate Millen hurrying in his direction with a troubled look on his face.

"Now what the hell," Remson muttered under his breath.

It didn't take long for Millen to get to it. Drawing near, breathing a bit heavily due to the quickened pace that brought him here, he said, "Boy, I'm glad to have caught up with you, Arn. Especially not having had to interrupt you—you know, while you were still inside."

"Why the need to interrupt me at all?" Remson growled. "I told you I'd look you up when I finished my dealings with Mamie."

"Yeah, I know. You also told me to keep a tight watch on that Leonard woman and those hombres now helping her," Millen pointed out. "Well, that's the thing. The problem. It's turning out to be mighty tough keeping an eye on 'em when they've split up and are swarming all over different parts of town."

"What do you mean 'swarming all over'?"

"Just what I said. The woman struck out one way, McGantry another, and that Case fella ducked off somewhere too, I couldn't tell which direction." Millen made a quick, jerky motion with one hand. "I quick-like got hold of Mojave and sent him to dog the woman while I went after

McGantry. Cleve is still laid up at Quincannon's, not fit to pitch in at all."

"So why ain't you still on McGantry now?"

"Because I know where he is and I expect he'll be there a spell," answered Mullen. "So, since it's only a couple blocks away, I figured I'd make a quick jump over to try and catch you here. Let you know what's going on."

"So where *is* McGantry?" Remson wanted to know.

"The Dust Cutter. Old Homer ain't even open for business yet, but McGantry managed to talk his way inside anyway."

"What the hell reason would he have for going back there again?" Remson scowled and puffed furiously on his cigar. "That damned Homer. He's older than dirt, been around forever. Sees and hears way too much. Plus he's half-assed pals with Brady, thinks it gives him some kind of special privilege even though he ain't nothing but a lousy saloon owner in a shit part of town. But still, like I said, he has a way of catchin' whiffs of most everything that goes on all around town."

Millen's forehead puckered. "Yeah, but there ain't no way he could know anything about where Drake and the girl headed for . . . is there?"

"It don't seem like it. But if anybody could, it'd be that old bastard." Remson's scowl deepened. "I've thought more than once about pinchin' off his goddamn wick that has burned too long. Now might be a good time to finally get around to it. It'd send a message to that nosy Leonard cow and her crew . . . and maybe to that meddlin' cuss Brady as well. If he'd have left McGantry in a stinkin' jail cell like I had him, I doubt any of this would be takin' place."

"So we're going over to the Dust Cutter now?"

Remson glared at him. "Not 'we'—just me. I'll do what needs doin'. Maybe I'll be lucky enough to catch McGantry still there too. In the meantime, you run down Mojave again and see what the woman's been up to. Then, soon as you can, get a bead on that other fella, that Casey rascal to find out what he's been up to. Use Muldoon if you have to, since Cleve ain't of no use."

"Jeez, I don't know," said Millen, looking uncertain. "Might be hard to budge Muldoon away from the Ignacious just on my say-so. You know how doggone stubborn he can be."

"If you need him and he gives you any sass," growled Remson, "you damn quick remind him what-all is at stake here. If this whole Crawford thing pans out, we'll all be sittin' fine as princes not too far down the road. But if Muldoon don't want to do his part—especially since he had the woman and Case stayin' right there under his nose—tell him I'll see to it he won't *ever* have to budge away from the Ignacious and he can stay behind and rot there when the rest of us move on!"

"Okay, okay. I'll handle it," said Millen.

"See that you do." Remson paused to look longingly back over his shoulder at Madam Mamie's place. "I made a new deal with Mamie and, come evenin', I got a new belly warmer due to show up at my place. She's a Jamaica mama with teats the size of grain sacks and a pair of thighs like the drumsticks you'd dream of gettin' off a prize turkey. I want to be home to enjoy her as soon as she gets there and I don't want none of this troublesome business lingerin' to get in the way of my full attention. Understand? Now hop to it so we can get this cleared up and done with!"

Chapter Nine

Sue Leonard's resolve was now beginning to waver somewhat. Results at the third and supposedly final doctor she visited had turned out the same. Which was to say she was initially denied any specific patient details—until her distressed pleading with a nurse and receptionist finally caused them to relent enough to assure her that no one fitting her inquiry had been treated there. Having once again determined at least that much, she was on her way out the door when an elderly lady seated in the waiting area stopped her.

In a conspiratorial whisper, the lady said, "The kind of situation and injuries you're describing, dearie, sounds like something that might more likely be brought to the attention of Doc Quincannon rather than these better established practitioners. Have you checked with him?"

"Quincannon?" Sue echoed. "I've checked with all the other doctors in town. But I don't recognize that name. Who is he?"

Maintaining her secretive whisper in spite of a disapproving frown being aimed her way by the receptionist, the lady explained, "Quincannon is a former Confederate medic who is shunned by much of the community in general and the other town doctors in particular. They have their reasons and I'm not one to say they aren't justified. But nevertheless, Quincannon does perform a service to the sick and injured, folks who are down on their luck and living more on the fringe of things. No offense, but it sounds like your man might fit that category and therefore perhaps was directed to Quincannon for the care he needed."

"Yes. Perhaps," said Sue, her mind racing, thinking that the medic the woman was describing sounded very much like someone an injured ambushing skunk might seek out. "Where can I find this Dr. Quincannon?"

The old woman didn't know the exact address but she was able to provide a street name and the general section of town where she'd been given to believe Quincannon could be found. Once in the neighborhood, she suggested, Sue ought to be able to inquire among the locals and be guided the rest of the way.

Feeling a renewed sense of hope that she might yet be able to turn up something worthwhile, Sue set out in search of the lesser-known doctor described by the old woman. Somewhere out toward the west end of Yucca Street, she'd been told, was where she would find him. What hadn't been mentioned—possibly, to give the benefit of doubt, something the woman may not have known—was that as Yucca Street stretched farther to the west it became increasingly more run down as far as the condition of the buildings lining it with no shortage of rough-looking characters coming in and out of them. The warning, Sue realized, should have been in the reference to these as being "folks down on their luck and living more on the fringe of things."

At any rate, she had now ventured into their midst and, despite her wavering resolve, was too stubborn to call it off and turn back. Of greater concern, frankly, was the "shadow" that had previously attached himself to her in the more established part of town. She had by now identified him with certainty—a quick-moving, average-sized individual with stringy black hair and a coppery hue to his features that indicated he had some Indian blood in him. At the moment, however, more distinct than his native coloring was the bluish-purple stain of two blackened eyes and the unnatural swelling and tightness of a nose that Sue's medical training recognized as having been recently broken and its nostrils stuffed with cotton. Though this clearly wasn't the one who'd ended up with a gouged eye from the attack on Lone, Sue strongly suspected her shadow might be one of the other two who had participated and paid a price for choosing the wrong victim. Which made his attention to her now all the more ominous. Was he stalking her as a means to try and get some revenge on Lone?

Sue weighed her options for how best to

proceed. She had to believe that if this Doc Quincannon was truly a healer and caregiver of any note then he ought to also be a source of aid if she convinced him she was in danger. For this reason, as well as her stubborn pride, she continued on. Another elderly woman, emerging from the doorway of a bakery just ahead, struck her as a safe enough local resident to make an inquiry of. The woman was stoop-backed and wrapped in a threadbare shawl, carrying a small straw basket with the noses of two cloth-draped loaves of bread poking out of it.

Sue spoke to her, saying, "Pardon me, grand-mother."

The woman's face whipped around and a pair of tiny dark eyes flashed fiercely out at Sue. "Who you calling 'grandmother,' you impertinent brat? I ain't your grandmother—I ain't no brat's grandmother!"

"I-I'm sorry," stammered Sue. "I only wanted to—"

"I don't care what you wanted! Quit bothering me." The old woman suddenly clutched the basket tight within the wrap of her shawl and wailed, "Don't you dare try to take my bread either! It's mine and you can't have any!"

Sue's mouth hung open, so shocked by this reaction she didn't know what to say. Before she could find any words, the bakery door popped open again and a plump, balding man in a flour-dusted apron came hurrying out. He spoke soothingly to the excited woman. "Muriel, Muriel. Calm down, dear, everything is all right."

"That little brat tried to take my bread!" Muriel exclaimed, her flashing eyes still aimed at Sue. Then, her bottom lip thrusting out like that of a pouting child, she added, "But I won't let her have any. She's a stingy, mean brat, I can tell!"

"It's all right now, Muriel," the man assured her. "I won't let the lady take your bread. You go on home, everything will be fine."

Muriel obediently turned and started away. But over her shoulder she said, "You tell her to stay away from me. I need my daily bread giveth to me, the Lord says so!"

As she moved out of earshot, the plump man turned to Sue with a sheepish grin. "Sorry about that. Muriel is really quite harmless. She's just, ah . . . just . . ."

"Just very fond and protective of her bread," Sue finished for him, smiling.

"Okay. We'll go with that." The baker's grin took on a wry twist. "I try to keep an eye on her but stuff like this still happens every once in a while. She lives just around the corner, she'll be okay now. To be fair, she doesn't have much so the loaves of no longer fresh bread I let her have for a few pennies so she won't see it as charity are kinda important to her."

"I understand. You're a good neighbor," Sue told him.

"I'm also a heck of a good baker. I'd invite you in to sample my wares, but I have a strong hunch you did not come to this part of town—where you clearly do not belong, if you'll pardon my saying—seeking the taste treats from Margelino's oven."

"That may be true," Sue granted. "But only because I was regrettably unaware that such existed. But now that I do—"

"Now that you do," Margelino cut her off somewhat gruffly, "you still need to get yourself out of this place before *you* become a tasty treat for one or more of the, er, unsavory types who roam the streets hereabouts, especially with evening not far off. Excuse the unpleasant picture that might paint, but facts are facts. What the devil is a lady like you doing on Yucca Street anyway?"

"Right about now I'm asking myself that same question," Sue admitted. "I came looking for a doctor by the name of Quincannon. I wasn't given an exact address but I was told—"

"So that's it," Margelino declared, interrupting her again. "I should have known. Doggone careless gals and the gutless men who won't stand by them! By the look of you it can't be much, but how far along are you?"

Sue was now totally baffled. "What are you

talking about? How far along toward where? I told you I came looking for Dr. Quincannon. I was trying to ask that lady, Muriel, for directions."

"I understand that. I also understand why young girls like you seek out Doc Quincannon. But it's not my place to judge. Nor do I mean to impose where I'm not wanted. I just don't want to see you harmed any farther."

Sue's bewilderment made her once again momentarily speechless. Until, abruptly, she realized what was being implied. "Good grief, Mr. Margelino!" she exclaimed. "If you're suggesting I am with child and that I came here looking to . . . you are very wrong and very rude in your assumptions!"

Now it was Margelino who was stunned into momentary silence. When he found his voice, he said, "If you are not here because of . . . well, what I thought . . . I terribly regret rushing to a wrong conclusion, miss. Please accept my apology. It's just that, in the past whenever a young woman such as yourself came around looking for Quincannon it was always only for . . . well, never mind that now. Again, please accept my apology."

Sue regarded him sharply for a long moment. His earnest expression and the sincerity in his voice won her over. Plus, his was the only thing resembling a friendly face she had seen for some time. The handful of people passing them by as they stood talking showed nothing more than sullen indifference. "Very well," she said to the baker. "I guess you can't help it if past experiences have conditioned you to expect a certain outcome. I accept your apology. But I am still in need of directions for finding Dr. Quincannon."

"In that case," Margelino replied, "in addition to my apology I hope you will accept my offer to personally show you the way. It is only a few more blocks but I would feel better if I accompanied you."

"Why are you going out of your way to be so nice to me?"

Margelino spread his hands. "Because it is as I said at the outset. No matter your business here, I can tell you are the type of young lady who does not belong on this end of Yucca Street. So I am concerned for your well-being while you are here."

"That's very gallant of you," said Sue. "But, feeling the way you do about this area, may I ask why you yourself remain a part of it?"

"Because," Margelino answered with a faint smile and a *what-can-I-say?* hand gesture, "I am a stubborn Italian. My beloved late wife and I opened this bakery nearly twenty years ago, before the neighborhood turned bad. Now she and our blessed daughter are buried in a small nearby cemetery, where I will one day rest beside them. Until then, I will stay here and do what I do and show that one does not *have* to be something less even when things around you go on a downward slide."

By the time he was finished speaking, Sue was aiming an admiring smile at him. She said, "It would be my honor, sir, to have you accompany me. But what about your shop?"

"Don't worry. I have trusted people who will take care of it while I'm away," Margelino assured her. "Come then, let us go find the doctor."

As they began walking, Sue said, "With you being so much help, I feel I owe you an explanation for why I *am* wanting to see Dr. Quincannon."

"Only if you wish. My motives—to see you safely come and gone—remain the same, regardless."

Despite this stated disinterest, Sue nevertheless related to him the fabricated story she'd been using elsewhere, about checking out a vague report of serious injuries sustained by her estranged husband. She finished by saying, "One of the reasons we separated is because he took to hanging out with the kind of crowd that was sure to be the cause of him getting hurt or in trouble. Or both. Should he truly be badly injured, what kind of healer is this Quincannon . . . I mean, in view of the other things you've indicated he dabbles in?"

Margelino pursed his lips thoughtfully before responding. "I can't say I approve of many of Quincannon's professional or personal practices. But, at the same time, he does provide services to citizens of Yucca Street they would otherwise suffer without. I have to give him that."

They left it at that for the remainder of their walk.

At fifty-seven years old, Sylvester Quincannon was a former Southern aristocrat who had grown deeply disillusioned and bitter toward the world in general and his life in particular. The failure of the Confederacy, to which he had committed himself wholly, was the beginning of his soured outlook. Then came the loss of all his family holdings in the aftermath of the war, followed by the rebuke of the woman he loved who no longer had use for a penniless man without prospects. Ensuing years of drifting, drinking, feeling sorry for himself and drinking even more to dull his remorse unfolded next. Until he ended up here on Yucca Street in Cheyenne, Wyoming. The only thing that allowed him to hold his head up any degree of dignity at all, when the rotgut didn't have it hopelessly drooped, was telling himself that here he was at least able to put his medical training to some use. Yes, his clientele were low class and often at odds with the law, but his practice was still of noble ilk and he himself was doing nothing illegal . . . well, except for performing the occasional abortion. But even that, he justified, was a needed and necessary service that saved the ruination of young maidens who didn't deserve to have their lives shattered by a moment of emotional weakness. And the payment for performing those deeds, usually backed by prominent families seeking to avoid scandal, helped finance the treatment he was able to give the downtrodden of Yucca Street who often had little in the way of paying for themselves.

Existing for some time now on these flimsy remnants of pride and self-worth, this afternoon Quincannon suddenly found himself faced with the prospect of possibly having to abandon even that thin veneer.

"Goddamn it," Mojave Jones hissed impatiently, with his battered face shoved close to Quincannon's. "This is something that might matter big to Remson. You understand? Do I have to tell you how much you do *not* want to piss off Remson by refusing to help?"

"I-I'm not refusing anything," Quincannon stammered. "I just don't understand what I'm supposed to do . . . what I *can* do."

"I told you plain enough," Mojave insisted. "The woman and those helping her have been a thorn in our asses ever since she came to town.

Now she's on her way here, gonna show up any minute. I don't know why, what exactly she's up to, but the fact she's looking for you at all don't seem like a good sign to me. I think Remson will want to know about it. So all I need from you is to make sure you keep the bitch here, once she shows up, long enough for me to go fetch Millen or Remson. One or the other, maybe both. Is that so stinkin' hard to understand?"

"But how am I supposed to keep her here if her business with me reaches a conclusion and she wants to leave?" Quincannon wailed. "You expect me to *force* her to stay?"

"That's exactly what I'm saying," Mojave snarled. "I ain't got time to do your thinking for you. You're supposed to be the big brain, the *doctor.* Stick one of your magic needles in her ass and knock her out for all I care. All I know is that she'd better be here waiting when we get back or your drunken ass might be the one on the line. Now I gotta go. She oughta be rapping on your door any second, you'd damn well better figure out a way to do what I'm telling you!"

With that, Mojave turned and disappeared out the back door through which he'd entered. Staring after him with a tormented look on his face, Quincannon stretched out a trembling hand and wrapped it around the ever-present whiskey bottle that was never far from reach . . .

Chapter Ten

The address Margelino led Sue to turned out to be a small, two-story wood frame house located on a narrow corner lot. Giving Sue a somewhat hopeful sign was the fact that it appeared notably better kept up than the surrounding buildings. Another hopeful omen was the fact that she no longer could feel or spot any sign of the copper-skinned man who had been following her. She wasn't sure what to make of that other than to think the presence of Margelino must have discouraged the shadow at least enough for him to back temporarily off. She didn't mention him to Margelino for the time being, but her thoughts nevertheless strayed ahead, weighing the option of possibly asking the friendly baker to stick with her until she was back in friendlier territory. Which, considering how protective he was being, he might already be planning himself.

Margelino's knock on Quincannon's door was answered, unhurriedly, by the doctor himself. Not surprisingly, his dubious practice did not include the amenities of a receptionist or nurse. The man was a tall, lean specimen, very pale, with faded blue eyes and a pattern of fine blood vessels spider-webbed over each sunken cheek, marking years of heavy drinking. Sue's nose immediately picked up the scent of bleach and lingering medicinal odors coming from inside, and the smell of whiskey on Quincannon's breath when he spoke.

"Margelino," Quincannon said, a touch of surprise in his tone. "A rare occasion it is for you to come knocking on my door."

"Expect it to remain a rarity," the baker replied coolly. "But, as with most things in life, there are exceptions."

Quincannon's gaze shifted to Sue and she sensed a sudden uneasiness in his eyes that she found rather curious. But he quickly countered it with smooth words of greeting. "And quite a lovely exception you have brought with you, neighbor. Please come in and tell me the nature of your visit."

The room they entered was tidy and furnished very sparely. At one end was an examining table covered by a crisp white sheet, with a pair of thinly padded chairs pushed against one wall and, lining the other three, glass-fronted cabinets containing various bottles of medicine, liniments, rolls of gauze wrappings, and so forth. At the other end was a kitchen area with a two-burner stove, food cabinets, a table and a pair of wooden chairs. There was no sign of anything resembling a parlor or leisure area, though a curtained-over doorway in the wall directly across from the entrance might have led to such.

Closing the door behind them, Quincannon motioned Sue and Margelino toward the chairs in the examining area and said, "Please, be seated. Then tell me the nature of the ailment that brings you here, and which of you is unfortunately stricken."

Sue sat, Margelino remained standing.

"Actually," she spoke in response, "our reason for being here is on my account. Mr. Margelino was kind enough to accompany me when I got lost. But my purpose for seeking you out is not due to any illness."

Once again Sue saw the uneasiness flicker in the doctor's eyes. And this time when he replied his voice lost much of its smoothness. "Really? I find it unusual for anyone to call on me if not for a medical purpose." Then, around a nervous smile, he added, "Not that I fail to be pleased and flattered by a visit from someone so fetching."

"The girl is merely looking for some information," Margelino stated with gruff impatience. Turning to Sue he then said with a touch of the same gruffness, "Go ahead and cut to it. No sense spending any more time here than necessary."

For a moment Sue bridled at being ordered in such a manner. But then, reminding herself how helpful the plump man was being and realizing how distasteful he found it to be in Quincannon's presence, she calmed herself. "Very well," she said, favoring the doctor with a plaintive look.

"What I came to ask of you is information on a patient you may have recently treated. The person in question is my estranged husband who—though we are separated at the moment—I still care about. His name is Fred, Fred Kurtz. I received a secondhand report that he was injured in a saloon brawl either late last night or very early this morning. My impression was that his injuries were serious enough to likely require a doctor's attention. I have spent much of the day making inquiries of the town's other doctors, trying to locate Fred and determine his condition. You are my last resort."

Quincannon listened to this with a tolerant expression. His voice conveyed more of the same when he replied. "In speaking with the other doctors, Mrs. Kurtz, I'm sure you must have encountered the policy of anyone in our field not being allowed to break patient confidentiality without some kind of prior authorization."

"Yes, yes. I know all that," Sue said. Her tone had a sharpness to it but inwardly she was once again amused at hearing herself called "Mrs. Kurtz"—the actual Fred Kurtz being the curmudgeonly old bachelor who wore a town marshal's badge back in Coraville. Continuing with the fabrication, she protested, "But I am his wife!"

"Though estranged," Quincannon was quick to point out.

Sue sighed and shifted from being borderline shrill to a more pleading approach. "Can't you at least confirm, without divulging any specifics, whether or not you've recently treated anyone such as I described? And, if so, what kind of condition he's in? The other doctors were all willing to share that much—that they *hadn't* treated any such patient."

In the midst of asking this, Sue saw Quincannon's eyes once again take on that uneasy glint and then dart, for just a split second, toward the curtained doorway on the other side of the room. Her heart quickened with the conviction that the source of the medic's uneasiness could be found behind that curtain and in all likelihood it was the ambusher with the gouged eye.

Issuing his own resigned sigh, Quincannon responded to her plea by saying, "All right then. In view of your distressed state, I too will relent to the extent of revealing to you that neither have I treated any injury that fits your description. To ease your mind further, I might even go so far as to suggest that this vague report you received must have been exaggerated or perhaps in complete error."

"It would be nice to think that," Sue allowed. "Considering how Fred *hasn't* turned up for medical treatment anywhere, I guess it's safe to assume he must not be too badly hurt after all. That gives me a good deal of relief. We thank you for affording us your time, Doctor." She rose from her chair, her mind once again racing ahead with thoughts of getting back to Lone as soon as possible to report her belief that *here* was where one of his ambushers could be found.

"No. Wait!" Quincannon blurted this objection so abruptly it gave both Sue and Margelino a start. Then, forcing another nervous smile, he tried to soften what had sounded like practically a command. "I mean . . . please. Please don't be in such a hurry to leave. I get so few callers who aren't here for medical reasons, many of which are, er, in the nature of rather unpleasant emergencies. It would be nice to, uh, sit and simply visit with someone for a little while. I was just about to have my afternoon tea. I prefer tea but, if you'd rather, I could make some coffee instead. Yes, coffee. We could sit and, uh, chat for a bit over cups of fresh coffee."

Margelino scowled fiercely. "What the hell are you talking about, Quincannon? What's got into you?"

"I was just trying to be friendly. Neighborly."

"We've been neighbors for nearly a decade, but never friends," Margelino said. "And I don't see any reason for that to change."

The doctor's voice became strained trying to hold back an angry retort. "There might be a basis for it if you didn't have to be so rude and crude. Especially in the presence of a young lady."

"Your history with young ladies," snapped the baker, making no attempt to hide his disdain, "is one of the main reasons I will never have any use for you."

Now Quincannon's face flushed with unchecked anger. "Damn you! Those accusations have never been proven, and you know it!"

"Says you. I know enough to believe otherwise." Margelino placed a hand on Sue's arm and started for the door, adding, "You go ahead and enjoy your tea, but we'll be leaving now."

"Not so fast—you ain't goin' no damn where!"

The harsh command, issued in a deep, guttural voice, came from the curtained doorway on the side of the room. The faces of Sue, Margelino, and Quincannon all whipped around to look that way. What they saw, partly emerged through a split in the curtains, was a man of average height and build. He was barefoot and clad only in dingy long johns, holding a converted Navy Colt in his right fist, extended out at waist level. Under an uncombed thatch of reddish-brown hair, the man's right eye was wide and wild-looking; his left eye was covered by a bulky gauze patch held in place by bandage strips wrapped around his forehead and left ear, tied at the back of his head.

"Cleve!" gasped Quincannon. "I didn't know you were awake."

"I been awake," Cleve snarled. "It's time for a dose of that laudanum shit, but I'm out of it back there. I heard most of what Mojave told you and then, just now, I heard your pathetic attempt to do like he said in order to keep these two here . . . an invitation to tea, for Chrissakes! It's a good thing I *was* awake so's I could come out and get the job done proper." Though his words were addressed to Quincannon, as he spoke neither his eye nor the muzzle of the Colt ever wavered the slightest from being aimed directly at Sue and Margelino.

"Who the devil are you to be aiming a gun at us?" Margelino demanded boldly.

"Who I am," Cleve was quick to respond, "is a beat up, foul-tempered sonofabitch who won't think twice about usin' this cutter to blast out your liver and lights for just a smidgen of a reason. And, in case you don't get it, you just used up the only smidge I'm in the mood to allow."

"Take it easy, Mr. Margelino," said Sue. "I think I'm the one he's mainly interested in."

"So the little lady is smart enough to figure out that much," sneered Cleve. Then, his mouth twisting menacingly, he added, "Too bad the nosy bitch ain't smart enough to know when to back away from things that ain't none of her stinkin' business!"

Beside her, Sue felt Margelino stiffen. She clamped a hand on his forearm and held him in check.

"I would add," Cleve continued, "that the same holds true for the two hounds she's got followin' her around, pantin' to do her bidding like a couple of obedient puppies. But that ain't no way the case for one of 'em, the big, square-faced bastard they call McGantry. The last thing I want—me personally—is for *him* to back away. Not until I get my crack at evenin' the score for what he done to me!"

At that, Sue was unable to hold herself in check. "You deluded, miserable fool," she scoffed. "I hope you do exactly that—try to even the score with McGantry. You got off lucky the first time. You tangle with him again, you'll *wish* all you came away with was a gouged eye."

Cleve slapped the curtains away with his free hand and took a lunging step toward Sue. "Shut your mouth, bitch, or I'll lay this pistol barrel across your jaw. I got it figured Remson and Millen will probably want to use you as bait to suck in McGantry and your other lapdog. So you gotta be in one piece. But that don't mean the piece can't be dented up some."

"That's not going to be conducted here, is it?" wailed Quincannon. "I mean, when the others show up you'll take these people somewhere else . . . right? Somewhere else to do whatever is deemed. No one would consider my place for doing the kind of thing you're implying . . . *Would they?*"

"Shut up," Cleve said irritably. "What's with you . . . got a queasy stomach all of a sudden?

Jesus, after some of the stuff *you* have done here?"

"Everything I do falls under the umbrella of medical procedures," Quincannon argued. "That's far different than—"

Cleve cut him short. "Yeah, yeah. Save it for the judge. Speakin' of medical procedures, how about fetchin' me a fresh batch of that laudanum? My eye's killin' me. I hope Mojave gets back with somebody pretty soon."

Quincannon went to one of the glass-fronted cabinets and began extracting what he needed in the way of ingredients.

All during the exchange between the two men, Sue had been watching closely for some opening, some chance that might allow her to make a grab for one of her guns. But nothing presented itself. Cleve's fierce one-eyed glare never diverted, not for a second.

If anything, with the doctor now otherwise occupied, Cleve's attention seemed to focus even more intently on Sue. With the menacing twist returning to his mouth, he said, "I'm actually kinda glad my eye is still hurtin'. It keeps me in the right mood for dealin' with your man McGantry when I get my chance. Would you like to hear what I got in mind for him?"

"Go ahead and amuse yourself," Sue sneered. "The only advantage you'll gain over McGantry if you face him again is in your imagination."

"Call it what you want, but the payback I'm plannin' for that eye gougin' bastard ain't gonna be my imagination—it's gonna be his nightmare!" Cleve's eye shone with a heightened wildness and his breathing grew more rapid. "I got it all mapped real clear in my mind. First, I'm gonna blast his kneecaps to powder. Then his elbows. And when I got him squirmin' on his belly like a landed fish, then I'm gonna take my slow, sweet time pluckin' out his eyeballs one at a time." He paused to utter a throaty, nasty laugh before adding, "If you behave yourself, sweetheart, I'll try to arrange for you to watch the whole thing."

"You are a sick beast!" declared Margelino.

Cleve's eyes blazed. "You think so, baker man? And you know what you are? Dumber than shit, that's what. I gave you fair warnin' about not poppin' off your mouth no more else I'd gun you. We need the girl for bait, but nobody needs you for nothing. And it's only gonna take four of the cartridges in this smoke wagon I'm holdin' to deal with McGantry as planned. Meanin' I can burn one on you and still have one to spare. So that leaves just this question: Are you ready to do some beggin' your pardon and maybe convince me to give you one more chance? Or . . ."

Cleve's unfinished sentence hung in the air for a long, tense moment.

Until, from farther back in the room behind

the curtain, there came the sound of a door unlatching and opening.

Cleve's mouth curved into a sly smile. "Well, well. Sounds like the company we've been waitin' for has arrived. Guess you catch a break, pie maker . . . for a little while at least."

Chapter Eleven

As the clump of boot heels advanced in the room behind him, Cleve said over his shoulder, "Come on in and join the party, boys. Everything's under control out here, no thanks to our tea serving quack of a doctor."

The boot heels stopped clumping and a deep voice calmly replied, "Thanks for the invitation."

An instant later the roar of a gunshot hammered into the main room. Accompanying it was a tongue of red-gold flame licking out through the split in the doorway curtains and, hurtled from this, a .44 caliber slug came smashing into the cartridge cylinder of Cleve's Navy Colt. Cleve screeched with pain and surprise as the heavy gun was torn from his grasp and sent spinning away until it clattered against the opposite wall next to the front door.

"Aiiee, my hand's busted!" wailed Cleve, his knees buckling slightly and body twisting half around as he reached with his left hand to clutch his right, the one formerly wielding the shooting iron.

Lone McGantry emerged through the curtains in a long stride, growling, "Shut up, or I'll bust a hell of a lot more than that!"

He held his own smoking Colt on Cleve for an instant longer before sweeping it in a flat arc, past Sue and Margelino, until he brought it to bear on Quincannon. The latter, who had spun around at the sound of the gunshot with a bottle of some concoction in one hand, now gawked in wide-eyed terror at the sight of the gun aimed his way. The bottle slipped from his trembling fingers and he stammered, "N—No. Please don't shoot, I b-beg of you!"

"It's okay, Lone," Sue was quick to say. "He's harmless."

"That's a matter of opinion," Margelino muttered. Then, taking a step toward Cleve, he bit out through clenched teeth, "But for damn sure this foul-mouthed pig ain't!" And in concert with that statement he uncorked a beauty of a right cross that caught the mewling Cleve flush on the jaw and knocked him flat.

"Whoa!" barked Lone. "You can have all of him you want, pal—but only after I'm done with him."

Margelino stepped back, rubbing his knuckles. "I'm good for now. Go ahead."

Sue came forward and threw her arms around Lone. Pressing her face to his chest, she said, "God, was I glad to see you step through those curtains!"

Grinning, Lone slipped his free arm around her shoulders. "Sorry to make such a noisy entrance. But with his gun trained on you, it was the surest way. If I'd called out for him to drop it, he might've panicked and got trigger happy. So, since I had the angle with you safely off to one side, I just went ahead and separated him from his trigger."

"Which was a mighty fine sight to see," praised Margelino. "But will somebody please tell me what this is all about?" He pinned Sue with a hard gaze from under furrowed brows. "Am I to believe that this"—a jab of his thumb to indicate Lone—"is your estranged husband?"

Sue gave a short laugh as she stepped back from Lone. "No, Mr. Margelino, that's not the case. It's a tale too complicated to go into right now. For the time being please just accept my apologies for you getting caught up in and endangered by my pretenses." Then, her gaze sweeping back up to gaze urgently at Lone, she said, "We musn't tarry here. More of the men who ambushed you are on their way. The one called Mojave—"

"Don't worry about Mojave," Lone cut her off. "He's in the alley out back, clubbed unconscious and hogtied." After Sue drew back, her eyes wide with surprise, he continued, "I ran into that skunk on the way here. I first got directions from Homer to a flophouse where the three have been stayin'. When none of them was there, another fella I ran into told me he'd heard how one of 'em was bein' cared for by a doctor and he gave me new directions. Headed this way was when I spotted Mojave. Spotted him before he did me. I drug him into an abandoned building and we had a little chat. That's when he laid out for me what I could expect to find here if I slipped in through the back door. The only difference was that he said I'd find this one"—a nod toward Cleve— "in a drugged sleep back there. No matter, it still worked out okay. Though a little less so for Cleve."

"Did you get any other information from Mojave when you had your, er, chat with him?" asked Sue.

Lone nodded. "The stage to Laramie was the one Drake and Rosemary took. Mojave claimed not to know any destination past that. When I heard about the situation here, I didn't spend any more time on him. Once I had you in the clear, I figured, then we'd be able to chat at length with *both* of these polecats." He cut a glance over at Quincannon, who remained in a frozen pose in front of his medicine cabinets. "And maybe a third one, too."

The doctor shook his head vigorously. "Oh, no. No. I assure you I know nothing about the schemes of these two or any of the others. I take care of their injuries from time to time, true enough, but that's the extent of it. As far as anything—"

"Quit your damn babbling," Lone shut him up, "before you get so antsy you pee yourself. Just stand there and keep quiet unless I ask you something direct."

160

Quincannon's mouth clapped shut quick and tight and he went back to standing statue still.

Holstering his Colt, Lone made a gesture toward Cleve's gun lying over against the wall and said, "Somebody pick that up and hang on to it while I go fetch Mojave. Won't take me but a minute. Then we can bring the two varmints around and have ourselves a gab fest with the both of 'em."

Lone was turning to go back through the curtained doorway and Margelino was leaning over to pick up Cleve's gun, when the front door suddenly opened and Tate Millen started to enter. Several things happened all at once. Margelino paused in mid lean, looking up and promptly muttering a low curse at the sight of Millen. Lone hesitated part way through the curtains and looked around at the sound of the door opening. Sue gasped audibly, having no basis for recognizing Millen yet somehow sensing that his arrival was not a favorable development. And Millen, his gaze immediately falling on Cleve sprawled in the middle of the floor, halted his entrance and spat, "What the hell?"

For an instant, everyone froze just like that. But only for an instant. Then it all broke into chaotic motion.

Millen jumped back out of the doorway, slamming the door closed again with one hand and with the other clawing for the gun strapped to his hip. Margelino finished snatching up Cleve's Navy Colt then dodged to one side. Lone wheeled from the curtains and broke for the front door, drawing his own Colt as he did so.

"Stay back and stay down!" he ordered Sue and Margelino, quickly crossing the room and then pressing himself tight to the wall directly beside the slammed door. He held like that for a moment, listening intently. Then he slowly reached out with his free hand, twisted the knob, and give the door a hard shove. It swung outward.

Two shots roared from out in the street and a pair of bullets poured into the room, sizzling across its width and ripping through the curtains on the opposite side. Lone crouched low. Holding his Colt at the ready, he leaned slowly out and cautiously peered around the edge of the door frame. No more shots came.

Straightening up, Lone said over his shoulder, "The yellow cur is makin' a run for it! I'm goin' after him. You two stay here. Keep a tight watch on Cleve, take no chances with him. Lock all the doors and don't open up for anybody 'til I get back!"

And then he was gone. Out the door and racing up the street in pursuit of the fleeing Millen.

When it came to a foot race, Millen's shorter legs and stocky torso put him at a disadvantage against the taller, longer-legged Lone—not to mention the latter's powerful endurance and angry determination. Offsetting these somewhat, however, was Millen's greater familiarity with the area. If he could stay ahead of Lone long enough to make it back to a busier stretch of Yucca Street, he might be able to lose himself among other residents or duck out of sight into a building or alley somewhere. Lone knew he had to close the gap on him before that could happen.

For the remainder of the block in which Quincannon's house was located, Millen pounded down the middle of the street. Over half of the buildings on either side looked empty, abandoned, and no other people were in sight. That started to change in the next block, though, and at that point Millen veered off toward the left side of the street. He ran past a man watering a burro at a wooden trough and barreled between a pair of indignantly shrieking women. Lone was steadily closing on him, but not fast enough. And now, with other people scattered about, he couldn't risk taking a shot.

Near the end of the block, Millen made a sudden turn and darted in through the battered, crookedly hanging batwing doors of a nameless saloon. Lone was close on his heels. Just as he was getting ready to make his own charge through the batwings, he heard Millen hollering on the inside: "There's a crazy bastard out to kill me! Help! Somebody stop him!"

Lone plunged into a dim, smoky, low-ceilinged rectangular room that stank of spilled booze and sour body odor. There was a plank bar off to one side, a handful of mismatched tables and chairs in the middle. Some of the chairs now lay scattered and tipped over from Millen's reckless dash through the place. Lone was just in time to see him running down a short hallway at the far end then disappearing out a back door.

As far as any customers in the joint being available to respond to Millen's desperate call for help, there was only a rickety old man propped up against the bar and two droopy-headed drunks at one of the tables. All looked bewildered and disinterested and too soused to be of any help even if they'd been inclined to try. A beefy, bearded hombre in a barkeeper's apron, however, appeared to be a different matter. He was coming around one end of the bar with a mean scowl on his face and a billy club in one meaty fist.

Barely breaking stride, Lone swung his Colt in a slashing backhand that cracked the barrel hard across ear and cheekbone and sent the would-be clubber staggering back until he fell against a shelf of bottles, many of which shattered and came raining down on him as he collapsed to the floor. Lone plowed on for the back door, scattering several additional chairs as he went.

At the end of the short hallway, Lone held up before barging on out. It occurred to him that Millen might take a notion to stop running and use the opportunity to lie in wait. Once an ambusher, always an ambusher.

The exit door had been left slightly ajar. Once again Lone crouched low and pressed himself back behind its frame. The narrow hallway didn't give much cover, but enough. Reaching out with his free hand, he shoved the door open wide.

Sure enough, a shot instantly rang out and a bullet screamed in, slicing a long furrow down the hallway wall. Lone immediately leaned out and blindly fired back. All he really sought to gain was a quick scan of whatever the layout was behind the saloon. What he saw was an expanse of flat, weed-choked ground reaching back about twenty yards and spreading a little over half that distance to either side. Straight back was a half-collapsed section of weather-grayed wooden fence. Between it and the rear of the saloon building were scattered various pieces of junk and broken-down equipment. Among these was a rusty plow, a wagon bed without wheels, half a dozen rotted wooden kegs, a couple of wheelbarrows lying on their sides, and in the middle of it all a battered one-horse surrey with tall, spoked wheels and a precariously hanging flat canopy high over the driver's seat. A haze of powder smoke hovering in the air on the back side of this conveyance told Lone that there was where Millen had fired from.

As Lone ducked back after taking his shot, another slug came blasting in through the doorway.

Immediately to the right outside the door, Lone had also spotted a good-sized pile of split wood. There was about three feet of space between the outer wall of the building and the near side of the pile. Enough room for a man to maneuver in behind and use the heap of wood for cover.

Lone leaned out again and triggered two rapid-fire rounds, hammering them into the near side of the surrey, giving cause for Millen to keep ducked down behind it. Then, in a single fluid motion, Lone sprang out of his crouch and streaked at an angle out the door and in behind the woodpile. He was dropped safely in place before Millen got off another shot. Wood chips kicked up and rattled against the side of the building above his head.

As his fingers nimbly plucked fresh cartridges from his shell belt and replaced the spent ones in his Colt, Lone called out tauntingly, "You're a holy terror when it comes to shootin' wood and empty doorways—but you can't hit shit otherwise!"

"All it takes is one bullet, you meddling bastard," Millen hollered back, "and I got that very one waiting for you!"

Lone shifted to the other end of the woodpile

before calling out again. "That cuts both ways. But if you play it smart and cough up some information, I'll let you and your bushwhackin' buddies live. I ain't interested in little minnows, I want the big fish!"

Now it was Millen's turn to give a harsh laugh. "Like my old grandmaw used to say—Want in one hand, crap in the other and see which gets full first! All you're gonna get out of me is one of these .45 slugs I already offered you."

While Millen was talking, Lone had the chance to eye the surrey more closely. He saw something that gave him an idea. The flat, fringed canopy high over the driver's seat was tilted sharply down on the back corner and it appeared only two of the thin struts holding it up were still intact. Maybe, with a little luck . . .

Resting his gun hand on a solidly wedged chunk of wood, Lone took careful aim and stroked the Colt's trigger. Once. Twice. The two remaining struts blew obligingly apart and the canopy tilted then dropped down on the back side of the carriage.

"Ow! Goddamn!" howled Millen's voice.

Lone didn't hesitate. The falling canopy might have stung a little and had a startling effect, but it wasn't heavy enough to have done any real harm. What the former scout had in mind next, as he surged to his feet and went tearing around the end of the woodpile, was to deliver a consider-

167

ably more damaging blow to the momentarily distracted Millen.

It was just short of a dozen yards from the woodpile to the surrey. Lone covered the distance rapidly in long, powerful, leg-churning strides. Then, just short of reaching the conveyance, he dropped his right shoulder low and rammed the base of the driver's box with a full head of steam. The impact caused the lightweight surrey to shudder, lift, then flip back and over onto its opposite side—and thereby also onto a screeching Tate Millen.

Chapter Twelve

Once Lone had disarmed and dragged a bruised, whimpering Millen out from under the tipped-over surrey, he got him up on his feet and prodded him at gunpoint out toward the street. He didn't return back through the saloon but rather skirted around the end of the building.

Even though this end of Yucca Street was a rugged part of town, two armed men running loose, plowing through one of its business establishments, and then engaging in a prolonged exchange of gunfire, was still enough of a disturbance to warrant wide attention from the citizenry. By the time Lone and Millen reached the street, a score or more of buzzing, grumbling people were clustered out front of the saloon with more on the way from farther up. Lone found himself uncertain when it came to judging their overriding mood—whether it was merely mob curiosity luring them or if there was some sentiment against him, the outsider. He scanned facial expressions and looked close for any sign of weapons. Hoping to make sure nobody got any notion to try and interfere, he brandished his Colt prominently behind Millen's head and swept everybody with cold, flinty eyes.

That's when his gaze fell on a tall individual

crowding his way forward through the pack. A deputy marshal's badge glinted on the tall man's chest. For a moment, Lone tensed all the more . . . until recognition of Deputy Marv Brady caused him to expel a sigh of relief.

Not that Brady looked to be in a particularly pleasant mood when he stepped up and planted his feet in a wide, confrontational stance. "I was hoping like hell I was wrong," he said through clenched teeth. "But as soon as I heard there was a fresh bucket of hell getting kicked down the middle of Yucca Street, I had a bad hunch who was gonna turn out to be doing some of the kicking."

"The man's a menace, a raving maniac!" wailed Millen. "He chased me and shot at me and—"

"Shut up," Brady cut him off. "I want any noise out of you, I'll ask for it. Otherwise keep quiet."

The deputy's eyes cut back to Lone. "Well? How about it? What's the story? I was hoping that by now you and the woman would be gone from town."

"We'd like nothing better," Lone told him. "Trouble was, we were lackin' a clear direction to head off in. But now, with the less than eager cooperation from this piece of crud and two of his pals who are waitin' for us down at Doc Quincannon's place, we're fixin' to get that information and maybe a few extra tidbits."

"Ain't none of us telling you shit!" spat Millen. Then he immediately shrank back from Brady's glare.

After pursing his lips thoughtfully for a moment, the deputy brought his gaze back to Lone. "All right. Looks like we need to take a walk down to Quincannon's and sort this out," he said. Turning to the still-gathering crowd behind him, he raised his voice a little louder and announced, "Okay, everybody, the excitement's over. Nothing more to see. We're going down the street a ways and finish settling this. No call for the rest of you to stay clumped up trying to stick your noses in. Go on about your business, back to whatever it was you were doing. Git!"

Reluctantly, grumbling their disappointment and dissent, the knot of gawkers began breaking up and meandering off.

"Now. After you put that gun away," Brady said to Lone, "we can commence heading for the doc's place."

When they got there, it was Margelino who answered Lone's knock. He had a wary expression on his face and Cleve's gun in his hand. When he saw Brady, his eyebrows lifted in surprise and he exclaimed, "Deputy Brady!"

Brady's expression also registered surprise as he followed Lone and Millen inside. "Mr. Margelino," he said. "I didn't expect to see you mixed up in this."

"That makes two of us," Margelino replied with a rueful grunt.

Once through the door, Brady scanned the room thoroughly, taking in Sue, Quincannon still standing meekly in front of his medicine cabinets and then, over in the kitchen area, Cleve and Mojave (who had been brought in from the alley) tied back-to-back in the wooden chairs. "Jesus," the deputy muttered under his breath.

"You see? They're all maniacs!" Millen wailed anew. "They're rounding us up and treating us like animals. The whole bunch of 'em needs to be—"

Brady silenced him with the jab of a finger. "I warned you once to keep quiet, didn't I? Don't make me tell you again." Then he spun on Lone and said, "But from *you* I want to hear plenty! What in blazes is going on here? I hope to hell you've got a good explanation."

So for the next handful of minutes, Lone laid it all out. Since Brady was already familiar with the whole underlying matter of Lone being on hand to aid Sue in trying to catch up with her brother, he started with the previously unmentioned ambush from the night before. Then he told of the "shadowing" and the suspicions of how their pursuit of Drake and Rosemary, as a means to intercept James, was being discouraged and diverted. He explained how seeking to identify the ambushers was an attempt to learn, through them, where Drake had taken Rosemary. Margelino proved invaluable in his backup testimony about the incriminating threats and admissions made by Cleve during the time he'd been holding Sue and the baker at gunpoint.

Brady listened intently, with few interruptions. His expression remained somber, mostly unreadable. It seemed clear, however, that the input from Margelino carried significant weight.

When he'd heard enough, the deputy raked his gaze over Millen, Cleve, and Mojave, saying, "You three have been skimming on the edge of the law for too damn long. Sounds to me like your sorry asses have now blundered full over the line."

"You ain't even heard our side of things!" protested Millen.

"What would be the point? If I wasted time listening, all I'd hear would be a pack of lies."

"You ain't got the whole say on the law around here," Cleve sneered. "Might be when Arn Remson gets wind of—"

"Shut up!" Millen cut him short.

"No. Let him speak," said Lone. Pinning Cleve with a hard glare, he demanded, "Go ahead. Let's hear it! Tell us more about what difference Fatso stickin' his nose in any of this would make."

"Walk careful, McGantry," Brady advised sternly.

"Why?" Lone growled. "That badge-totin' lard ass is every bit as dirty—maybe even dirtier—

than these three peckerwoods. And you know it!"

Before anybody else could say more, Margelino spoke from where he stood looking out the front window. "Whatever difference Remson might or might not make, it looks like we won't have to wait long to find out. He's coming down the street now."

All eyes swung to the speaker and then shifted to the front door. In the sudden silence, the low murmur and grumble of several voices—same as had emanated from the crowd formed earlier out front of the nameless saloon where Lone ran down Millen—could be heard growing closer outside.

"Now we'll see what we see," smirked Cleve.

Brady gave him a venomous look but didn't bother with any response.

A moment later, the door thundered under a heavy knock and Arn Remson's voice called from the other side. "Doc Quincannon! Open up—what's goin' on in there?"

Brady tipped his head to Margelino, indicating for him to open the door. When the baker did so, the ponderous Remson bulled his way through and then paused a couple steps in to sweep the room with a fierce scowl. Through the open door, the dozen or so gawkers who had trailed along in Remson's wake went suddenly quiet, listening to try and hear whatever transpired next.

Remson pinned Brady with a blazing glare.

174

"What kind of shit show are you runnin' here, fella? What the hell are you up to?"

"It's called clearing the undesirables off the streets of our town," Brady replied evenly. "It's the kind of thing those of us who wear badges are supposed to do. Or have you forgotten?"

"What kind of smart-assed crack is that?"

"Wasn't nothing smart-assed about it," Brady snapped back. "It was a plain and simple statement of fact. In case it wasn't plain enough, let me try again. I'm in the act of placing these three lowlifes"—he swept a hand to indicate Millen, Cleve, and Mojave—"under arrest. The charges will be assault and battery, malicious intent, kidnapping, reckless endangerment, and being butt ugly eyesores to the community. And maybe some more if I can think of any on my way to the jail!"

"You're crazy! You can't do that."

"Just watch me."

The fire went out of Remson's eyes. They turned ice cold instead and his heavy-lipped mouth twisted in an ugly, menacing way. "No. I *won't* watch . . . I won't let you. This is one too many times you've bucked me, you snot-nosed pup. Now back off. Learn your place, and get ready to keep it from here on out." He shifted back half a step and the fingers of his right hand curled above the hogleg riding on his hip. "Otherwise, make your play and we'll settle this once and for good."

"Not so fast," declared Lone. "Not 'til I've settled *my* score, Fatso!" So saying, he stepped ahead of Brady and, in a single smooth blur of motion, drew his Colt and slashed it savagely across Remson's meaty jaw. The big deputy buckled at the knees and dropped straight down, collapsing into a heap.

Brady stood frozen and wild-eyed for a second. Then he turned angrily on Lone. "Damn you, you had no right to interfere!"

"I just kept you alive, mister," Lone barked back. "You think too much of that damn badge, of upholdin' law and order in a proper manner. I could see it in your eyes. You'd've hesitated an extra second, frettin' about such, and in that second this cold-hearted bastard would have blown your gizzard out. If I'm wrong, prop him up again after I'm gone and go ahead with it. But I'm damned if I'll be stickin' around to watch."

"And just where do you think you're going?"

"West. Laramie," said Lone. "We learned enough today to know that's where Drake and the girl went from here. I'd hoped to try and find out more, but we'll settle for that." He glanced over at Sue to see if she gave any sign of objecting. When she didn't, he went on. "Just give us time to round up Johnny Case and get outfitted, we'll be gone before sunset. I can't say I'll be sorry to put this town of yours behind me, and I'd imagine right about now you wouldn't mind havin' us out of your hair."

"After I've had some time to think about it, I might come to feel different," allowed Brady. "But no, right about now seeing you three making dust outta here don't seem like a bad idea at all."

"But we're leaving you with your hands awfully full," Sue pointed out.

"I'll manage," Brady assured her. "Like I said, it's time and past time this pile of garbage was cleaned off our streets."

"What about Remson?" Margelino wanted to know.

The muscles at the hinges of Brady's jaw bulged visibly before he grated, "It's past time for him to be dealt with too. If the marshal won't back me on that, then maybe it's time for me to also put Cheyenne behind me."

"I'd hate to see that," said Margelino.

"So would I," replied Brady. "But we'll have to find out."

Lone eyed him with a glint of heightened respect. "That's all well and good. But don't forget your own warning to me about him. I'll turn it back on you now. Don't make the mistake of thinkin' Remson won't try to get even and, when he does, don't expect him to do it straight-up."

Brady nodded solemnly. "You've made your message clear . . . now didn't you say something about kicking up dust out of here?"

PART TWO

Chapter Thirteen

Johnny Case regarded Lone across the flickering campfire flames and said, "So are you going to stay sore at me all the way to Laramie?"

Lone took an unhurried sip of his coffee before replying. "Ain't sure what you're talkin' about. When I'm sore at somebody, they don't usually have to guess about it."

"Well you like to've bit my head off for not mentioning sooner about Remson roughing up old Homer. And you've been brooding ever since."

"I don't *brood*."

"Actually, yes you do," spoke up Sue from where she also sat by the fire.

Lone gave her a look.

The three of them were camped about five miles west of Cheyenne, as far as they got after riding out of town once they had purchased trail supplies and mounts for Sue and Johnny, which they were able to obtain from the same livery where Lone had boarded Ironsides. This flurry of preparation, coming tight on the heels of the events on Yucca Street, hadn't left a lot of time for small talk other than quickly filling Johnny in on what Sue and Lone had learned and what else transpired to warrant their sudden departure.

It was only after they were out on the trail that Johnny got a chance to relate the results of what he'd been able to turn up during their separation. In truth, his findings were fairly insignificant as far as the particular matter he'd been sent to look into—the question of whether or not the hotel clerk O'Feeney might have set up Lone for the previous night's Edge Street ambush. Johnny came away convinced O'Feeney had played no part, confirming what had already been generally suspected going in. It was after that that the basis for the discussion now taking place occurred. Thinking he might catch Lone still at the Dust Cutter, Johnny had gone there to touch base with him. Though Lone was already gone, what Johnny walked in on was Arn Remson threatening old Homer for talking too freely. Johnny's interruption put an end to it before any serious harm was done. Even at that, however, when Lone heard of the incident he had reacted with fierce anger.

"Okay," he said now with the firelit faces of both Sue and Johnny gazing expectantly back at him. "What's ranklin' me—what you two call brooding, I guess—ain't got nothing to do with bein' sore at Johnny. It's myself I'm sore at. On account of thinkin' back on how I had that cowardly tub Remson right there in front of me and all I did was give him just a single whack to the jaw. Damn it all, I should've never stopped at that to begin with—and especially not now, not after hearin' the way he went after ol' Homer."

"But things had already turned plenty rough there at Quincannon's and out on Yucca Street," Sue pointed out. "If you would have gone any harder after Remson at that point, no matter how much he had it coming, I fear we would have lost the sanction of Brady and not been able to get away from there so easy."

"I suppose not," Lone allowed grudgingly. "But it sticks in my craw that Homer cooperatin' with me is what caused him to almost get hurt. And I worry now that, even though we've moved on, a sidewinder like Remson might hold enough of a grudge to go back and give him a hard time regardless."

Johnny frowned deeply. "That's a mighty disturbing thought. And I can't argue that Remson don't come across as being the kind to act that very way. But short of making him dead, how could you ever go about being certain he'd never resort to such?"

Sue's eyes widened. "Good Lord. I understand the concern, but I hope no one is seriously suggesting anything that drastic. I've already got a brother who's a murder suspect—that's quite enough, thank you." She focused her gaze on Lone. "Besides, if Brady follows through on the way he was talking, it sounds like he means to see Remson and his tactics brought to an end.

That ought to give the fat bully plenty else to worry about without thinking any more about Homer, wouldn't you say?"

"Be nice to believe that's how it'll go." Lone set his jaw. "Either way, it's how we're gonna have to leave it. Can't go back and change anything now. We've still got plenty left to worry about on ahead."

"Speaking of which," said Johnny, "how far is it to Laramie?"

"Day and a half's ride," Lone answered. "Might've been quicker by stagecoach, the way Drake and James's wife went, but I figured we would draw less attention moseyin' in on horseback."

"Makes sense. Except, once we're there, ain't we gonna end up drawing attention anyway when we begin asking around to pick up some kind of lead on the ones we're pursuing?"

"Might turn out that way. But, for starters, it happens I've had some past dealings with a few folks in Laramie," Lone explained. "They're saloon types, like ol' Homer, who tend to know a thing or three about most all the doin's around— especially if it's tied to something big like we suspect might be behind all the finaglin' Drake went through back in Cheyenne to block anybody from followin' after him and the girl. With a little luck, I'm hopin' these folks I'm talkin' about might be able to point us in a direction that will save us diggin' from scratch all over again."

"Man, that would be a welcome break," said Johnny. Then, eyeing Sue, he added with a touch of remorse, "If only we can catch some kind of similar break that helps turn up James."

Sue's mouth pressed momentarily into a tight, straight line before she replied, "I remain convinced that somehow—don't ask me exactly how—James's determination will lead him to Rosemary. If we reach her, he will show up."

"I hope you're right," said Lone, "because right now that's the only angle we've got to play for gettin' a line on him. It's our whole reason for continuin' after his wife and Drake."

Sue gave a firm nod. "I know. I stand by believing it will pay off."

Lone drained the rest of his coffee, tapped the grounds out of the empty cup, then announced, "Well, the best thing we can do for now is grab a good night's rest so we can head out early and fresh in the mornin'. I'll go make a final check of the horses." He stood up. After a glance at the cloudless, star-splattered sky overhead, he added, "Suggest everybody lay out your bedroll with an extra blanket. This clear night is gonna turn mighty brisk before the sun shows again."

"Twenty years. You hear what I'm sayin'? Twenty years I been wearin' a badge for this stinkin', ungrateful town. That goes back near to when you three was still sucklin' on your mama's teat." As he railed on, Arn Remson paced furiously back and forth across the patch of weedy ground behind his cabin. Smoke from the cigar he was puffing left a hazy trail in his wake and drifted across the faces of the three men who stood watching and listening to his rant. "Cheyenne wasn't much more than a wide spot in the trail," he continued. "Filled with buffalo hunters, saddle tramps, and hardcases passin' through from all parts of the West. And if you ventured very far outta town, there was some sonofabuck of an Injun waitin' to lift your hair."

Long shadows of late evening stretched across the bare lot and cut at sharp angles throughout the structures of the surrounding neighborhood. Lights glowed in the windows of some of these buildings and also in a single window of Remson's place. The varying patterns of shadows that fell over the facial features of Tate Millen, Cleve Boyer, and Mojave Jones where they stood leaning against the back side of the cabin, made their expressions all the more somber, almost grim.

"Me and Jeremy Cade put on deputy badges the very same day, pinned there by ol' Cork Conlon hisself," Remson went on. Though his voice carried loud and clear, there was a bitter, personal undertone to it that almost seemed like he was reminiscing to himself as much as talking to the others. "Cork said what the law was, and me and Jeremy was young and mean and tough enough to dish it out just like he wanted. Our ways was rough, but nobody complained 'cause the ways of those we had to tame was rougher. The town started to grow and prosper, but that didn't mean all the bad elements got cleaned out. Not right away. Came the night the Ridgeway gang showed up in town and Cork took both barrels of a Greener twelve-gauge to the back. Near cut him in half, from between his shoulder blades on through to his brisket.

"Me and Jeremy ran the gang down afterward. Held each of the bloody bastards to account, and I don't mean by bringin' none of 'em back to stand no trial, neither. Not a damn one. Town made Jeremy marshal after that. That was okay with me. I stuck by him and we tamed things down all the more."

Remson paused in a splash of dim light and his expression took on a look of anguish. "Got too damn tame," he spat. "Pretty soon we was up to our ears with a mayor and a city council, and a city attorney, and a damn newspaper editor . . . all who started breathin' down our necks and questionin' the very tactics that made the town safe enough for them show up and start flappin' their gums to begin with. Jeremy was able to adjust. Able to accommodate the lily-livered do-gooders. Told me I'd better do the same. But whenever some rough customer came along"—here his lips peeled back in a disdainful sneer—"guess who all of a sudden got called on to deal with 'em in any way necessary?"

His three-man audience smirked and muttered their support for what he was implying.

"Then came the hirin' of that damn back stabbin' Marv Brady." Remson's tone grew even more bitter. "He started undercuttin' me right from the first. Makin' me look bad every chance he got, queerin' most of the side deals I had goin' that put a little extra jingle in my pocket and never should've been no skin off his nose at all. I ought to have cut his water short right then. But I made the mistake of bein' too cautious. And it all piled up and came tumblin' down on me this afternoon followin' that shit show at Quincannon's.

"When Marshal Jeremy got back to town and heard it all laid out, he looked at me—*at me,* who'd been sidin' him through thick and thin over all these years!—and said he was ashamed of my conduct and questioned whether I was still fit to wear a badge. Well, I damn quick answered his question for him. I flung my badge down on the desk, told him to take it and pin it somewhere where the sun don't shine, then marched out the door!"

"That was a salty damn move, Arn," said Millen.

"Way it had to be," declared Remson. "I've wasted way too much of my life in this damn town. With the deal cookin' in Promise Valley, I just move out a little sooner is all. And now that I've bailed your sorry asses out, you're free to ride there with me."

"But what if Drake and that lawyer fella ain't ready for us yet?" questioned Cleve.

"Then they'd damn well better *get* ready," Remson answered. "Even before this, I've greased the way for Drake often enough different times when he passed through here. He owes me some accomodatin' in return."

"Besides," pointed out Millen, "we got to go as far as Laramie anyway, to head off those three troublemakers who squirted out of town ahead of us just a little while ago."

"Aw shit," groaned Cleve. "We have to tangle with that McGantry cuss yet again?"

"No, you can bow out and stay behind with Muldoon if you want," Remson told him. "But that means you bow out once and for good from the whole Promise Valley deal. Don't come suckin' around later tryin' to get back in."

"Now damn it, Arn," Cleve protested. "I didn't say nothing about ducking out. Cut me a little slack, for crying out loud. That big sonofabitch near cost me my eye . . . might yet . . . makes a fella a little bit leary, that's all."

"Maybe so. But it'd make *me* all the more

determined to want another crack at him," said Remson, rubbing the bruise left on his jaw by Lone's gun barrel. "Matter of fact, I already got my own hankerin' for that. Stick with me, we'll both get our chance. And we won't have to wait to get to Laramie, neither."

"What do you mean?" asked Mojave.

"I mean," Remson answered, "I aim to go after those three troublemakers and stop 'em on the trail—before they ever make it to Laramie."

Millen's brow puckered. "Why not take the morning stage and get to Laramie ahead of them? We could be waiting to take care of 'em there as soon as they show up."

Remson shook his head. "No good. Might cause too much of a scene if we did it that way, maybe draw attention that could put to risk the Promise Valley business. We already let things get out of hand here. Uh-uh. We catch up with 'em on the trail, leave their bones in a far-off gully somewhere, and they can't make no trouble for nobody no more."

"But they're already headed out. What about the jump the got on us?" questioned Mojave.

"Only by a couple of hours. I figure they've already stopped for night camp by now, and they got a woman ridin' with 'em remember." Remson made a dismissive motion with his hand. "We get an early start in the mornin' and ride hard, we can catch up in no time."

"So that's our plan then?" Millen's tone made it clear he damn well knew the answer and didn't like it much.

"You got it," Remson confirmed. "Meanin' you fellas need to line up some horses and trail grub for us. Meet me here first light tomorrow and we'll ride out. Say your goodbyes to Cheyenne between now and then."

"What are you gonna be doing?" Cleve wanted to know.

Remson grinned lewdly and jerked his thumb toward the cabin. "I got me a two-hunnert pound Jamaica mama inside who's gonna fill my time real nice until I'm ready to switch to another saddle come mornin'."

Chapter Fourteen

Weather-wise, the first full day on the trail was nearly ideal. Once the sun rose and dispelled the night's chill, it became warm but not too warm, there was the faintest of breezes, and the rich blue sky was dotted with a handful of wispy, slowly skidding clouds. Lone took the lead, setting Ironsides to a steady, familiar pace that had carried the two of them over many miles during the former scout's drifting years. More began falling away this day. Sue had proven herself in the past to be a competent rider, as was Johnny, so neither they nor the mounts they'd selected had any trouble keeping up.

The terrain they covered alternated between expanses of rolling grassland and rocky, moderately rugged stretches. Iron Mountain loomed to the north and the Medicine Bow range could be seen sprawling farther west. They spotted several clusters of cattle as they rode, skirted wide of the few ranch buildings that came in sight.

Talk was sparse as the hours passed, even during the periods they paused to give the horses a breather and the brief lunch stop they made. The task at hand occupied each of their minds fully and any more fretting or speculating beyond what they'd already hashed over was pointless.

Reaching Laramie held the hope—the *demand*—to provide more.

As evening began to descend upon them, Lone felt more than satisfied with the day's progress. He reckoned they would easily reach Laramie by the middle of the following morning. That prospect, combined with a particularly appealing spot for a night camp presenting itself, was enough for him to call a somewhat earlier halt than otherwise intended. Said spot offered good graze for the horses, a spring pool for water, a stand of cottonwoods for campfire fuel, and a curving spine of jagged rocks to break the biting wind that had begun kicking up out of the northwest.

"This'll do right nice," Lone announced. "We'll tuck ourselves in here, give ourselves a good meal and a good rest. Be in Laramie in the mornin'."

"Sounds good to me," Johnny was quick to reply. Leaning back in his saddle and reaching to press the palm of one hand to the small of his back, he added, "I plumb forgot how long it's been since I spent a full day on horseback. But there's parts of me that have been sending regular reminders for quite a few miles now."

"I know exactly what you mean," said Sue with a wry smile. "What's worse, being a lady prohibits me from rubbing the parts that are reminding me the strongest."

Lone grinned. "I expect a touch of privacy could be arranged for you to rub your, er, sore parts. Especially since I got some liniment in my saddlebags that works pretty good for such things. We'll call it payback for the gunk you been smearin' on my back. Though, in your case, I reckon you'll have to do your own smearin'."

"Hey, if you got some stuff that works good, don't forget to include me too," said Johnny. "And I ain't so shy as to need no special fussing over who sees me do my smearing on."

"Well that hardly means the rest of us *want* to see such a sight," Sue snapped promptly in response.

A moment later all three were chuckling at this exchange. The small bit of lighthearted banter was a welcome shift from the stern, introspective quietness that had gripped them most of the day and it carried over into preparation for night camp. Lone first produced the liniment he'd spoken of and availed it to the others, who took turns disappearing in among the cottonwoods to apply it. Then, while Lone tended to the horses, Johnny laid out the gear and got a fire going as Sue began working up a meal. Daylight had nearly faded by the time they finished dining on beans, ham hocks, and pan-fried biscuits. Before settling back to relax and enjoy cups of post meal coffee, Sue insisted on treating Lone with some more of the liniment she'd purchased in Cheyenne.

"These welts and bruises on your back are healing remarkably well," she commented. "You must have hide like a buffalo."

"They'd be healin' even better if I had the satisfaction of knowin' I'd paid back proper those who gave 'em to me," Lone replied.

"From what I saw," said Sue, "you repaid them pretty well."

"And don't forget, I also got in a few licks on your behalf," mentioned Johnny.

"I guess," Lone allowed. "Still seems like they got off too easy, especially that fat skunk Remson."

"Keep in mind there are likely more skunks ahead to be dealt with. One for sure being Earl Drake," Sue reminded him, putting bitter emphasis on Drake's name.

After a couple reflective sips of his coffee, Lone said, "Speakin' of what lies ahead makes me wonder some more on what's behind. Occurs to me that, throughout the day, I never did no serious checkin' of our back trail."

Johnny frowned. "Not really no call to, was there? I mean, any of those who'd take an interest in us—Remson and his boys—got left pretty well sewed up by Deputy Brady. Didn't they?"

"Seemed like. But, then again, that would've partly depended on the marshal seein' things the same as Brady. By all reports he's a fairly decent fella, yet at the same time he's given too much free rein to Remson and his bully-boy tactics in the past."

"Even still," said Sue, "do you really think there's a chance that Remson and his thugs would set out after us?"

Lone's forehead puckered. "Can't say it seems likely. But the thing is, it's always been a practice of mine to keep an eye on my back trail. Havin' *not* done it today leaves me feelin' antsy. So, since there's a fair piece of twilight left, I think I'll go ahead and cure that antsiness by takin' a little ride and makin' a sweep back for a ways. Won't take long. Just to be sure."

"That makes you a lot more anxious to climb back in the saddle than I am," said Sue.

"Means he must have buffalo hide in places other than on his back," added Johnny.

Lone grinned. "Not just buffalo hide. Whang leather and gristle too. That's me from head to toe." In a single smooth motion, he rose from where he'd been sitting cross-legged before the fire. "You two just sit tight, I'll be back in a short. Save me some hot coffee."

Nearly ten hours of steady riding had Arn Remson sore all over. His back and shoulders felt like one giant, throbbing toothache had invaded his whole torso. His bulging gut was cramped and queasy as a result of the sloshing around it got from the swaying motion of being on horseback. And the only reason his legs and feet didn't hurt worse was because he was pretty sure they'd gone numb several miles back. Much as he hated to admit it, too many years of being a "townie" had softened him badly to the rigors of long stretches in a saddle. What the hell had he been thinking—heading out like he was twenty again instead of more than double that? Not to mention all the extra pounds packed around his middle.

But he was in the thick if it now, him and the other three as well. The only saving grace was that he could tell all of them were in just as much misery as him.

Cleve made no bones about that when, as soon as Remson signaled a stop for night camp, he exclaimed, "Thank sweet Jesus!"

All four men slid stiffly and awkwardly down from their saddles and spent the next handful of minutes, amid a chorus of groans, standing there stretching and twisting in various ways to work some of the kinks out.

"I feel," declared Millen, "like I been shot at and missed but shit at and hit!"

"So now you feel just like you look," Mojave quipped.

"Maybe so. But I'll always look good standing next to you," Millen came back.

"If you two are done tradin' compliments,"

grumbled Remson, "how about pitchin' in and gettin' started on settin' up our camp. A warm fire and some hot grub will make everybody look and feel better."

Pulling the cork on his bottle of laudanum and raising it to take a swig, Cleve said, "I got something right here that'll help do the trick for me—on the feeling good part anyway."

Remson scowled. "Hey now. How much of that stuff you bring along?"

Cleve finished taking his drink and then cocked a brow, looking suspicious. "What difference does it make?"

"The difference it makes is wantin' to know how good it works. Does it knock down pain like they say?" Remson wanted to know.

"Well . . . yeah. It's pretty potent stuff."

"There you go then. I'm achin' from my ass both ways," admitted Remson, "and it's plain to see that so is everybody else. Ain't none of us used to forkin' a saddle for a long stretch like we've took on here. So why you bein' such a hog with some elixir that'd help us all?"

Putting the cork back and clutching the bottle somewhat possessively, Cleve said, "Quincannon give me this on account of my tore-out eye misery, remember? I got that *on top* of the aches from this ride-out you dragged all of us on. That means I need it the worst."

Millen and Mojave were now crowding in

closer, also taking an interest. "Ain't nobody lookin' to take the damn stuff away from you or sayin' you can't even have extra due to your extra misery," said Remson. "All I'm suggestin' is that you could share some of it. You can see we could all use a dose of the relief it'd give."

"That's a fair point," agreed Millen. "You got plenty there."

"Quincannon made you that fresh batch just yesterday," added Mojave.

"So what?" Cleve countered sullenly. "He didn't make enough for three other mouths to guzzle down. This eye hurts like a bastard, in case you'd like to know—even *with* this stuff. I can't afford to run out."

"We ain't gonna drink you dry, for cryin' out loud," Remson told him. "We just want a snort to ease our aches and pains long enough to get settled in for the night. Jesus. And we'll naturally be passin' around a jug of whiskey later on to settle ourselves some more. Besides, if we run your supply too low, we'll fetch you a refill first thing when we hit Laramie in the mornin'."

Grudgingly, Cleve gave in. He held the bottle out to Remson, saying, "All right then. I'm outnumbered and outvoted. But I'll warn you, the taste of that devil's brew is surely no treat."

"That's a good sign," said Millen. "My dear saint of a mother, who would never lie to me,

199

told me that the worse a medicine tasted the more good it would do."

"In that case," exclaimed Remson, puckering his face into a fright mask as he lowered the bottle after taking a swig, "this shit must be the greatest medicine in the world! Gawd! Because it tastes like something straight out of a sewer pipe from Hell itself!"

"I tried to warn you," said Cleve.

Millen reached for the bottle. "Aw, come on. It can't be that bad." After tipping it high and gulping a big swallow, he lowered it and made his own tortured face. "I was right. It ain't that bad—it's worse!"

When he went to pass the bottle, Mojave shook his head. "No thanks. I'll stick with some good ol' reliable redeye a little later on."

They then went about pitching their camp. To help get a fire going, Millen gathered up some twigs and branches and then kneeled to provide a wind block for Remson as he nursed a small pile of kindling into flames large enough to take on more fuel. "You really think we'll make Laramie okay by tomorrow?" Millen asked, starting to feed in some of the twigs.

"Oh, hell yeah," said Remson. "By my reckonin' we oughta be able to noon there. In spite of near bustin' our town-soft asses and backs to do it, we covered a good stretch of distance today."

"In that case, what about those we're following after? You think we closed on them any?"

Remson scowled. "We got to have, them bound to be slowed by a woman travelin' with 'em and all. I was hopin' we might catch sight of 'em by now, but even scannin' with my field glasses I ain't seen nothing. While we still got some light, keep an eye peeled to the west for maybe a wisp of campfire smoke. Barrin' that, come dark one of us needs to go up on that rise yonder and look for sign of a fire."

"What if we *do* see something? We go after 'em then?"

"What do you think? Catchin' up with 'em and endin' 'em pokin' into Drake's business once and for all would be a sight easier out here than after we get to Laramie, wouldn't you say? And closin' in on 'em in the dark would for sure be easier than bracin' 'em in the daylight." Remson leaned back, squinting against the smoke now curling up from the fire. "But first we got to *spot* the damn meddlers before we can do anything at all!"

"Don't worry, Arn. One way or other, we'll catch up and finish dealing with 'em," Millen assured him.

"We'd damn well better. Now more than ever we got too much ridin' on that Promise Valley deal goin' through," growled Remson. Then, raising his voice to make sure the other two also heard, he added, "Are we all clear on that? I don't care how sore anybody's ass or back or eyeball is, by this time tomorrow we plain *got* to have that Leonard woman and her two hounds took care of and out of the way. Understood?"

Lone was almost ready to turn and go back when he saw it. Drawing rein atop a gravelly slope and peering due east, there it was. A small, pulsing dot of light. A campfire. About a mile and a half out, in the middle of nowhere—but also smack in the middle of their back trail.

The former scout swore under his breath and then wasted a couple minutes trying to convince himself it might be nothing at all connected to his group. Could be a lone drifter, such as he himself had been many a time in open country like this. Maybe some hunters. Or maybe some brushpoppers out rounding up strays for a big ranch somewhere in the vicinity. But, for all that, it *could* also be trouble tracing back to what him and the others stirred up before leaving Cheyenne.

All boiling down to there being only one way to find out for sure . . .

Chapter Fifteen

Sue and Johnny were still awake and waiting when he got back to camp. Lone wasted no time giving a terse report, biting out the words through clenched teeth. "They're there alright. All four of the mangy polecats, tucked in a shallow draw just under four miles back."

"Remson too?" asked Johnny.

"Just like I said. All four. Remson, Millen, Cleve, and Mojave. The big toad from the pond is right there in the thick of 'em."

"Things back in Cheyenne must not have worked out to Brady's liking," said Sue, frowning.

"No way of knowin'," Lone allowed. "Could be this pack got tossed out on their ears. Could be they took out on their own. No matter how or why, we got 'em on our tail now. Makin' 'em our problem to deal with. Again."

Sue held out a cup of coffee she'd poured for him. "You got something in mind?"

"Been thinkin' on it all the way back." Lone took the coffee and had himself a drink. "Way I see it, we got no option but to shake 'em *off* our tails. The sooner the better—and this time permanent-like."

Sue's brows pinched together. "You don't mean . . . ?"

"If I meant that," Lone snapped, "we'd right now be talkin' about four corpses. And don't think doin' it that way didn't cross my mind. But no, I'm willin' to give the varmints one more chance to keep their lives. Mainly, because I want another crack at gettin' more information out of 'em. That means Remson in particular. The other three don't amount to much more than hired guns, and we was only gonna get so much out of them, no matter what. But a chance to now get our hands on the big toad . . . I figure he's in plenty deep on knowin' the whole picture of whatever's behind needin' so bad to keep Earl Drake and Rosemary in the clear. We squeeze that out of him, I'm thinkin' we'll gain a lot of ground on where we need to get to."

"You reckon we'll be able to get him to talk?" Johnny asked.

Lone took another drink of his coffee. When he lowered the cup, he cast his gaze down at the fire and said in a low voice, "If need be, I got ways to be pretty persuasive."

Sue and Johnny exchanged looks but said nothing.

Lone swung his eyes back from the fire and said, "When I left their camp they were finishin' up their supper and startin' to pass around a jug of hooch. Moanin' and groanin' about how tuckered out and saddle sore they all was. I figure, by the time we get back, the lot of 'em oughta be sleepin' sound as hogs beside a slop trough. Shouldn't be too hard for us to slip in, strip 'em of their guns, and have 'em under the muzzles of ours before they're awake enough to know up from down."

"You make it sound awful slick," replied Johnny. "And I ain't saying it won't go just that way. But we'll still have two to four odds trying to keep 'em corraled and under control after that."

"*Three* to four odds," Sue was quick to correct him.

"Aw, come on," Johnny protested. "You don't think you're gonna ride out and—"

"I certainly do," Sue cut him short. "We've been through this before, Johnny. I'm in this to the hilt. I *started* all of this, remember? And I've proven by now that I'm not some shrinking violet who's going to stand by patiently and let others do all the dirty work to get results."

Two pairs of pleading eyes swept to Lone. He focused on meeting Johnny's. "Like the lady said, we been through this before. Maybe I ain't crazy about it either. But, number one, how we gonna keep her from followin' us short of leavin' her hogtied? Number two, like you hinted at yourself, we could use another gun. And she *has* proven her mettle and this *is* her show that we each signed on to. Seems to stack up pretty clear in her favor, and we ain't got a lot of time to waste arguin' over it."

Johnny puffed out his cheeks and blew an exasperated sigh. "Okay. Mark me down as not being in favor of it. But, like you said, I signed on to this show so I guess I gotta fall in line like a loyal soldier."

Lone chuckled. "Spoken like every grumblin' trooper I ever spent time in the Army with. Come on, let's go get horses saddled for you two."

With a three-quarter moon and a canopy of bright stars to light their way, Lone led Sue and Johnny on a re-trace of the back trail sweep he'd made a short time earlier. This took them due east to the gravelly slope where he'd first spotted Remson's campfire, then a wide swing south and around until they came at the camp downwind out of the southeast. The chill wind that had begun to kick up near sunset was still gusting out of the northeast, but it hadn't grown appreciably stronger.

A hundred yards short of the camp they dismounted and staked their horses. Reaching the lip of the shallow depression in which Remson and his crew were camped, they bellied the last few feet and held there to study the scene. Four bedrolls were arranged in a ragged semi-circle around the campfire. The latter had died down to mostly pockets of glowing red coals with a few stubborn flames licking up here and there. Across the way, off to one side of some tanglebush and a pair of weathered cedar trees, four horses were picketed.

Lone concentrated on the four sleeping forms wrapped in their blankets. Their faces were all obscured by dense shadow but he reckoned he could still identify the individual lumps. The biggest, thickest one was clearly Remson. Each man had his rifle lying visibly on the ground right beside him. Two of them—Millen and Cleve, if Lone was judging their forms accurately—had removed their gun belts and holstered pistols and these could be seen hanging on the saddles that were their headrests. Meaning Remson and Mojave still had theirs either still strapped around their waists or otherwise held close inside their blankets with them.

Lone pointed this out to Johnny in a low, close whisper. "When we roust 'em out of their blankets, we'll have to watch those two real tight."

Johnny nodded his understanding.

Lone next leaned his face close to Sue's and spoke again in a very low whisper. "Okay. Johnny and me are gonna move in, just like we talked about. We're gonna try to strip away their guns without wakin' 'em. While we're doin' that, you position yourself so you got a crossfire bead on 'em. Once they're rousted and get a look at that gut shredder you'll be aimin', I'm countin' that'll put a stop to any frisky notions that might otherwise crawl into somebody's pea brain."

Sue gave a firm nod. The "gut shredder" Lone had referenced was a twelve-gauge, double-barreled Greener shotgun provided from his own gear for her to use. It was a big step up from the double-barreled derringers she was also still carrying, but she wielded the long gun with confidence.

At a chin jerk from Lone, he and Johnny moved forward. Slowly, silently, they made their way down the slight incline, angling off to one side and then curling back in on the sleeping men. While they were doing that, Sue eased straight down and took up a position about six feet short of the nearest blanket-wrapped form. She kneeled on one knee and balanced the Greener across the thigh of her raised leg. If she fired even one barrel of the powerful gun from where she was braced, the blast would sweep across all four men and do vicious damage. The spread might even partly catch Lone or Johnny, but that was an acceptable risk if there was cause for her to shoot. Lone trusted her judgment not to do so unnecessarily.

As Lone and Johnny drew closer to the bedrolls, the snoring and sleep murmurings coming out of the men inside them grew so loud that the need for stealth was all but eliminated. *Hell,* Lone thought to himself, *I could have ridden Ironsides down here until he was standing straddle over this bunch and they'd never of heard him above the noise of their own snoring.*

Nevertheless, he and Johnny took all caution when reaching out and quietly lifting away the rifles from beside the bedrolls and then depositing them well out of reach. Next they did the same with the two visible gun belts. That done, wielding their own Winchesters that they'd carried with them down the slope, they each took a wide-legged stance just back from the heads of the sleeping men.

After signaling his intent to Johnny with a faint head tip, Lone reached down with the muzzle of his Yellowboy and flipped back the covers from around Remson's head and shoulders. "Rise and shine, Fatso!" he hollered in a loud voice. "Ain't no amount more of beauty sleep ever gonna help your ugly mug anyway!" To emphasize his words, as Remson's eyes opened and his head started to lift groggily, Lone jacked a fresh round into the Yellowboy and waved the muzzle just inches under Remson's nose.

"Heeyah! All of you varmints wake yourselves up!" Johnny shouted to the others, also using his rifle barrel to flip the covers off Mojave. "Where's your manners—company has come calling!"

As protests and curses began to erupt from the rousted men, Lone shouted louder still to make sure he was heard over them. "Understand this!

Anybody reaches for anything but your ears is askin' for a bullet! And if you think you want to risk that, look over at the Greener barrels aimed your way and see if you want to take a chance on what comes outta them!"

The sputtering and grumbling continued, but quieted considerably.

Remson glared fiercely up at Lone. "What the hell's the meanin' of this! What right have you got to—"

"Shut up!" Lone cut him off. "We're the ones with the guns that you're on the wrong end of. That means we got all the rights and you got none!"

"The hell with that! You goddamn—"

This time Lone stopped him with a short jab of the Yellowboy's muzzle, cracking it against the bridge of his nose. Remson yelped and clapped the palm of one hand over his face.

Lone raked his eyes over the rest of the rousted men who had all pushed themselves to sitting positions by now. "Alright, here's how it's gonna go," he said. "You're all gonna shut up and listen up and speak only when spoken to. And if a question is asked of you, you'd damn well better answer and answer straight. You all had your chance to stay back in Cheyenne and stay out of this. But now you've gone and horned into our business some more, so don't whine and cry if you get the horns rammed back at you!"

"Don't let this big bastard bluff you, boys," growled Remson, his words wet-sounding from the thick worm of blood running down his nose and over his lips. "He's got nothing on us and there's nothing he can do to—"

When the Yellowboy's barrel struck Remson this time, it was a hard swat across the side of his head. Hard enough to stun the heavy man and knock him back flat.

Now it was Lone who spoke in a growl, addressing the other three. "I got a particular dislike for this tub you're lettin' lead you around, so if he wants me to keep provin' I *ain't* bluffin' then I'd kinda enjoy it showin' him some more. But unless you're purely as dumb as him, the rest of you got the chance to cooperate and avoid some of the same treatment."

There was a faint pause before Millen, who was closest to the gaping twin bores of Sue's Greener, spoke. "I don't know about the rest of you fellas, but I'm smart enough to know when I got no cards left to play. We should've cut our losses and stayed in Cheyenne. I already tangled once with this jasper and came up on the short end. I don't think he's bluffing at all, and I ain't ready to cash in my last chip out here in the middle of no-goddamn-where!"

The other two, while not saying so in words, grumbled a general assent.

Lone nodded. "That's showin' at least a small

sign of smarts. Johnny, go ahead and—careful-like—relieve Mr. Mojave of his gun belt. While you're at it, Remson too. Then shake out those lengths of rope we brought along . . ."

Chapter Sixteen

Like most bullies—which Lone had a hunch would be the case—Arn Remson's tough exterior crumbled quickly enough when he found himself on the receiving end of punishment rather than being the one dishing it out. Oh, he held up for a while to some general slapping around. But, with his three henchmen securely bound and able to do nothing but helplessly watch, it only took a few swipes from Lone's Bowie blade, heated cherry red in the coals of the freshly stoked campfire, before Arn began freely spilling everything he knew or could speculate about the scheme Earl Drake was involved in and why it had been so important to block all pursuit of him and the girl.

When the grim business of getting Remson to talk was finished and the last of the burned flesh stink had been blown away by the gusting wind, Lone laid out further instructions for dealing with the four polecats. All were stripped of everything but their trousers. Then, barefoot and shivering in the chill night air, they were bunched together and re-tied to the cedar trees. Their guns and all of their gear was bundled up in their bedrolls and loaded on the horses, which Lone, Sue, and Johnny would be leading away.

Once all of this was ready, Lone stood facing

the knot of men, feet planted wide and Yellow-boy braced on one hip. "You wretches might think this hard treatment," he grated. "But keep in mind that, if things had gone the other way, you know damn well you'd've left our bodies for scavenger pickin's, likely without the bother of even shovin' us into a gully somewhere. So you're lucky to still have your lives, pathetic as they are. One of you ought to find a way to wiggle free of those ropes by sunrise. Then you'll have a long, uncomfortable hike before you find a ranch or a couple out-riders or some such. Be a challenge to come up with a yarn to explain the fix you're in, won't it?"

He paused, showing a thin wolf's smile for just a moment. Then his mouth went tight again and his eyes turned even colder and harder than before. "But whatever you tell anybody else, best make sure you convince your own selves of this: You're damn lucky to be left alive and if you want to stay that way, make sure you never cross my path—or that of my friends here—ever again. You come lookin' to bother either of them after this, I'll hunt down every mother's son of you. And if you come after me and I lay eyes on any of you, no matter where or when, I won't hesitate, I won't think twice, I will simply burn you down on sight. Now, if all that has sunk in real clear, me and my friends will say good night and be on our way."

Which is what Lone, Sue, and Johnny then proceeded to do. They led the gear-laden horses back to where they'd left their mounts staked, climbed in saddles once more and returned to their own camp. Ordinarily, one might have expected that the ride back would be filled with eager discussion about all the new information Remson had given. In this case, however, there was hardly any talk at all.

Lone understood plainly enough why. His methods for getting Remson to talk and to make sure he was telling it straight had been more than a little shocking to both Sue and Johnny. Though they hadn't protested openly at any point, the look on their faces (and the way Sue turned her head a time or two) left little doubt as to their discomfort—and perhaps downright disapproval. Yeah, he understood; but at the same time he felt a little bitter about such a reaction. He'd tried to warn them up front what it might take and they should had their own clear realization by now that the kind of ruthless men they were dealing with, especially Remson, would hardly bend to kid glove treatment.

So that's the way it was. Lone was willing to let it ride for the duration of the trip back. That would give Sue in particular some time to sort things out in her head. She was the reason he was here. Though he by now had his own investment of sorts in this thing, if she decided his ways no longer fit with what she'd been expecting, then he'd be willing to turn Ironsides back toward home and let it go at that.

When they got to camp and the horses were all picketed, Lone stood before Sue and Johnny. "We got two or three hours left before daybreak," he said. "I suggest we use it to get what shuteye we can before headin' out again, this time for a place called Promise Valley based on what Remson had to say."

Sue regarded him. "You'd actually be able to sleep after . . ."

Hearing her words trail off set Lone's teeth on edge. Okay, here it was. Time to trot it out into the open and get it settled. "After what?" he said with some bite to his tone. "After the way I went about questioning Remson? That it? If it is, spit it out of your craw and say it plain."

Sue's face flushed, maybe in anger, maybe something else. "Jesus, Lone, what do you expect? I wasn't ready to see that side of you. You were so . . . so . . ."

"Harsh? Savage? Go ahead and say it. I can take it because I know what I was, what I can be again if and when I have to. It's a side of me that was honed a long time ago in places and under circumstances far more savage than the likes of Arn Remson could ever endure." Lone's eyes bored into her as if lit by a strange, faraway fire. "It's not me at my core, Sue. But it's a part I had to develop to survive. And, whether you want to admit it or not, it's a part you recognized and why you sent for me in the first place to help try and save James. Think about that."

The flush drained from Sue's face but she had no response.

Lone cut his eyes to Johnny. "You got anything to say?"

The ex-deputy met his gaze evenly. "No, I reckon not. Like you said, one way or other we need to start thinking about a place called Promise Valley."

Lone nodded. "Okay. I'm gonna go ahead and grab some sleep." His eyes returned to Sue. "Come daybreak, you can have your mind made up on whether or not you want me to stick with the show."

"Naturally I want you to stay. We need you . . . and all that that entails. I'm sorry for the way I acted before. It's just that I-I was startled by what occurred. I realize now it was necessary for the type of individual you were dealing with. And the information you got out of him was not only valuable but it saved us what might have otherwise taken days to learn. Days . . . when every minute might be crucial for James."

These were the words from Sue that greeted Lone when he woke with the sun and first crawled out of his bedroll. She was already awake, if she had slept at all, and had a pot of coffee cooking on the fire.

Lone ran his fingers back through his hair, clapped on his hat, went over and squatted beside her. "I'm glad you reached that decision," he told her. "I did some thinkin' too, and saw where I could've better handled things. Not so much with Remson, I don't mean. But I could've at least taken him aside somewhere and . . . well, had my talk with him. It was crude and even a little cruel—to you, I'm sayin'—to do it the way I did. I truly regret that, Sue."

"It's done," she said, meeting his earnest gaze. "The thing now is to capitalize on what was learned. We must focus on getting to Promise Valley and now hope that it holds the promise of fulfilling my belief that if we catch up with Rosemary there we will also find James."

"It continues bein' the only angle we've got on him," allowed Lone.

A tousle-haired Johnny, rousted from sleep by their talk, came over to join them. "You ever hear of this Promise Valley before, Lone?"

The former scout shook his head. "Can't say as I have. All I know is what Remson described, how it's about two days ride to the northwest and at its heart is a town called Promise City."

"Where we will find," added Sue, repeating more of what Remson had had to say, "a shifty lawyer named Lavin who is behind the scheme

218

Earl Drake is helping him work that is supposed to gain them control over most of the valley and whatever wealth it holds."

"Sounds like mighty big shucks for a place nobody ever heard of," commented Johnny.

Lone smiled thinly. "Maybe so. But keep in mind that, one time or other, folks could have said—and did—the same thing about places like Deadwood Gulch, Tombstone, Sutter's Mill, and so on." He shrugged. "Maybe this snake Lavin knows something others just ain't yet aware of."

"Whether he does or not isn't our concern," Sue said solemnly. "All I want is to get my brother out of the way before he gets ground up by whatever scheme Lavin and Drake have got underway."

Chapter Seventeen

Niles Lavin interlaced his well-manicured fingers atop his office desk and regarded the man who had just taken a seat in the padded leather chair positioned in front of the desk. "Well?" said Lavin. "You just came from the Crawford place . . . how are things settling in there?"

The man in the leather chair, Earl Drake, finished lighting a long, thin cheroot he held clamped between his teeth. He puffed the cheroot to life, shook out the match, and blew a perfect smoke ring before replying. "As a fine old Southern gentleman I once knew was fond of saying . . . everything is fine as frog's hair. The old couple remain thrilled and overjoyed by the safe return of Rosemary from her alleged kidnapping, and their treatment of yours truly for handling the ransom and release is so deeply heartfelt it damn near makes me feel guilty for shading the poor fools."

Lavin smiled slyly. "But not so guilty, I trust, that you'd consider giving up your cut of the ransom payment?"

"No, your trust in thinking that is plenty safe. The small slice of decency I have left in me that generates occasional pangs of guilt does not come anywhere close to getting in the way of accepting a piece of fifty thousand dollars."

Lavin's smile broadened. He was a solidly built man in his middle forties. He had a rather plain face but held with a certain bearing that made it seem something more. A high forehead was topped by thick, slightly wavy hair streaked with silver-gray at the temples. He had quick, intelligent eyes, a thin nose, and an expressive mouth. His attire of a well-cut business suit, crisp white shirt, and blue string tie marked him as a man of taste and some degree of affluence. The well-appointed office surrounding him, advertised by the shingle out front and the lettering painted on its windows as that of an attorney at law, completed the picture of one who has attained success in his life and career. In Lavin's case, however, what only a very few close confidants knew was that he had a huge appetite for even more success—and the conversation currently taking place with Drake was part of a complex plan for achieving it.

Around his widened smile, he now said, "It's encouraging to hear that a spurt of decency from you isn't something I need to be concerned about. Your conniving and cleverness has proven useful many times in the past, but never more so than the way you thought to turn that stupid runaway girl's flight into a kidnapping hoax that kept the Crawfords hanging fire long enough for you to get her back and keep our overall scheme on course. Plus bring in a tidy unexpected bonus."

"That's me. Scalawag extraordinaire," chuckled Drake. "My years as a detective for the Pulford Agency, before you hired me to represent your practice full time, introduced me to a parade of characters—on both sides of the so-called Law, just for the record—who educated me on a wide range of cleverness and connivery." He was a lean, well-muscled number a few years short of forty. Roguishly handsome, with a neatly trimmed pencil mustache, slick black hair, razored sideburns, and a frequently flashed cocky smile to go with a generally cocky attitude.

"Proving that beneficial skills can indeed be learned outside of musty books and lecture halls," Lavin said dryly. "But getting back to the girl . . . are you confident she has her head on straight now and won't be pulling any future antics to jeopardize all we have riding on the line?"

Drake blew another smoke ring. "I made it painfully clear that any more such nonsense would be paid at a very steep price. Not only by her but also by everybody and everything— from that idiot she used to call a husband to some dumb horse we left behind in Cheyenne—she ever held dear. I'm counting on that, along with the Basteen brothers now on duty as her constant bodyguards, to keep her sufficiently in line."

Lavin frowned. "How could you threaten fur-ther harm to her abandoned husband when you've already done so? You did finish him off, didn't you?"

Drake looked annoyed. "I told you. I *shot* him. It would have been a kill shot for certain if that damn half breed pal of his hadn't shown up and shouted a warning just as I was drawing a bead on the husband. I had to shoot the breed first because he was pulling a gun. When I got my second shot off at hubby, he was making a run for it. I know I hit him, but it wasn't clean enough to put him down. I couldn't give chase because too many people were pouring out of the saloons in response to the gunshots."

"Sounds to me like the stubborn fool could still be alive."

"Damn slim chance," Drake insisted, even more irritably. "He ended up carrying around a bullet and a murder charge for the breed. Where could he turn? The fact no sign of him showed up again seems pretty damned convincing to me that he crawled off into a gully somewhere and bled to death." He drew hard on his cheroot then blew out a churning cloud of smoke. "No matter, the girl doesn't know any of this, so it makes my threat to her still solid."

Lavin appeared mollified. "Okay then. Let's return to the girl and the Crawfords . . . how is the old couple taking to having the Basteens on hand?"

"It's an adjustment, of course. Mrs. Crawford

ain't at all comfortable with the hoglegs they pack everywhere they go. But I explained to her," Drake described, "how it's a necessary precaution against any more nasty kidnappers making another try for Rosemary. Her fear of that and her trust in my judgment is allowing her to go along okay."

"There's the key," said Lavin, his expression darkening. "The stubborn old bat just *keeps* going along and continuing on. What about her failing health that the damn doctors claimed was heralding her doom clear back six months ago?"

"It's the same old story," Drake replied with a shrug. "She has her good days, she has her bad ones. When Rosemary was missing, ol' Irene sank mighty low. But now, since Rosemary's return, she's perked right up again. Just like she did when I brought Rosemary around in the first place."

Lavin rose from his chair and strode to the window where he stood gazing down on the main street of Promise City. It was a quaint, tidy, bustling small town scene. Ordinarily, Lavin would drink in this view and take considerable satisfaction in counting the number of businesses he owned controlling interest in—covertly, in most cases, through a handful of different companies he wasn't known to be the head of. At the moment, however, he felt more restless than satisfied. "I can be a very patient man, Drake," he said over his shoulder. "I've proven that by how long I've allowed to slowly, methodically tighten my grip on properties in this town and the outlying valley. But always there was progress, even if slow and grinding at times. Yet now my biggest, most crucial move . . . acquiring the Crawford holdings . . . is starting to feel stalled, like it isn't moving at all."

"I don't think that's the case, Mr. Lavin. Not really." Drake frowned. "This thing with Irene Crawford—she *is* mighty sick and frail. I've seen it, so has everybody who's around her much at all. Even though she's bounced back some right at the present, that kidnapping thing really took a toll. Irene's a tough old gal, pioneer stock and all, but I'd say she's been whipsawed near to a frazzle."

Lavin turned to look at him. "So you don't think we ought to once again consider . . . helping her along?"

"I not only don't think it's necessary to consider that yet," Drake said, "but if you mean trying to use Rosemary again, then I for damn sure don't. That's the one thing almost certain to turn her rabbit again and we'd end up losing ground instead of gaining any."

Lavin scowled irritably. "I thought you said you had her put back in line?"

"Up to a point, yeah. But asking her to pinch out the old lady's wick is *over* the line. We found that out the first time, and it ain't no different now," Drake insisted. "Rosemary has grown about as fond of Irene as the other way around. It'll be hard enough for her to hold it together when the old gal checks out natural. She'll manage that much, though. But expecting her to help it along? Forget it." He wagged his head firmly.

Lavin expelled a breath out through his teeth. "Okay. You've convinced me. I guess I have to play the patience game a while longer." He sat back down and placed his hands on the desktop again. Only this time they were balled into fists. "But I'm determined that my patience *will* pay off, Drake!"

"Oh I believe you, Mr. Lavin," Drake assured him through a puff of smoke. "I'm counting on it too."

Chapter Eighteen

Lone, Sue, and Johnny rode steady for two solid days. They stayed in the saddle practically every minute from sunup to sundown, grinding out the miles. To keep it up without being too hard on their horses, they hung on to the three best animals of the four they'd taken from Remson and his crew. This allowed them to change back and forth to fresh mounts at regular intervals. The fourth horse they turned loose in good grassland where it would be able to join up with a wild herd or end up getting roped and made part of a ranch remuda somewhere. The guns and gear they'd confiscated—minus cartridges and grub supplies they could make use of—they dumped into the first suitably deep creek they came to. Shedding the weight of the guns and everything else non-essential helped to lighten the load on the horses. Under different circumstances, Lone would have kept the guns to try and make some resale money off them when they came to a town or settlement. But since they were traveling through unfamiliar territory, he didn't want to take the time for haggling or to risk drawing suspicion from some ambitious badge toter.

Early on the second morning, they came to an outlying trading post run by an old buffalo hunter named Strode and his squaw wife Walking Bird. A stop there proved well worth the time. Inasmuch as they'd originally set out for only a short trip to Laramie, their grub supply was pretty meager, even augmented by what they got from the confiscated gear. So the chance to stock up some more in that area was quite welcome. It was a source, too, for some grain to feed the horses they were pushing so hard. What was equally welcome was the information they also gained about Promise Valley. The trading post was near enough and Strode had been around long enough so that he was well versed on its history.

It all dated back to the mid-Forties, he related, only a few years ahead of the big gold rush. A small wagon train of settlers headed for California reached the wide untamed, unnamed valley rimmed by a small mountain range called the Estelles to the northwest and cut through by a river called the Little Finger. After camping there for a night, one member of the group—a man named Ezra Crawford, traveling with his wife and two toddler sons—took a good look around the next morning and decided that a body didn't need to go any farther to discover a fine place to put down roots. According to the story that eventually built up, Crawford said words to the effect that here was land with good grass for raising cattle, good soil for farming, and plenty of water—making it a place that held a fair promise to succeed and build a good life for anybody who wanted to put forth the effort. And that's what he intended to do. Hence the name Promise Valley (and eventually Promise City as things grew and thrived) was born.

Three other families from the wagon train decided to remain along with the Crawfords, the rest moved on. In the years that followed, Crawford succeeded even better than he'd envisioned, he and his sons building a big cattle ranching operation that laid claim to a quarter of the valley along its northwest boundaries. But that still left plenty of room for others. Two of the original families failed and moved on; the third stuck it out, though on a much smaller scale than Crawford. More folks then began arriving. Some of them also failed, but more found it to their liking and stayed. Out of this grew the necessity for a town.

"From all reports," Strode summed up, "it seems like a nice, peaceful place to live and folks are generally happy there."

"Sounds like," allowed Lone. Then, deciding to take a chance and probe a little deeper, he said, "Reason we're headed that way is on account of we ran into an hombre named Drake back in Cheyenne who spoke of another fella by the name of Lavin who's supposed to be hirin' on help out in Promise Valley at pretty decent wages. You hear anything about that?"

"Naw, 'fraid not," Strode answered with a shake of his head. "The valley's still far enough away so's I don't really hear a lot of current news or know much of any names out that way. One thing I know is that there's been talk on and off about bringin' a railroad spur into Promise City someday, but ol' Ezra's always talked it down. Maybe this Lavin fella has finally won him over and that's what this talk of jobs is all about."

"Maybe," Lone said. "Never did any railroad work before. But I reckon a job is a job as long as the pay is right, eh?"

Strode grinned through his whiskers. "Don't ask me. This child never worked for wages a day in his life."

Niles Lavin and Earl Drake were once again occupying Lavin's office. Although it was only the middle of the day, a lamp was burning on a corner of the spacious desk. This was in deference to the dense cloud cover that had rolled in outside, its churning gray mass threatening rain and turning what had been a bright morning into an afternoon as gloomy as dusk.

The expressions on the faces of the two men were also nearly as dark and brooding as the sky without. Drake was once again sitting in the padded chair hitched up in front of the desk; Lavin was on his feet, pacing restlessly.

In his hand, the attorney clutched a recently

received telegram, addressed to Drake and signed by Tate Millen. As he paced, Lavin kept raising the piece of paper and glaring at it fiercely. Its message read:

THINGS HERE TURNED BAD. STOP. REMSON OUT OF IT. STOP. LEONARD WOMAN AND TWO MEN HEADED THERE. STOP. WATCH OUT FOR BIG MAN ON GRAY STALLION. STOP. NAME OF MCGANTRY.

"Damn and double damn," Lavin fumed. He stopped pacing and spun on Drake. "What kind of incompetent fools did you leave behind in Cheyenne? I thought you had things sealed off so that stupid husband of Rosemary's and his meddlesome sister could never follow you here?"

"I've used Remson and the men he employs several times in the past when I had cases in Cheyenne," Drake replied defensively, "and they always worked out okay. I don't know what went wrong this time. If they'd followed everything the way I had it laid out, there should have been no problem."

" 'Remson out of it.' What the hell does that even mean?"

"How the devil am I supposed to know?" Drake reached into an inner pocket of his jacket, withdrew a cheroot and a match. "By the wording and the fact it was Millen who sent the wire and not Remson, I'd judge something must have happened to the tub. He could have got injured or maybe wounded. Hell, maybe dead. Whatever the answer, that's not nearly as important as the fact that that damn Leonard pain in the ass and her followers are on the way here."

"You think I don't know that—don't realize how much trouble they could stir up for us? How does she keep adding helpers? Who are they and what stake do they have in any of this?"

Drake got his cheroot going and blew out the match. "When I left Cheyenne, she only had the one fella trailing her around," he said. "Way I heard, he was from the same town as her and her dopey brother. Friend of the family, wanting to help out, the way it looked. Wanting mainly to get in good with the sister, was my guess."

Lavin scowled. "So, at that point, whoever this McGantry is, he was no part of it."

"Never heard the name, never saw nobody who fit that description."

"You'd recognize the woman and the other fellow, though. Right?"

"Right."

"But if McGantry showed up and you happened to see him neither on his horse nor in the company of the other two, you could look right at him and not recognize him at all," Lavin stated. "He sure as hell isn't the only man in Wyoming who fits the description of merely being *big*. He could already be in town. He could be walking by right outside on the boardwalk this very minute and we would have no idea it was him!"

"Calm down, Mr. Lavin," Drake told him. "He's not in town yet. Can't be. Since Millen knows the color of McGantry's horse, means he—and the others too, you've got to figure— are riding in and not coming by stage. So they couldn't have made it by now."

"So we've got time to prepare for their arrival. There's at least one break for us."

"Uh-huh. And as to getting prepared, I've already put some things in place for that," Drake said with a degree of smugness. "If those three are coming in after some days on the trail, one of the first things they'll likely want to do is look to their horses. I've put men standing watch on the only two livery stables in town. If they come in together, a woman traveling with two men on horseback isn't exactly a common thing. So that will stand out, in and of itself. If they decide to split up before coming in, then the big man on a gray stud will be the key to watch for."

Lavin appeared to relax some and nodded eagerly. "Excellent thinking. Excellent." But then, almost immediately, his expression tightened with renewed concern. "Yet even still, no matter that we identify they've arrived, once they're here and began asking questions and

233

poking about, I'll be at risk for having attention drawn to everything I've worked so hard to line up with so much careful discretion."

"Two things to consider about that," Drake was quick to point out. "Number one, their main interest is in finding the woman's brother. James Risen, is his name. Even if they start spouting that out, it won't mean anything to anybody."

"But since they're coming here, isn't it possible they've also picked up at least your name in the process?" Lavin said. "What if—"

"Hold on," Drake cut him short. "I said two things, remember? The second thing is this idea I have for not giving them a chance to say or ask a damn thing. The minute we know they're in town, we turn the tables on 'em and have them fighting for their stinking lives."

Lavin's eyebrows pulled together. "How do you propose to do that? We can't just open fire on them for no reason."

Drake smiled slyly. "I'll have a good reason. A damn good one . . . I will recognize them as the dirty lowdown rats who kidnapped Rosemary!"

Chapter Nineteen

After leaving Strode's trading post, a cloud cover moved in out of the north just past noon and by the time Lone signaled for night camp a cold, drizzling rain was coming down. With no wind to speak of, they found decent shelter under a flat, rocky ledge thrusting out from a high cliff face. There were cedars and aspen trees crowded close around, providing adequate dry fuel for a fire. Sue got one going and set to making coffee while Johnny laid out their sleeping gear and Lone saw to the horses. In short order, they were huddled around the flames in their slickers and soogans, drinking hot coffee and eating the beef on sourdough sandwiches and fresh cinnamon rolls they had purchased back at Strode's trading post.

"Man," said Johnny, "you reckon this is how good all Injun squaws cook, or you figure Walking Bird is some kind of exception?"

A corner of Lone's mouth quirked up. "Why? You thinkin' about goin' courtin' on some Indian rez when you get back to South Dakota?"

Johnny paused with his sandwich raised partway to his mouth, getting ready to take another bite. "That wasn't exactly where I was headed when I asked that question," he said. "But maybe it's something to consider. I ain't getting any younger. I already lost the prime years of my life chasing after Sue and getting nowhere. I need to watch out or I might end up some old hermit stuck with eating my own lousy cooking for the rest of my days."

"Are you saying you'd blame me if it came to that?" Sue wanted to know.

"Well, you sure never gave me the chance at a better option like I was hoping for." A moment after he said this, Johnny held up his free hand in a palm-out gesture signaling to take it easy. "But forget I brought it up. I said my days of pestering you were over and I meant it. We better stick to talking about this business we're in the middle of here."

"Sounds like a right smart idea," Lone agreed.

"In that case," said Sue, "how about considering Mr. Strode's speculation about a railroad spur coming to Promise City? There's a lot of power and money involved in bringing the railroad to a place. Something like that would certainly fit with the talk of this Lavin, if he's in the thick of making it happen, suddenly wielding a lot of clout thereabouts. And if Ezra Crawford, who's painted as having been the he-bull of the valley up to now, remains opposed to such a thing— well, you've got the makings of a classic power struggle that would be ripe for a snake like Drake to slither in and offer to help work some leverage for whoever's willing to hire his services."

Talking around a bite of his own sandwich, Lone said, "You make all those names fit together in a convincing way. But only as long as you remember it's all hung on a string of speculation. What we're gonna have to do once we get to the valley and the town is see if we can start tyin' off some loose ends in that string. And all the while we'll need to keep an eye peeled in case one of those loose ends hopefully has James also there grabbin' for a hold of it."

"It sounded a lot tidier the way I laid it out," Sue replied. "But you're right about needing to also watch for James in the mix of things. Thank you for remembering to add that."

"Like you were ever gonna forget it for more than a few seconds." Lone washed down his bite of beef and sourdough with a swallow of coffee. "One thing's for certain, we'll have plenty to watch for when we get there. If Strode's directions were accurate, we should make it before noon tomorrow."

Johnny stuck his hand out into the rain. "Sounds good to me. Let's just hope it ain't all sunk underwater by the time we show up."

"A certain form of being underwater doesn't sound at all bad," said Sue somewhat wistfully. "I've been days on end without a bath and I fully intend to soak in a hot, sudsy tub as soon as possible once we reach Promise City."

• • •

The rain stopped sometime during the night and when the sun rose in the morning it shone through a still breaking cloud cover with larger and larger patches of clear sky showing through. In the dawn light, lingering raindrops glinted like a thousand tiny pearls on the grass of the low hills that rolled out away from the cliff where Lone and the others had made their camp.

They woke at first light, ate a quick breakfast of leftover sandwiches and fresh coffee. Then they cleared camp, saddled the horses and hit the trail again.

The chill of yesterday afternoon and the night's rain quickly lifted as the sky cleared completely and the warmth of the morning sun poured down on them. After about three hours, upon passing over a stretch of gradually upward sloping ground heavily dotted with trees and underbrush, they came to the rim of the incline and suddenly found themselves looking out over a vast depression, oblong in shape, spreading out for miles and miles as far as the eye could see. To the northwest a hazy jumble of mountains; to the south a barely discernible hint of buildings, maybe a church's bell tower thrusting up. In between, grassy expanses, stands of trees, vague indentations marking the winding path of a watercourse.

Drawing rein and resting a forearm down atop

his saddle horn, Lone drawled, "Well, folks, I think we're gettin' our first look at Promise Valley."

"Quite a sight," muttered Johnny.

"Indeed," said Sue, her tone somewhat hushed. "It's not hard to understand what Ezra Crawford saw that made him decide there was no need to travel any farther."

They gazed out quietly for a few beats. Until Lone cleared his throat and said, "Okay. Now that we're here we need to discuss how best to proceed. I been rolling some thoughts on that around in my head."

Sue looked over at him. "Go ahead. Let's hear them."

"It occurs to me that I'm the only one of us Earl Drake wouldn't recognize on sight. He for certain would spot you, Sue," Lone pointed out, "since you were in Cheyenne askin' questions before him and Rosemary lit out. Your showin' up likely played a part in him settin' Remson and the others to work blockin' you or anybody else from closin' in on him again after he was gone."

"What about me?" said Johnny. "I didn't tip my hand about followin' Sue and havin' any interest in her search until you were there too."

"You maybe didn't tip your hand to Sue," Lone corrected him. "But you *were* foggin' her, keepin' an eye on her. Meanin' that once Drake knew about her and sicced Remson's crew on her, there's at least a fifty-fifty chance they also spotted you. Too risky not to consider."

"So where are you leading with this?" questioned Sue.

"Just this. If all three of us ride into town together, no matter how slick we set about tryin' to find some things out, if Drake spots one or both of you then his alarm bells are gonna go off and I'm bettin' things will turn hard against us mighty quick." Lone eyed Sue and Johnny levelly. "If Drake went to the trouble of leavin' a barricade up in Cheyenne, think how solid a one him and Lavin, the big cheese, have likely got in place here."

"So what does that leave? What are you suggesting?"

"That I go into town alone and do some careful sniffin' around, hopefully without gettin' myself noticed. Once I've had a firsthand look at things and maybe picked up a useful bit of new information, then I rejoin you two and we plan our next move from there."

"And we just wait here doing nothing?" Sue asked, her tone conveying she wasn't particularly pleased with that notion.

"Actually, no," Lone responded. "You'd remain out here in open country, yeah—but you wouldn't have to sit your saddles and do nothing. Seems like it'd give you a chance to make a sweep to the northwest and have a look at the big Crawford spread that's supposed to be off that way. You could scope it out from a distance, using my field glasses, or maybe you'd want to ride in closer under some pretense." Lone grinned. "Think what a kick you got out of play-actin' back in Cheyenne, Sue. You could come up with some new story and take a crack at it all over again."

"Yeah, but I ain't no play actor," grumbled Johnny.

"And when I tried it before, no matter how much fun you seem to think I was having," said Sue with a sharply arched brow, "you might also recall it darn near ended up getting me killed."

Lone grunted. "Hell, ain't that what we're all continuin' to do anyway? Askin' for—or at least riskin'—the chance to get ourselves killed by stickin' our noses in where dangerous hombres don't want us?"

"But all in the name of trying to find and save my brother."

"And goin' to check out the Crawford spread, however you go about it," Lone insisted, "is still a part of that. Don't you see? If there's a power struggle goin' on, like you suggested, between Lavin tryin' to bring in a rail spur and Crawford meanin' to hold him off—then maybe you can spot some signs of it, some confirmation. I can't say how that might fit to findin' James. Only if Rosemary's somewhere out here and James has managed to follow her here, the way you keep believin', then the more we know about the whole picture, the better. Tyin' off loose ends, remember?"

Johnny puffed out his cheeks and expelled a breath. "Whew. This is getting awful complicated for a plain old South Dakota lad. Back when I was wearing a badge for Marshal Kurtz, breaking up saloon brawls, jailing drunks, keeping angry wives from splitting hubby's skull with a frying pan or meat cleaver for coming home drunk . . . that was all real simple and straight-forward. Nothing like this."

"You're not ready to give up, are you?" asked Sue.

He met her gaze. "No, I ain't saying any such. No matter what I agreed about no more pestering, you oughta know better than that . . . I'd never quit on you, Sue."

Their eyes held for an extended moment before Sue turned back to Lone, saying, "You make some valuable points and, as usual, you have reasonable suggestions for addressing them. If we proceed as you say, how much time are we talking—when and where would we meet back up?"

Lone rubbed his jaw. "Well, been my experience that the loosest talk a body is likely to find in most places—the way to pick up on the general mood and hear about the latest goin'-ons—is evenin' talk in saloons. So, to give it a fair shot, I'd need to be in town at least the rest of today and tonight. And if the Crawford spread is as big as Strode made it sound, then you two will need about the same amount of time, the rest of today's light anyway, to give it a good lookin' over. So that stacks up for bein' tomorrow, say about noon, as a re-joinin' time." He twisted his head one way then the other, looking around. "And since this seems like a reasonably out of the way spot, might as well make here where we come back to. How's that sound?"

Sue took a minute to consider. Traded looks once more with Johnny, then nodded. "Sounds workable . . . if you can make it in and out of a series of saloons without getting in a fight and thrown in jail." Lone wasn't sure if she was being serious or not. Before he could retort in any way, she added, "But we'll take the risk and go with it."

"Sure," said Johnny dryly. "You stroll leisurely around town, probably enjoy a nice sit-down supper, then sample good whiskey and cold beer served by flirty bar maids in however many different saloons they got . . . while me and Sue put in more saddle time, eat more camp cooking, sleep another night on the cold, hard ground. Sounds like a real swell trade-off."

"Look at it this way," Lone countered, "you'll be moseyin' down through that valley in the company of a pretty gal, breathin' fresh, clean air. Meanwhile, I'll be stuck in a saloon, chokin' on stinkin' cigar smoke and bay rum slapped on eye-waterin' strong by cowpokes wantin' to smell sweet enough to attract interest from the house dollies."

Sue rolled her eyes. "Oh, you two poor things. All I've got to say is that if my camp cooking isn't good enough for you, Johnny, then you can go hungry. And as for you, Lone McGantry, I don't care how much cigar smoke you have to endure or any of the rest. But if I find out you take time for a hot bath before I get a turn at one, the way I've been looking forward to but now have to postpone for who knows how much longer . . . I will never forgive you!"

Chapter Twenty

It was just short of noon by the time Lone and Ironsides had angled down through a corner of the valley and arrived in Promise City. Before parting with Sue and Johnny, they had staked the three spare horses in a copse of trees just back from the overlook where they would be returning to on the morrow. There was plenty of grass and a puddle of water from last night's rain to sustain the animals until they got back.

The main street of the town was muddy, also from the rain, churned with wagon ruts and horse tracks. Otherwise the modest-sized community appeared very tidy and neatly laid out, as if to a thoughtful plan; not the haphazard jumble that marked the way many western towns got built up. The false-fronted businesses lining Crawford Street and the houses spread off to either side were mostly wood frame structures, a few of stone or brick. Lone spotted the bell towers of two churches, located at opposite ends, and the gaudily painted fronts of three saloons interspersed among the other stores and shops in between. The need for Promise City's menfolk, and especially the wranglers and hired hands from the outlying ranches and farms, to let the wolf howl a little, had also evidently been recognized in its careful planning.

Lone slowly rode the length of Crawford Street, giving things a general look-over, then circled back to a livery stable he had noted a short ways down a side street. WOODROW'S LIVERY read the letters painted on a one-by-twelve board nailed over the double front doors of the barn.

When Lone rode up, a lanky black man in faded bib overalls and thick-soled work boots came out to meet him. He was running a large, spotted hanky back over the sweat-dotted dome of his cleanly shaved head.

"Mornin' . . . just barely," greeted the man. "You wantin' to board that fine lookin' animal?"

"That's the general idea," Lone told him. "You got room?"

"Plenty. My name's Woodrow, and I guarantee your big gray will get real proper treatment. For how long you thinkin'?"

"Overnight, for starters. I'll have to see beyond that."

Woodrow stated his rates. Lone dismounted and paid him.

Before putting his billfold away, Lone said, "Past few years I been punchin' cows back Nebraska way. Fella I was workin' for had a couple bad winters, though, and had to cut back his crew. I was one of the ones he let go so I decided to drift some, look over more of the country. But that don't mean I'm livin' high while I'm lookin', if you know what I mean. You say you got plenty of room in your barn—any chance you'd rent me an extra forkful of clean straw where I could bed down later tonight?"

Woodrow grinned. "Fifty more cents ought to be enough to arrange that. I'll leave a clean, empty stall right next to your gray . . . long as you promise not to do no careless smokin' and burn the place down."

"I don't smoke, careless or otherwise," Lone assured him.

Woodrow slipped the money Lone paid him in a bib pocket, then asked, "You lookin' for work while you're hereabouts?"

"Could be. I heard talk in Cheyenne there might be a new rail spur comin' through these parts. Never done any railroad work before, always thought it might be interesting to try if ever I ran across any."

"Interestin'?" Woodrow's eyebrows lifted. "That might be one word for it. But back-breakin', muscle-tearin' pure cussedness be more accurate ones, and that's for sure."

"I take it you've had a firsthand taste?"

"Near five years. Pushin' track all across Kansas. Cost me a wife who ran off on account of I was always gone workin' long hours. Those long hours, though, earned me enough put-away money to come here and buy into this business, which I now own." Woodrow paused to run the hanky back over the top of his head again, more habit than necessity now that most of the sweat had already dried. "Lookin' back on hindsight," he continued, "I reckon both those things was for the better . . . but it don't mean I got a hankerin' to take on no naggin' wife again, and for dang sure not to ever work layin' track again."

"I guess you've given me second thoughts, leastways about the railroad part," allowed Lone.

Woodrow shook his head. "Ain't my way to tell another man how to set his course. I was just sayin' how some things went for me is all. Far as the railroad, though, it don't really matter for the time bein'. For you, I mean . . . on account of, what I'm tryin' to say is, there ain't no railroad work goin' on nowhere around here anyhow."

"I guess that settles that then. At least for the time being, like you said. Talk I heard in Cheyenne must've been just hot air."

"In the past they's been some stirrin' about bringin' a rail spur into Promise City. A couple different times. But nuthin' recent, leastways not that I know of. And I 'spect I'd've heard."

"I'm sure you would have, Woodrow." Lone handed over Ironsides' reins, saying, "Here you go, then. This big fella's name is Ironsides. Treat him good."

"You bet I will, mister. I'll put your saddle and the rest of your gear in that empty stall we talked about, next to his, and treat them good too."

"Obliged."

· · ·

When Lone had ridden the length of Crawford Street, Promise City's main artery evidently named after the valley's original settler Ezra Crawford, he had closely scanned the different businesses lining it but had taken particular note of two. One had been a brick building with an ornate shingle hanging out front and equally ornate gold leaf lettering on its windows all bearing the legend: NILES LAVIN—ATTORNEY AT LAW. That hadn't been surprising, he'd been expecting some prominent sign of that gent's presence. However, the other business that especially caught his eye, its name at least, was both surprising and very intriguing. It was a narrow, two-story wood frame building squeezed between a saddle shop and a barber. The plain lettering on its wide first-floor front window read simply: WURCZINSKI'S BILLIARD PARLOR.

Now there was nothing either surprising or intriguing about a pool hall existing in any town. Nor was a Polish name like Wurczinski totally uncommon. But that particular Polish name with that particular spelling struck a distinct chord with Lone. And if it possibly signified the individual he thought and hoped it might, then it could be a very good stroke of luck coming at a much-needed time.

Walking now, Lone strolled past the attorney's office one more time, just for the hell of it. But the shades were pulled on the front window so he couldn't see anything going on inside. He then proceeded on to Wurczinski's pool hall.

Entering, he found himself in a long, low-ceilinged room. Everything looked tidy and clean, though the lingering odor of cigarette and cigar smoke hung in the air. There were six tables positioned crossways at well-spaced intervals down the length of the room. Against the wall off one end of each was a small, round-topped table and a pair of chairs. On the opposite wall hung racks of pool cues. To the left of the entrance door, situated diagonally in front of the corner was a short bar with three stools in front.

Behind the bar, planted on an elevated perch to offset his five-foot-nothing height, thumbing through a copy of Police Gazette, was none other than Herman Wurczinski himself. Onion bald, jug eared, with a bulbous nose and neatly trimmed goatee and wearing a bright red vest over a lemon-colored shirt, all making him look exactly the same as the last time Lone had seen him at least eight years ago.

Lone paused for a moment inside the door, scanning the room and pausing an extra beat on its only two customers, a pair of elderly gents playing quietly at a table near the back. Deciding they looked harmless enough, Lone closed the door behind him then strode over to the bar.

Reaching out, he rapped a knuckle sharply on

the polished surface and said, "Alright, Herman, what's the dodge? Where you hidin' Griselda and the girls?"

Herman lowered his Gazette and looked up. At first his mouth made only a silent, perfectly shaped "O." Then he blurted out, "Lone McGantry, as I live and breathe! What whirling dervish of a wind blew you to Promise City?"

Lone grinned. "A fair one, Herman, you ought to know that. I always travel on a fair wind."

"Aye. Fair for you maybe—but not so much for the scoundrels it carries you *to*."

"You'd know about scoundrels, bein' one yourself."

Herman hopped down from his tall chair and stepped forward to extend his hand across the bartop, saying, "But I'm one who's never been sorry to see you." Despite his modest height, Herman was powerfully built through the chest and shoulders and had a paw nearly as big as Lone's. But, on this occasion, the former scout couldn't help noticing that the grip which always in the past fiercely tested his seemed to have lost much of its steam. Also, on closer examination, he noted that the shorter man's face appeared to have taken on a gauntness never there before.

As their handshake ended, Herman said, "I'll ask again, what brings you to this part of the country? I heard somewhere that you'd settled down and started a horse ranch back in Nebraska."

"That's true to some degree," Lone admitted. "But before we get into that and before you tell me what *you* are doin' here, what about Griselda? Never known her to let you very far out of her sight."

Herman winced at the question and his eyes filled with a sudden sadness. Lone immediately knew he was in for some bad news.

"Just under three years ago, old friend . . . my beloved Griselda left this world. Let me out of her sight forever and, God help me, took her from mine." The grief in Herman's tone was painful to hear.

"Jeez, Herm. I'm awful sorry to hear that," Lone told him sincerely. "I had no idea."

Herm wagged his head. "Life goes on. *I* must go on, as she would have wanted. But what also continues is the terrible emptiness."

Lone almost said something stupid about knowing how he felt, but quickly held himself in check. He hated hearing people say that to someone in a time of grief or mourning. No matter how genuine the intent of the sentiment, no person could truly know the feelings of another at such a moment or at any point in the aftermath.

Lone surely knew the pain and ensuing emptiness—having recently experienced it himself—of losing someone he deeply loved. His Velda had been snatched from him suddenly and tragically. But theirs had been a whirlwind of discovering and passionately embracing their love that had been cut short after less than a year. How could that compare to loss suffered by one of two people whose relationship had endured for decades?

Softly, Lone said, "I guess that answers why you left Laramie and came here."

"Aye. Too many memories crowded in on me there. Only made the empty feeling worse. Plus I wasn't up to handling the girls, not without Grissy. They didn't trust me to understand their feelings and, in all honesty, they were right. I had no patience with their petty complaints and the constant bickering among them . . . so when a buyer came forward offering a fair price, I took it and moved on."

For as far back as Lone could remember, Herman and Griselda had owned and operated a highly successful saloon and bordello in Laramie. Ironically, when it had looked like Laramie was the destination for Lone, Sue, and Johnny and Lone had mentioned he knew some people there who might be able to give them some valuable leads—it was Herman and Griselda he'd been referring to. To have been diverted from Laramie only to find Herman now present here in Promise City seemed very fortunate. Maybe.

"The hardest part," Herman continued now, "was leaving Grissy's gravesite behind. I go back at least once a year, though—for sure on our anniversary—to leave fresh flowers and . . . talk with her awhile. It helps me get through."

Not sure how to respond to that, the best Lone could come up with was, "That sounds mighty comfortin', Herm. For you and Grissy too, since I'm bettin' she's lookin' down on you."

"Thank you for saying that, Lone. I like to believe the same." The short man squared his shoulders, cocked his head a bit, and worked up a less somber expression. "But enough about me. That's my tale for being here. Let's get back to my original question about what brings you 'round to these parts?"

Chapter Twenty-One

Responding to Herman's stubbornly repeated question, Lone said, "The simple answer to what brings me here is that I'm doin' a favor for a friend."

"A friend in Promise?"

Lone shook his head. "No, not quite. This gets kinda complicated, but it all centers around a runaway wife and a husband who wants her back bad enough to go chasin' after her. Addin' to it is that it appears the wife has got herself mixed up with some pretty rough characters who are likely to greet hubby in a hard way if he shows and tries to 'front 'em. He ain't in no way carved from the kind of bark that'd give him much chance if it came to that. The friend I'm helpin' is the sister to the husband and she's hopin' I can sorta get in the way before her brother ends up hurt worse than by just a broken heart."

Herman's eyebrows were lifted by the time Lone was done speaking. "You're right, enough about it sounding complicated. Is the runaway wife worth all the trouble and risk?"

"That I can't say. Never laid eyes on the gal," said Lone. "My friend don't especially think she is. But what matters is that her brother does, and he's the one she thinks *is* worth the trouble."

"You could expect a sister to think that about her brother. But what kind of fellow is he in the eyes of others?" Herman asked. "What makes his wife so bent on getting away from him—does he mistreat her?"

"No, I'm pretty sure that ain't the case. I've had some dealin's with him—his name is James, by the way—and I can't say I took a particular likin' to him," Lone explained. "But I don't make him for a wife beater. Everything seems to point to her just havin' a wild streak, and him not bein' able to get over her."

"Aye. I've seen the like. Seen it break more than a few good men."

"Well that's what I'm tryin' to stop in this case."

"And somehow Promise City or Promise Valley figures into it?"

"That's what brought us this far. And now that I've found *you* here, I'm hopin' you can help me sift things out a little finer." Lone cocked an eyebrow sharply. "How about it? You got your ear to the ground when it comes to the goin'-ons around these parts the way you did back in Laramie?"

Herman considered the question with thoughtfully pursed lips before replying, "It's true I've always thought it wise for a man to maintain an awareness of the things taking place about him. And those feelings are no different in this setting than back in Laramie. However, the settings themselves *do* present some noteworthy differences."

"I didn't come here for riddles, Herm," Lone remarked.

"For one thing," Herman continued as if he hadn't heard him, "my setup here is obviously much simpler, drawing a less rowdy and less talkative crowd. I serve only beer from behind this bar, so that also helps keep things more tamed down. And, of course, there are no girls— who were a fountain of information back in Laramie due to the things their male admirers bragged about to help impress them all the more during, er, intimate moments."

"I came wantin' even less to hear those kind of details."

"But they're all important," Herman explained, "for you to understand that, even though I maintain my awareness—or keep my ear to the ground, as you put it—what I have knowledge of may be less than you're hoping for. Above all, you must realize that this whole quiet, peaceful valley does not generate much that can be 'sifted' any finer than what is on the surface."

What Lone realized even more was that his old friend was milking the situation for all it was worth. "Come on," he said. "Ain't no place so quiet and peaceful it don't have *some* secrets under its surface. And if they're there, I'm still willin' to bet you've caught at least a whiff of 'em."

"You flatter me."

"Suppose we try it this way: I toss out some names, you give me a reaction. But before we get to that"—Lone glanced down toward the men knocking balls around down at the far table—"is there somewhere a little more private we can go?"

"Have you had lunch yet?" Herman asked.

"No, I just got into town."

"Come then. You can join me up in my quarters, I'll fix us both something. Can't get any more lonely or private than up there."

"What about your customers?"

Herman waved a hand dismissively. "Those two will be at it for a couple more hours, they always are. If they want a drink or anything while I'm away, they know where to get it. Let me hang an Out To Lunch sign on the door to keep anybody else out. Then follow me, the stairs are down at the other end . . ."

Herman Wurczinski's second floor living quarters were roomy, sparsely furnished, very clean and orderly. Everything basic and simple. The only signs of excess were the number of framed pictures of his late wife Griselda, showing her at various ages, hung on the walls; and stacks of books occupying several horizontal surfaces.

In the kitchen area, Herman prepared each of them thick-sliced kielbasa sandwiches on rye bread, garnished with hot mustard and served with tall glasses of strong wine. They sat at the table and talked while they ate.

"Now I have a confession to make," announced Herman, smiling slyly around a bite of sandwich. "It has come to pass that I once again *do* have some ladies at my disposal who provide a good deal of information on area happenings."

"Why, you old dog. I should have known," responded Lone.

Herman held up a hand, palm out. "Tut-tut. Don't be too fast to jump to conclusions. I said 'ladies' and I wasn't using the term loosely. What I'm talking about, you see, is the most surprising development of a ladies billiard league that has formed and meets for competition at my place on alternating Tuesday afternoons."

"Women openly and regularly showin' up in a pool hall?" Lone echoed what he'd heard, unable to keep the surprise out of his tone.

"A *billiard parlor*," Herman was quick to correct him. "A mere 'pool hall' would be too scandalous to consider."

"Well pardon me all to hell."

Herman chuckled. "Don't worry. When the group first approached me with their proposal, I was as rocked back on my heels as much as anybody. But, in the end, I saw it as a kind of compliment. After I'd been in business for a while and word spread how I ran things clean and non-rowdy, some of the younger and more daring gals in town floated the notion that—as a way to socialize and fill their leisure time, and what with the ancient game of billiards not being an evil thing strictly in and of itself—it might be fun to try their hands at it. Oh, there was some grumbling from the churchy types at first. But that died down before long and, lo-and-behold, some of the older dames started joining in too. There are over two dozen regulars now. I serve them wine and tea and they have themselves a fine time."

"And attentive host that you are, you keep your ears open and overhear all the gossip bound to float back and forth among two dozen women."

"Ladies," Herman corrected him once again. Then he smiled and added, "Isn't that what you hoped to hear from me? Plus, although the wranglers and farm hands who come around at night aren't the boisterous, loud, boasting types you're more apt to find in the saloons, they still trade banter and rumors they've picked up here and there. They're not as rich a source as the ladies, but they can still be interesting at times."

"See?" said Lone, reaching for his glass of wine to counter the heat of the mustard on the bite of sandwich he'd just swallowed. "Now you're startin' to sound more like what I was hopin' for when I spotted your name on the window of your poo . . . er, billiard parlor."

The corners of Herman's mouth turned down. "But I'm afraid there still might be a problem."

After he'd cooled some of the fire in his throat, Lone lowered his wineglass and said, "How's that?"

"Like I said at the outset—this town, this whole valley, is so peaceful and quiet that if you collect a whole bucketful of its rumors and gossip, they still don't amount to anything you could consider close to scandalous or shocking. Not much of any significance, really. Certainly nothing recent that suggests the presence of a hardcase villain showing up with a woman of questionable morals. *That* would have gotten noticed, and I would have heard about it."

"You make this place sound like the Garden of Eden before Eve chomped into the apple," Lone growled. "No place can be that lily pure."

"I never claimed it was lily pure," Herman argued. "Of course there are some minor flare-ups from time to time. Neighbors or rival businessmen getting into petty spats, saloon brawls naturally. Even a touch of rustling once in a while, but seldom more than ten or a dozen head." Herman paused a moment, then added, "No doubt the biggest thing, crime-wise, ever to happen in Promise Valley was the recent kidnapping."

"Kidnappin'?"

"Yes. A terrible thing for the Crawfords to have to endure in their frail, advanced late years, their precious, belatedly discovered daughter-in-law taken from them. Thankfully, it got resolved and she was safely returned."

Something caused the hairs on the back of Lone's neck to crackle as if there was a fierce lightning storm brewing overhead.

"The whole matter was kept mostly hushed up. But I," Herman said rather smugly, "managed to catch wind of it. My respect for the Crawfords, however, has kept me from repeating anything about it until just this minute."

"When you say Crawford, you mean the big he-bull of the whole valley? The one who first settled here and got this whole shebang started?"

"The same. Finer people, him and his wife Irene, you'd be hard pressed to find anywhere," Herman stated earnestly. "It may sound trite, but I've come to believe that it is their simple, basic decency as founders that has spread and made this area the kind of place it is."

"That's mighty high praise," Lone allowed.

"Aye. And you know I'm not one to sugar coat a thing."

"Gotta give you that." Lone frowned in thought. "But goin' back to something you said . . . you called the Crawfords' daughter-in-law 'belatedly discovered.' What did you mean by that?"

"Oh, indeed that's quite a story." Herman took a big drink of his wine before continuing. "The Crawfords had two sons, you see. Riley and Theron. Fine lads by all reports, helped their father build his cattle ranch to its early success. But then the war came and both boys went off to join the fighting. Riley for the Blue, Theron for the Gray—one of the few ever pieces of discontent within the family, since Ezra and Irene, as most folks in the valley, were Northern sympathizers. But their love and respect for their son was strong enough for them to reluctantly accept his decision. In the end it was of little consequence as, sadly, neither boy made it back.

"What followed were dark years for the Crawfords. They endured, but age began to catch up and Irene especially grew gradually frailer and sicklier. Some said it was hurried along by grief over her lost sons. But then, only about a year ago, a ray of potential hope and joy shone in when an old war vet, a comrade of Theron's, passed through and visited the Crawfords to pay his respects. It was from him they learned the startling news that, before he died from his wounds, Theron was wed to one of the nurses caring for him."

"Why didn't the gal ever come forward and contact them herself?" Lone asked.

"That I don't know. Never heard. But what I do know," said Herman, "is that, once they heard about her, Ezra and Irene pulled out all stops and spared no expense setting out to find her. They put their lawyer, Niles Lavin, on the case and he hired a full-time private detective—you know, one of those Pinkerton types, only this fellow works exclusively for Lavin—to run down every possible lead. Lo-and-behold, about six months ago, he found her.

"I think Ezra and Irene were hoping a grand-child might also be involved. Someone to continue the bloodline. That wasn't the case, unfortunately, but finding Rosemary they still saw as a great blessing. They welcomed her into their home and into the family with open arms. To celebrate and announce the occasion, they threw a party out at the ranch and invited everybody in the whole valley. It was the grandest shindig anybody around here has ever seen. And the icing on the cake was that Irene and Rosemary hit it off so wonderfully that Irene's faltering health almost immediately took a turn for the better."

"That's a real touchin' tale," Lone muttered. "Tell me something. This private detective who works for Lavin . . . his name Earl Drake by any chance?"

"Why, yes. Yes, it is. You know him from somewhere?"

"Let's just say our paths have crossed. Tell me something more. The recent kidnappin' of the

Crawford daughter-in-law . . . Lavin and Drake involved in gettin' that resolved?"

"Of course. I don't know the exact details—like I said, they meant for it to be kept mostly quiet. Our town marshal and his deputy were involved, too, but it was the kind of thing pretty far outside of their experience. From what I do know, indications are that Lavin arranged a ransom pay-off and Drake conducted the money delivery and brought Rosemary safely back."

Lone's mind raced. *Rosemary . . . Drake . . . Lavin . . . the Crawfords.* All the puzzle pieces of the pursuit that had brought Sue, Johnny, and him this far. The only piece missing was James Risen. And he was the only one whose motive and how he fit was clearly known. How the others exactly meshed—with one another, and somehow with an alleged scheme for Lavin to take control of Promise Valley—was a jumbled mystery. But still, the pieces *were* identified, Lone told himself. All that remained now was figuring out the scheme they added up to and then coming up with a way to stop it and yank James out with his hide intact.

Yeah, that was all.

"What's wrong?" Herman asked. "You suddenly look deeply troubled, my friend. More so than when we started."

Lone set his jaw. "Yeah, Herm, it's true I got some troublin' thoughts tumblin' around in my head. And I hate to tell you, but before I'm through, I fear this peaceful valley of yours might see some of 'em play out in an ugly way."

Little did he know how soon that was about to start.

Chapter Twenty-Two

August "Gus" Teaford, the marshal of Promise City, didn't care much for Earl Drake. He found the man to be arrogant and often condescending. Those wouldn't have been Gus's words exactly, because his vocabulary didn't stretch that far (precisely the kind of thing Drake liked to subtly rub in whenever he got the chance). But the sentiment was there regardless. Trouble was, now that Drake had become a full-time investigator for attorney Niles Lavin, one of the town's most prominent citizens, Gus was stuck with needing to treat the hombre with grudging respect.

Truth be told, Gus wasn't all that crazy about Lavin either. In his case, he was always very friendly and courteous and outwardly proper in all regards. And right there was what troubled Gus about the man. He was *too* damn proper and polite, raising the old lawman's hackles almost like when he encountered a phony Bible thumper or snake oil peddler. Gus admitted to being past his prime, with fading eyesight and an arthritic gun hand, but he still counted his by-God bullshit detector as being sharp as ever.

The catch when it came to Lavin and Drake combined, however, was how they both were so favorably looked upon by Ezra Crawford and his wife Irene. And the Crawfords, in Gus's eyes just like most folks throughout Promise Valley, were practically deities. Anyone they thought well of deserved nothing less than to be treated in kind. And the thing—two things, actually—forever cementing the Crawfords' lofty opinion of both Lavin and Drake was the way the pair had served to first reunite the old couple with their long-lost daughter-in-law and then, later, to rescue her safely from a gang of ruthless kidnappers. These accomplishments were hard for even Gus not to admire and find commendable.

Yet for all that, the sight of the two men barging excitedly into his office a few minutes earlier had immediately disturbed the lunch he'd recently finished eating and turned it into an anxious lump in the pit of his stomach. Then, when they started spouting what it was that had brought them, the knot tightened up all the more.

"It's him, I tell you. I'm positive of it!" Drake was insisting vehemently. "I was on my way to lunch when I saw the lowdown cur, bold as could be, walking down the boardwalk on the other side of Crawford Street. I wasn't armed at the time, or I would have braced him right then and there. By the time I rushed to my hotel room, grabbed my gun and got back out to the street, he was nowhere to be seen. Damn the luck!"

Gus frowned. "Why didn't you come get me or my deputy right away? If there's any gun bracin' to be done on the streets of this town, that's a job for us."

"It was lunchtime, I wasn't sure where I'd find you," Drake was quick to reply. "I didn't want him to get away—I thought I could get back out in time to keep him in sight."

"Everybody in town knows I go home every day, just around the corner, to take my lunch," drawled Gus. Then, continuing to frown, he asked, "Did you say you was meanin' to brace this fella, or just keep him in sight?"

Drake's face reddened. "What difference does that make right now? We're wasting time talking when you need to get some men together and start scouring the street looking for the culprit!"

"You must remember, Marshal," Lavin interjected in a conciliatory tone, "that Mr. Drake is a man of action, as his past deeds have borne out many times. I think that explains why his responses might be different than those of an ordinary citizen. It also explains—very fortunately, I might add—why he was in the unique position to recognize the individual in question as the leader of the treacherous gang who recently kidnapped young Rosemary Crawford."

"Yeah, if that varmint is out there within reach to be nabbed, it for sure is fortunate Drake spotted him," Gus allowed. "But I'm curious about something, Drake . . . I recall you sayin' how, when you paid the ransom and got the girl back, all the gang members had their faces covered. That bein' the case, how is it you're so sure now that the hombre you just saw is one of 'em?"

Again Drake was ready with a quick response. "Because, for just a second during the ransom transfer, the leader's mask slipped and I got a look at him. Thank God he didn't notice me looking his way, or he would have killed me on the spot to keep me from being able to identify him. And that's exactly why I never mentioned before about having gotten that look. I didn't want to risk word getting out and having him come after me. I'm no coward, but I *am* cautious about protecting Number One."

"Really, Marshal," Lavin huffed. "Don't you think your time would be better spent discontinuing your grilling of Mr. Drake and instead commencing with the apprehension of the villain he is prepared to bring charges against?"

"Usin' all those fancy words in that long-winded spiel damn near used up as much time as my questionin'," Gus remarked dryly. Then, sighing, he rose up behind his desk. "But okay. Let's go round up my deputy and—"

He halted in mid-sentence as the front door opened and a tall young man entered. It was Ben Langford, Gus's deputy. Early twenties, six-four in height, well-muscled and as solid as if he'd been carved from the trunk of an oak tree. Ben was good with his fists and good with a gun and made a fine deputy for the aging marshal. Some thought, rightfully so, that Ben was just a tad slow upstairs. But that complemented the pairing all the more for handling the infrequent bouts of trouble they encountered. Gus supplied the experience and savvy, loyal and obedient Ben supplied the quickness and the brawn.

Somewhat dull though he might be, in this instance it only took Ben a moment to sense the tension in the room, especially when he saw Gus buckling on his gun belt. "What's goin' on?" he said.

Gus gestured. "Mr. Drake here has spotted one of the skunks who was in on the recent kidnappin' of Rosemary Crawford. He's somewhere in town, we need to go flush him out."

"Wow," said Ben.

Gus gestured again, this time toward the gun rack on the wall. "Grab one of those street sweepers and bring it along, just in case."

As Ben strode to the rack and took down a double-barreled Greener and a box of shells, Gus addressed the other two men. "Mr. Lavin, best go on back to your office and keep to safety. Drake, you'll have to come along so you can identify this bird when we do flush him."

"My pleasure, Marshal," Drake assured him.

"But if it comes to any gun work," Gus said sternly, "you leave that to me or Ben."

271

• • •

Lone had just exited the billiard parlor and was paused on the boardwalk out front, pondering what his next move ought to be. He wished he'd made different arrangements for rejoining Sue and Johnny. He was busting to share the things he'd learned from Herman, along with his subsequent speculations based on them. He was anxious to get some reactions and input in return. Waiting until noon tomorrow for that seemed agonizingly far off. What was more, hanging around town for the balance of the day and evening now seemed almost pointless. He wasn't likely to learn anything more of significant value, and too much poking and prodding by a stranger might even run the risk of drawing unwanted attention.

Barely had this thought crossed Lone's mind when, out the corner if his eye, he noticed three men headed down the boardwalk in his direction. They were walking abreast of one another and, causing Lone to bring his head farther around for sharper examination, was the fact that one of the men on the outside was holding a Greener shotgun down along his hip. He was tall, muscular, with a youthful face and a deputy's badge pinned on his shirt. The other outside man was older, shorter, pot-bellied, and wore a marshal's badge.

Lone took all of this in in a fraction of a second but felt no particular alarm as there was no reason for him to fear the law. The man walking between the two lawmen, however, was a different matter. Lone didn't recognize him from ever having laid eyes on him before. But his slick dark hair and roguishly handsome face, bracketed by razored sideburns and sliced by a precisely trimmed pencil mustache, too perfectly fit a description that Lone had been given for there to be any doubt—he was looking at Earl Drake.

In the same instant this recognition hit Lone, Drake reacted to the sight of Lone. He stopped short, braced his feet, and thrust one arm forward, pointing as he exclaimed, "There the sonofabitch is!"

The two lawmen pulled up short too, their eyes locking on Lone. Lone didn't know what the hell this was about but now he felt a warning jolt run through him. As he watched, the twin barrels of the deputy's shotgun started to rise and Drake's right hand went streaking inside his jacket for what Lone had no doubt was a shoulder-holstered gun. That was all the former scout waited to see. With lightning reflexes and speed, he spun a hundred and eighty degrees then plunged through the doorway and back into the billiard parlor.

A pistol shot sounded and a slug crashed into the doorframe a foot behind him. Simultaneously, as if Lone needed any further confirmation of who the shooter was, he heard a gruff voice holler, "Goddammit, Drake, I told you to hold your fire!"

Chapter Twenty-Three

Bursting into the pool hall, Lone rushed past the corner bar where Herman Wurczinski was once more perched on his elevated stool, shouting over his shoulder as he ran, "Stay out of it, Herm—I got bloodhounds on my tail!"

Breaking into long, distance-eating strides, Lone streaked alongside the row of billiard tables and made for the opposite end of the lengthy, narrow room. The old gents who'd been playing at one of the tables before had since left and there were no other customers in the place. At the back of the room was a cramped, dimly lit hallway that led to a door opening to the outside. Just short of this, on the left side of the hall, was another door that Lone knew—from having followed Herman through it earlier—accessed a flight of switch-back stairs leading to the living quarters above.

At the end of the cramped hall, Lone kicked the outside door open wide. But then, rather than pass on through, he left it hanging rattlingly ajar and instead opened the side door and ducked into the stairwell. Pressing that door closed again behind him, he held there at the bottom of the stairs, making no attempt to ascend for fear the creak of the steps might give away his ruse.

Pursuing footfalls clattered loudly out in the

hallway, accompanied by heavy breathing and muttered curses. Lone crouched still and silent, drawn Colt held at the ready in case one of his pursuers thought to try the side door. But, from the sound of it, their focus—exactly as he'd hoped—was only on the wide-open exit. The only thing that kept them from immediately using it was a voice of reason, the same gruff voice that had cursed at Drake back on the street, now cautioning, "Take it easy, boys. Don't be in too big a hurry in case he's waitin' out there with a bullet."

Several tense seconds ticked by. On the other side of the flimsy door, only a couple feet away, Lone could hear continued heavy breathing and the restless shifting of bodies. He gripped the Colt so tight his hand threatened to cramp.

Then, abruptly, a different voice out in the hallway said, "It's clear out there. He's on the run!" There immediately followed the thumping and thudding of boot heels as the three men went charging outside.

Lone breathed a sigh of relief and straightened up out of his crouch. He'd gained himself some time. He'd also gained some more puzzling questions to cram in with the others already crowding his thoughts. What the hell had Earl Drake said or done to sic the local law on him? And how had Drake known of his presence and been able to recognize him? But first and foremost what Lone had to focus on was successfully eluding his trio of pursuers in order to begin trying to sort out the growing knot of puzzlements. Caught in the middle of a strange town in broad daylight wasn't going to make that easy.

For a brief moment Lone thought about fleeing back out through the front of the pool hall. But that would only expose him to people on the street who could point him out to those chasing him. Drake's pistol shot was certain to have drawn its share of attention. Plus, he didn't want to have to exchange lead with anybody—well, except maybe Drake—if he could avoid it.

Damn. If he could only make it to Ironsides, then him and the big gray could outdistance any pursuit and he'd be able to find a spot out in open country where he could lay low and gather his thoughts. But getting back to Woodrow's livery without being spotted and possibly catching a bullet wasn't going to be easy.

Turning, Lone proceeded swiftly, silently up the steps once more to Herman's private apartment. He doubled back through the kitchen area until he reached a window at the far end, placing him again at the rear end of the building with a view over the back door that Earl Drake and the lawmen had gone pouring out of. He found himself looking down on a small, fenced-in backyard.

In the center of the yard was an outhouse with

wooden planks on the ground leading to it. To either side were bits of clutter, a couple broken-down pool tables and some scattered wooden crates and barrels. Lone's three pursuers were still down there, clumped momentarily together in animated conversation being led mostly by the marshal. Watching, Lone gathered that the trio had by now satisfied themselves he was nowhere in the yard, not hiding in the outhouse or behind any of the clutter. The marshal was waving his arms and barking orders. Lone couldn't hear what he was saying but it became quickly clear he was directing his deputy off in one direction—over behind the fence then circling around back toward the main street—while the marshal and Drake would be making a sweep off the other way. With those orders given, all scattered accordingly.

Lone pulled back from the window. He stood there for a minute, closing his eyes and carefully envisioning the layout of Crawford Street in general and then, in particular, where Woodrow's livery was in relationship to Herman's building. The street ran at an angle stretching from points southwest to the northeast. The livery where Ironsides was stalled was located near the northeast end, just a short ways up a nameless side street that jutted due north. Herman's place was about a block and a half down from there, on the same side of Crawford. So near and yet so far.

Lone considered going back down the stairs and exiting out into the now abandoned backyard. He might be able to work his way unseen up the back sides of the various businesses lining this side of Crawford Street. Providing, since that's the way Drake and the marshal had gone, they stuck together and continued on at a pace that would keep them ahead of him. If they split up or tarried to examine some area or building too long, he could risk barging right into them.

Lone thought about the way the marshal had been windmilling his arms as he shouted orders, seemingly indicating for his deputy to go off one way and sweep back around toward Crawford Street while he and Drake would do the same going the other way. If that was the case, skimming up the back sides of the businesses might still work out okay for Lone.

The former scout moved the length of the apartment until he reached a window at the front, looking down on the main drag. He parted the curtains and cautiously gazed out, hoping he'd perhaps see some sign of his pursuers boiling out somewhere below. He saw no such thing. What he did see, however, were two or three clusters of citizens—with more gathering from each end of the street—chattering excitedly and pointing toward the billiard parlor. Damn, Drake's gunshot had stirred up even more attention than expected. If Lone, a stranger, even if no one had previously gotten a good look at him, was now spotted on the move anywhere down below—in back of the buildings or in front—it was certain he'd quickly be viewed with suspicion.

Double damn.

But wait a minute. *If he was spotted on the move down below* . . .

With a wild idea spinning inside his head, Lone cut back through the apartment and went to a curtained doorway on the side wall. Through this was Herman's bedroom. Crossing to another window in there, Lone parted the curtains and looked out on the roof of the saddle shop next door. The space between the buildings was so narrow, scarcely four feet, that it couldn't really even be called an alley. And the distance down from the sill of Lone's window to the roof of the single-story saddle shop was just about the same.

Looking out farther, Lone could make out the tops of five or six more businesses in line beyond the saddle shop to the spot where he estimated the side street with Woodrow's livery was. Their roofs were at varying levels, but none that appeared—moving from one to the next— too high to scale or too low to drop onto. The gaps between the subsequent buildings were indeterminable but it seemed reasonable to believe they could be overcome. Lone was a big man, powerfully built and over two hundred pounds, but nonetheless quite agile. And he was feeling increasingly desperate.

Damn it all, he was going to try it! If his escape was blocked at ground level then, by God, he'd find a way *higher above the ground.*

Before he could talk better sense into himself, Lone shoved the window open wide and started through. First one leg over the sill, then squeezing his head and shoulders out next. For a moment he hung like that. His right leg hooked over the sill on the inside, his left boot heel braced hard against the outside wall, hands clamped at each side. The distances involved—the gap between buildings, the drop to the saddle shop roof, the bigger drop to the ground—all suddenly looked greater than they had from the inside when he'd made up his mind to do this. Jesus. But no matter, his other options still didn't look any better.

Gritting his teeth, he unhooked his right leg, shoved with both hands and pushed off hard with his right foot. Out and down he went. Air rushed over his face like a sudden gust of wind. He landed, went immediately into a shoulder roll, and came up smoothly to one knee. The only miscue was that his hat fell off. He stood up, clapped the hat back on, and everything was fine.

Now that he was on the outside, Lone could hear the excited chatter of voices rolling up from the street. He grinned. Let 'em chatter. He'd soon be leaving behind not only the noise of their flapping gums but also the frantic searching of his three pursuers.

Lone turned and started for the next roof.

Chapter Twenty-Four

Fifteen minutes later, feeling exhilarated though breathing a bit hard and having acquired a few fresh elbow and knee scrapes, Lone was right where he'd hoped to get to. Almost. After jumping from roof to roof up the line of businesses that came after the saddle shop (his "squirrel escape" he would later refer to it as), Lone now stood at the rear corner of the roof of a tobacco store located diagonally across the side street from Woodrow's livery.

With so many citizens having swarmed to the area down in front of the billiard parlor, there was hardly any activity taking place up at this end of Crawford Street. In fact, the side street running before Woodrow's place appeared totally empty. Having studied it long enough to satisfy himself of this, Lone laid out on his belly and began easing over the edge of the roof. He skimmed part way down a drainpipe, then pushed out to clear the rain barrel it fed into and dropped to the ground.

A quick trot across the street brought him to the wide double doors at the front of Woodrow's barn. One of them was propped part way open. Lone stepped through. He paused, letting his eyes adjust to the dimness inside. The smell of horses, hay, grain, and the faint tang of manure filled his nostrils.

"Woodrow?" he called. "Woodrow . . . you anywhere around?"

There was the faint scuff of a footfall in the deep shadows off to his right. Half a second later, a voice growled, "I got a round right here, mister. A .45 caliber one. You make a wrong move, I'll introduce you to it the rest of the way."

Lone froze, moving only his eyes. Cutting them in the direction of the voice, he could see nothing but shadows—while he was clearly backlit in the partly open doorway. He had no chance to try anything.

Making matters worse, a second voice spoke from the shadows on his left. "And if that ain't enough, I got the .44 caliber cousin to that .45 over here. So you get those hands up by your ears or you're gonna meet a family you don't want no part of."

Lone raised his hands slowly. "If this is a holdup," he drawled, "you boys are gonna be mighty disappointed . . . no matter how much firepower you're packin'."

"Shut up," snapped the first voice. "Our payday is set, no matter what you got or ain't got in your pockets."

"Yeah," added the second hombre. "You think we'd expect much out of somebody who climbs down off a roof like a monkey out of a tree?"

"Squirrel," Lone said.

"Huh?"

A combination of his vision adjusting and the two men easing forward somewhat out of the deeper shadows allowed Lone to be able to determine their features. He recognized neither of them. The one to his right was tall and lean, with mean eyes and an elongated upper lip over a weak chin. To the left was a stocky, moon-faced number, an equally menacing glint also showing in his eyes. Lone quickly sized them up as a couple of cheap gun toughs.

"Never mind if he's a monkey or a squirrel, Tevis," said the tall one. "All he is to us is a package for delivery to Drake."

Tevis emitted a laugh that sounded almost like a girlish giggle. "That's right, Hoyt—like a Christmas present with a bow tied on it."

"Speakin' of tied-on bows . . ." Hoyt turned his head to glare down along the row of horse stalls, toward the opposite end of the barn. He hollered in a demanding tone, "Hey, Woodrow! Where's that goddamn rope I told you to fetch me? I need it, and I mean pronto!"

Lone could now see some activity, mixed with the agitated whinnying of a horse, taking place in one of the stalls about three-quarters of the way down. Woodrow's voice called back, shouting to be heard over the din the horse was making,

"Be right there, Mr. Grimes. I got me this fussin' horse critter I need to—"

"I don't give a goddamn about no horse," Hoyt Grimes cut him off. "Knock the troublesome nag in the head with a pipe if you have to! Just get your black ass down here with some rope—now!"

Moon-faced Tevis Morton wagged his head in disgust. "Shuffle-footed damn Blacks. Can't count on any of the lazy bastards to do nothing in a hurry."

"Well this one better had," growled Grimes, "elsewise I'm gonna—"

Now it was Grimes who got cut off. By the shrill scream of a highly aggravated horse. The eyes of Lone and the men who had the drop on him all swung sharply toward the stall where Woodrow had been having trouble with a "fussin' horse critter." What they saw was a tall, sleek bay suddenly spring out of the stall and instantly hurl itself in a powerful surge straight for the slice of sunlight pouring in through the open barn door.

"Whoa! Look out!" wailed Woodrow, stumbling out of the stall and into the middle of the barn's center aisle. "Look out for that runaway!"

Even without Woodrow's warning shout, the men clustered in front of the barn doors saw their danger from being directly in the path of the wildly fleeing horse. And they reacted in the only way they could—to scatter frantically out of the way. Grimes jumped off to Lone's right, Lone and Morton went the opposite.

In that moment, Lone realized he now had a chance to avoid not only getting trampled but also to escape out from under the guns of Grimes and Morton. Going into a low dive, he twisted his body so that he hit the ground on his left hip and shoulder. This left his right hand and the Colt holstered on his right hip unencumbered. Instantly, before his body even stopped skidding on the dirt, the Colt was in his fist and he was extending his gun arm up toward Morton.

Morton had sprung backward in an awkward half stagger, but remained on his feet. To give the devil his due, it was immediately clear that the moon-faced man also recognized how the unexpected disruption provided Lone an opening. But while his realization might have been immediate, his ability to try and do something about it was too slow. He swept his eyes and his already drawn gun in search of Lone, not realizing he had gone to the ground. When Morton's searching eyes dropped and he attempted to bring his gun in line, it was too late. Lone's Colt roared and sent a .44 slug ripping into his stomach.

Morton doubled forward and his body shuddered from the impact of the bullet. His trigger finger spasmed and sent a round gouging into the dirt a foot wide of Lone. The former scout fired a second time. This slug pounded once more into Morton's gut, folding him forward the rest of the way and pitching him face first onto the ground.

As Lone and Morton were trading shots, the bay horse barreled past and through the partly open door. As it burst free of the building, it kicked away the short length of two-by-four that had been propped against the door to keep it from closing and sent the door swinging back wide. A wash of bright afternoon sunlight poured in, turning the cloud of dust left by the fleeing horse into a boiling, brown-gold mass filled with sparkling dust motes.

For a tense moment, neither Lone nor Grimes—the remaining gun tough on the other side of the barn aisle—could see through this dust screen. Lone rose to one knee and went statue still, poised with his Colt raised and ready, straining to peer through the bright, swirling cloud.

An overanxious Grimes called through from the other side. "Tevis? You okay over there?"

Even though it wasn't smart to voice-locate himself, Lone responded. "Tevis is havin' a little trouble answerin' right now on account of tryin' to swallow the bullet caught in his throat."

Seconds later, the dust cloud dissipated enough for each man to be able to make out the vague shape of the other.

"You sonofabitch!" Grimes shouted, thrusting his gun hand forward and hurrying his shot.

Lone once again stroked the Colt's trigger smoothly, even as he felt the burn of Grimes's bullet scrape the tip of his earlobe. He saw a blossom of bright scarlet burst to instant full bloom in the middle of Grimes's forehead, and then the tall man toppled back and down.

Lone slowly straightened up. With curls of bluish powder smoke taking the place of the dust now fading out of the wash of sunlight, he stood automatically replacing the spent cartridges in the cylinder of his gun. As he finished reloading, the sound of approaching footfalls and accompanying hoof cloppings caused him to turn his head and look down the barn aisle. What he saw was Woodrow leading a fully saddled Ironsides toward him.

"Had me a hunch," Woodrow drawled, "that when you showed up again you'd be in more of a hurry to ride off than what you first intended. So I took the liberty of gettin' this big ol' gray ready for you."

"Well your hunch sure was right," Lone admitted. "Mind tellin' me what it was based on? And do you know anything about this greetin' party that was waitin' for me?"

"They's one and the same," Woodrow explained. "It all started right after you left before. That Grimes fella had been hangin' around for the past couple days, mostly over around by the tobacco store across the way. I thought he was sniffin' 'round a certain gal works there who ain't above doin' a little side business of her own, if you get what I mean. What I didn't catch on was that the shifty-eyed snake was keepin' an eye on my place over here . . . I found out the truth soon enough, though, when he came scaldin' over right after you left and had a Mr. Earl Drake with him. You know Drake, do you?"

"Sorry to say. But we're headed for the day when it's gonna be a lot sorrier one for him."

"Uh-huh. Nobody better deservin'."

"So what happened after Drake got here?"

"Grimes brought him in and showed him your horse." Woodrow scowled. "Marched right past me—smack in my own place—like I wasn't even there or didn't matter no more'n dirty beddin' in one of the stalls."

"That's the way men like Drake thinks and acts, Woodrow. They see other people as nothing except things to be used or shoved aside."

"Well he got plans for shovin' you aside in a mighty permanent way," Woodrow said. "When Drake saw your gray, he got half mad and half excited and said, 'Yeah, that's got to be the one!' Then he made Grimes describe you and next told him how you was a lowdown kidnapper who didn't deserve to breath the same air as decent folks."

"A kidnapper?" Lone echoed. Then, gritting

289

his teeth, he said, "So that's it. I'll be a sonofa-bitch."

"You and Drake agree on that much," Woodrow remarked dryly.

Lone looked at him. "You believe I'm a kidnapper, Woodrow?"

" 'Spect I wouldn't be helpin' you if I did. What I *don't* believe is nothing comes out'n the mouth of Earl Drake."

"That's my good fortune. What else can you tell me?"

"After they got done lookin' at your horse and labelin' you a kidnapper," Woodrow related, "Drake hurried off, tellin' Grimes he'd be sendin' somebody back to side him. That turned out to be Tevis Morton over there, who had the idea to stand lookout from up in the loft, which is how he spotted you comin' over the rooftops. When he showed up, Morton brought word how Drake made it clear they should try to hold you for him if they could, but go ahead and kill you if they had to."

Lone chuffed. "Nice to be loved, ain't it?"

Woodrow gave him a chuff right back. "You talkin' to a black man in a mostly white town. You ain't tellin' me nuthin'." Then, brow puckering, he added, "Though I can't say I been treated bad here in Promise City. Even still, before he left, Drake made it clear once more he was one of the exceptions by remindin' me I better know to keep

290

my mouth shut about everything I seen or heard else the town would be minus a Black it never needed in the first place."

"Gonna be hard to keep quiet after all this," Lone said, gesturing to the dead bodies.

Woodrow spread his hands and said innocently, "I'm just a simple livery man who knows how to look after horses, that's all. It's a miracle I escaped gettin' killed my own self what with these crazy white men bargin' into my place flingin' bullets in every direction."

Lone grinned. "You got that down pat, don't you?"

"Maybe so," Woodrow allowed. "But best you hightail it out of here before your bullet-riddled hide gets included in the mix. All this shootin' must've been heard even above that hubbub farther down the street, and is bound to bring the swarm this way."

Lone swung up into Ironsides' saddle. Looking down, he said, "One more thing. About that fussin' horse critter that got away from you at such a convenient time . . ."

"That's Beulah. She's mostly a good horse. But sometimes," Woodrow explained with that innocent look once again layered on thick, "I plumb forget how mother-in-law mean she can turn if you try to curry the knots out of her tail and give a sudden, too hard jerk of the comb."

Lone grinned again. "Uh-huh. Better be careful

about things like that. They say a body's memory is the first thing to go."

"Goin' is what you need to do. Better knock on it."

Lone took his advice. Wheeled Ironsides and sent him bolting around the corner of the barn, then headed hard for out of town.

"And if you see Beulah somewhere out there," Woodrow called after him, "tell her to get her ass home in time for supper!"

Chapter Twenty-Five

Niles Lavin was pacing again. As he strode past the front of his desk, he suddenly brought the edge of his right fist down and slammed it hard on the polished surface. "God *damn* it!" he exclaimed, his face red with frustrated anger. "How could that big bastard have slipped away in broad daylight without anybody seeing a whisker of him after you and our intrepid law officers chased him into that pool hall?"

Standing over by the office window, leaning with one hand braced on the side frame as he glared out at the street taking on the gloom of descending evening, Earl Drake grated, "You tell me and we'll both know. One minute he was right there in the middle of town with dozens of people streaming in tight from all angles—then he was gone. Like he stuck a feather up his ass and flew. Next thing anybody knows, he's gunning down Grimes and Morton at the stable where they was put especially to stop him."

"Yeah, a fine couple of stoppers they turned out to be," Lavin sneered. "You had your chance to stop him too. But your shot missed—again. Just like you missed killing the crazy husband back in Cheyenne, leaving him to also still be running loose for all we know."

Drake turned sharply from the window. "Best climb down off your high horse with me, mister. I don't take that kind of tone from you or nobody!"

Lavin stopped pacing and struck a challenging pose. "Oh, don't you? You find my tone so offensive you'd turn your back and walk away from your share of the grandest takeover you'll ever get close to?"

"Try me," Drake challenged in return. "I'm not some petty courthouse clerk you can boss around or a desperate client willing to pay through their ass for your services because they think you walk on water. *I'm* the one who's been paddling the canoe keeping you and this grand plan of yours afloat. Remember?"

The two men locked heated glares and held like that for several beats.

Until the rigidity finally sagged out of Lavin's shoulders and he expelled a grudging sigh. "Alright. Very well. We must both keep cool heads, especially at a moment like this. You'll forgive me if I spoke too harshly. But you, above all, surely understand the threat and the stress from this, this *McGantry* scoundrel!"

"Yes, I do." Drake looked very somber. "And, trust me, I've anguished every second since missing that damn shot. But here's the thing . . . other than the frustration of coming so blasted close but failing to take down that big oaf, today didn't really hurt our overall scheme."

"How do you figure?"

"Well we succeeded in branding McGantry a kidnapper, didn't we? That much stays solid. And him killing Hoyt and Tevis makes him even more of an outlaw. He won't dare show his face around here anymore. And that's got to queer things for the woman and the other fella too. So if none of 'em can come around for fear of being accused of kidnapping or accomplices to a murderer, how are they going to ask any questions that could stir up trouble for us?"

"By God." Lavin's eyebrows lifted. "When you put it like that, we don't come off looking so bad after all, do we."

"Maybe even better than we hoped, as far as fearing the trouble McGantry might bring."

"What about Marshal Gus? He buying all of this?"

"Like a baby gobbling candy," Drake said with assurance. "Too late in the day to start out now, but he figures to take a posse out first thing in the morning to try and cut McGantry's sign. I plan on going along just in case they have any luck. I get another shot at that big bastard with a long gun, I guarantee I won't miss a second time. And I'll see to it the other posse members are worked up for wanting to spill his blood almost as bad."

"Gus might have something to say about that," Levin suggested.

"He can try. I pump those other fella's heads

full of thoughts on what that nasty old kidnapper had in mind for the Crawfords' sweet little Rosemary," Drake boasted, "and then on top of that hammer how he cold-blooded gunned down their drinking buddies Hoyt and Tevis . . . hell, by the time I'm done, I'll have Gus himself primed for a necktie party."

"Maybe. But I wouldn't count on it."

Drake shrugged. "We'll have to see. I know most of the boys ol' Gus picked to ride out with him in the morning, and I know where they do their drinking. Might be I'll spend some time in those same establishments tonight and do some generous round-buying to grease the wheels on what passes for their minds in order to have them rolling in the right direction ahead of time."

"You sly bastard," Lavin said around a throaty chuckle.

This got another shrug from Drake. "Like I said, we'll have to see. First we need to catch that damn McGantry and, frankly, I have a lot more doubt about that than I do about talking the posse men into a blood frenzy. Can't say why, but I got a hunch he's got even more savvy out in open country than the luck and trickery he had here in town today."

"You almost sound like you have a kind of respect for him," said Lavin.

"Respecting an enemy ain't a bad thing," Drake

told him. "Makes you try harder, stay sharper, in order to come out on top."

"Sound outlook," agreed Lavin. "But that still leaves me with one concern."

Drake looked at him questioningly.

Lavin said, "The colored man at the stable where Grimes first called you to confirm McGantry's horse and then where Grimes and Morton ended up getting killed . . . does he—what's his name, Woodburn or something like that?"

"Woodrow."

"Isn't there a chance this Woodrow might have seen or heard too much and therefore could be a risk we can't afford to have blurting out something to our disadvantage?"

Drake laughed dismissively. "Trust me, I personally put the fear in that Black boy to *not* see anything he'd be sorry for. He got the message so clear that Black turned *white*. You got no concern about him."

"Something stinks, Ben."

This was the announcement that greeted Deputy Ben Langford when he carried a freshly poured cup of coffee over and placed it on the desktop in front of where the marshal sat scowling in thought.

Ben formed his own scowl. "Jeez, I don't know what it could be, Marshal," he said. "I scrubbed both cells real good yesterday and first thing this morning I swept and dusted the office. Ain't hardly been nobody—"

Marshal Gus cut him short. "No, I don't mean that kind of stink. I mean this whole business about Earl Drake recognizin' that kidnapper we went chasin' after and lost."

"Oh, yeah. That was a piece of bad luck for sure," Ben agreed earnestly. "First us losing him and then especially having him gun down those fellas at the livery stable."

"Yeah, and there's a big part of what's cloggin' my nostrils." Gus took a drink of his coffee. "Two men are dead and the one who shot 'em is the same hombre we was chasin'. No gettin' around that much. Woodrow confirmed it. But the question cloggin' my honker is: Why was Grimes and Morton there layin' for that fella?"

"Mr. Drake said he sent 'em there as a sort of backup to stop the kidnapper from escaping."

"But what made him think the kidnapper might go there if he had cause to try for an escape?"

"On account of that's where the kidnapper's horse was."

"And how did Drake know that?" Gus kept prodding.

Ben looked a bit puzzled and also uncomfortable about why the marshal was peppering him with all these questions. "Because Grimes saw him ride in on that big gray stud and leave him at Woodrow's place. And Mr. Drake had asked both

Grimes and Morton, some days back, to be on the lookout for a stranger on a big gray stallion. Mr. Drake explained all that to us, remember?"

"Yeah, I remember," Gus said tartly. "But what I don't get is what made Drake think there was any reason one of the Crawford girl's kidnappers—the leader of the gang, no less—would be bold enough to come back anywhere around here. What reason would he have? And why only the leader? And why, if he wanted somebody to keep an eye out for a stranger on a big gray stud, didn't Drake bother mentionin' it to me or you?"

Ben had gone back to the office stove to pour his own cup of coffee. Turning again to Gus, he said, "Jeez, Marshal, the way you're coming up with all these questions . . . it sounds like you got some kind of suspicion about Mr. Drake."

"I never liked that pompous jackass, Ben. You know that."

"Yeah, you never made no secret of it." Ben's usually mild expression hardened some. "I understand. Hard to like somebody who goes out of his way to make snotty remarks and seldom tries to hide how he looks down his nose at a body."

Gus said sternly, "You're half a foot taller than him, Ben. In more ways than one. Don't ever let me catch you feelin' looked down on by the likes of him."

"It's just that I know I'm a little slow, and

sharpies like Drake have a way of reminding me—"

"Goddammit, knock that shit off. You're one of the best deputies I ever had and I'd rather have you back me in a tight than anybody in the territory. You think I'd put up with you if you was 'slow'? Don't insult me!"

Ben's mouth spread in a shy grin. "Okay, Marshal. Thanks for saying so."

Gus harrumphed gruffly. "Okay. Now that we got that straight, let's get back to the business at hand. It ain't that I exactly *suspect* Drake of anything. But, at the same time, I can't shake the feelin' of there bein' something fishy about this sudden interest and identifyin' of the kidnap gang leader. Too many things bein' brought to light that for some reason was never bothered bein' mentioned before."

"Yeah, I'm beginning to see what you mean," said Ben. "And it occurs to me Drake was awful quick to take a shot at that kidnapper fella after you told him plain to take it easy about such."

"Uh-huh. Another thing . . . Drake said the first time he spotted and recognized the kidnapper, he couldn't do anything because he wasn't armed. Tell me: Since Drake has come to town, you ever before known him *not* to be heeled?"

"Not hardly."

"It's almost," Gus said, "like he wanted to make sure he had witnesses who knew that fella was—

or at least was *claimed* of bein'—the kidnapper, before he put a bullet in him."

Ben's face pulled into a deep frown. "So what do you suppose could be behind all this . . . fishiness, as you call it?"

Lowering the cup after taking an unhurried sip of his coffee, Gus said, "I don't know, son. I do not know. Yet. But I damn sure aim to find out."

"We still taking a posse out in the morning?"

"Got to. There's two dead men who deserve no less."

"You figure Drake will come along like he said?"

"Not a doubt in my mind. And here's the thing about that . . ." Gus paused to look up and regard Ben very directly before finishing. "While I'm ridin' at the lead, lookin' to cut sign, I want you to hang back and keep an eagle eye on our Mr. Drake. Got it?"

Ben nodded. "Clear as can be."

Chapter Twenty-Six

Lone camped that night just back from the grassy overlook where he, Sue, and Johnny had first reined up to gaze out on Promise Valley. Jesus, had that been only this morning? It seemed much longer ago. He'd done a lot of circuitous riding, to mask his trail in case anybody from town tried following him, before returning there. The thought of going back to the spot had felt oddly comforting, seeking out a place of even meager familiarity.

Lord knew he had encountered his share of *dis*-comforting things ever since leaving there those few hours back. He wondered how Sue and Johnny had fared during the same span of time. Better, he sincerely hoped, even if it meant experiencing nothing of any consequence. Thinking of them was probably another reason he'd been drawn back early to where he was to rejoin the pair. There was the chance they might have returned early too.

That wasn't the case, though. The spare horses they'd left staked out were still there, but that was all.

Lone stripped down Ironsides and staked him with the other horses. Then he built a small, hidden fire in the copse of trees and got some coffee cooking. When he went digging in his saddlebags for the coffee makings, he was surprised and pleased to find that Woodrow had stuffed some vittles into one of the pouches. Corn bread, two jars of canned berries, and a thick bundle of smoked fish. Lone was surprised at how hungry he was, though the tastiness of the fare no doubt accounted for much of that. It took a healthy dose of willpower not to eat all of the berries, but he managed to set aside part of them—along with some corn bread and half the fish—for breakfast in the morning.

All during the meal and well after he stretched out in his bedroll, Lone's mind churned. Replaying all that he had learned in town, then mixing that with what he surmised and speculated, then flipping and turning the whole works to try and examine it from different sides and angles.

What Lone saw as fact was that James Risen's estranged wife Rosemary had been willingly drawn into the ruse to convince the elderly Crawfords that she was their hitherto unknown daughter-in-law. The veteran soldier who had passed through earlier, claiming to be a wartime buddy of the Crawford son Theron and initially planting the notion that Theron had taken a wife before dying of his battle wounds, was obviously a plant to set the ruse in motion.

The ruse was an important part of the larger

scheme—details as yet unclear—for Niles Lavin to eventually acquire the Crawfords' vast holdings (along with others he likely already secretly held) and thereby claim virtual control over the whole valley. Toward what goal beyond that remaining unclear.

Rosemary's alleged "kidnapping," Lone was about eighty percent convinced but couldn't be certain, was the result of her getting cold feet about her part in the proceedings and fleeing back to James in Coraville. Maybe she truly meant to try and mend the marriage, maybe she was only looking to hide out for a while. Before either could be determined, Drake tracked her down and forced her to come back to Promise Valley with him. To resume her daughter-in-law role and do her part to cover up her absence by going along with the phony kidnapping tale Drake and Lavin had concocted so their overall scheme could continue.

This much Lone felt he had a pretty solid handle on.

Unfortunately, that still left plenty of questions swirling like smoke he couldn't begin to grasp.

How had Drake been able to recognize him?

How could he have even gotten a clue Lone was on his way to Promise Valley? Lone had been sure Remson's crew was left too much in shambles to even *attempt* pursuit, let alone succeed in getting here to spread word. The only explanation—a possibility Lone hadn't thought of but couldn't really have stopped, short of leaving the four men dead—was that one of them must have somehow made it to where they were able to send a telegram.

And what of the marshal and deputy who'd so willingly joined Drake in giving chase to Lone? Were they in the pocket of Drake and/or Lavin, the way Remson had been back in Cheyenne? Herman Wurczinski hadn't hinted at any such; but then, neither had Herman seemed to have any trouble accepting Drake and Lavin as stalwarts who'd done great service for the Crawfords.

And there was a potential question that no one was willing to consider in the slightest: What of the Crawfords? Herman had said they were like deities. Could any two mortals truly be so noble and good? What if they themselves were hiding something on the shady side—some secret learned by Lavin that made acquiring their holdings worth more than what was merely evident on the surface, enough more to warrant so much intricate scheming and conniving?

Questions. Puzzlements. Wisps of smoke a body couldn't clamp his fist around. Lone cursed them under his breath until he finally fell asleep . . .

Lone rose with the sun. After re-kindling the fire and setting a fresh pot of coffee to start cooking, he took his field glasses to the overlook and spent several minutes scanning the valley. He concentrated first on the town, looking for any sign of activity that might indicate the formation of a posse. He spotted nothing, but even with the magnification of the glasses his ability to see very far into the heart of the building cluster was limited.

Maybe it was too early, but it would come as a surprise to Lone if the marshal didn't mount some attempt to try and pick up his trail. After all, he'd left two dead men in his wake. They might not have amounted to much, but they were still men. And they'd clearly indicated they were somehow on the payroll of Earl Drake. Meaning possibly in association with the marshal too? Plus there was the "kidnapper" charge that probably made Lone even more of a wanted man.

Swinging away from his focus on the town and its immediate vicinity, Lone made a sweep of the rest of the valley. Though he knew it was too early to expect any sign of them actually being on the approach, he nevertheless was hoping for some indication of Sue and Johnny. Maybe a curl of campfire smoke in the distance. But there was nothing.

He returned to his own campfire and moved the pot of now boiling coffee out on the edge coals. Before taking his breakfast, he went to tend Ironsides and the other horses. Inasmuch as the rain puddle that had been present yesterday was now used up, he took one of the water bags out of the stack of gear and from it repeatedly filled his hat, which he held for each of the animals to drink out of until the thirst of each was satisfied. Then he re-staked them a dozen yards farther back to where they hadn't already cropped the graze down too short.

That done, he returned once more to the fire and settled down to enjoy the rest of the vittles Woodrow had provided. As he ate, his mind once again filled with the churning thoughts and questions he'd gone to sleep on. He was anxious to rejoin with Sue and Johnny partly because he simply wanted to see them again, to know they were okay, but also because he wanted to share with them his discoveries and speculations in order to get their reaction. Also, he was keen to hear if they'd found out anything—especially if they'd taken their explorations as far as actually visiting the Crawford spread. If they hadn't, then Lone reckoned that was the next stop they should all consider making. With the town now effectively shut off to them, that seemed about the only option left short of stumbling across James in the valley somewhere in between.

When he was done eating, Lone took his field glasses, along with a freshly filled cup of coffee, back to the overlook. As before, he saw no sign of posse activity anywhere in the vicinity of the town. Not that he particularly wanted a pack of riders hunting his hide, but he found it mighty curious that there wasn't. Though it was possible, he told himself, they might have ridden out while he was otherwise occupied and were now simply traveling temporarily out of sight within the intervening hills and gullies.

Pondering this curiosity, he swung the aim of his binoculars elsewhere across the valley with somewhat sour and limited expectations. But hold on! He had to halt the sweep of the powerful lenses and actually shift them back some. Yes, there it was again. Movement not too far off to the northwest. A rider coming fast. Headed straight toward him, toward the overlook. He dropped momentarily out of sight into a grassy depression, then popped up to become visible once more.

Lone's pulse quickened and he cursed under his breath as he fought to get the focus of the glasses properly adjusted. Then, abruptly, the features of the rider became distinct. It was Johnny!

Lone's elation was short-lived, though, as he realized there was no sign of Sue. What could that mean? Had something happened to her? He did more sweeping with the binocs, searching the area behind Johnny, thinking perhaps she was just lagging behind. Nothing. Still no sign of her.

By the time Johnny came riding up the slope to the crest of the overlook, Lone was waiting with a knot in his stomach and a look of intense concern on his face.

The wide grin Johnny was wearing offset this somewhat, but not entirely. "Boy, am I glad to see you!" sang out the ex-deputy. "We were hoping you'd show up here sooner than the noon deadline."

Lone didn't waste any time asking, "Where's Sue?"

"Don't worry. She's fine," Johnny assured him. "In fact, it's even better than that—we found James!"

Chapter Twenty-Seven

The James Risen who looked up and met Lone's eyes as Lone followed Johnny through the doorway of the weathered old line shack looked far different from the man first encountered up in South Dakota back in the spring. Gaunt, hollow-eyed, unshaven, clad in rumpled, soiled trail clothes as opposed to his former stylish attire. The only thing unchanged was the full head of pale hair, though now uncombed and falling in limp strands over his forehead.

After quickly taking in this sight, Lone cut his gaze over to Sue, who sat beside her brother on the edge of one of the shack's rough-hewn cots. She looked tired, but otherwise lovely as ever in Lone's eyes. Plus there was an added glow about her, something that hadn't been present these past days and what Lone promptly recognized as having come from finding her brother relatively safe and sound.

"Lone," she greeted him with a wide smile. "Thank God Johnny had no trouble finding you and we're all back together again!"

"Let me add to that," James said. "I know you and I haven't always seen eye to eye, McGantry, but Sue and Johnny have explained how much help you've been trying to help them help me out of this mess I've dragged everybody into, and . . . well, I'm truly grateful."

Twisting his mouth wryly, Lone replied, "I'll allow as to how it's good you've turned up safe, James. But, like I already filled in Johnny, before anybody gets too grateful for any part I played, you'd better stay sat down while I tell you about my trip into Promise City. Afraid I didn't exactly smooth the path for us gettin' the rest of the way out of here."

On the ride from the overlook to this seldom-used line shack out on the fringes of the Crawfords' C-Slash range, Lone and Johnny had traded tales of what each had experienced after parting ways the previous day. While Lone's account, which he now began relating to Sue and James, was plenty colorful, it almost paled in comparison to the wild report given by James after he'd revealed his presence to his sister and Johnny.

He picked up from the point of Chico Racone's shooting and his story went like this:

> After separating from Chico to unsuccessfully go check out the alternate saloon in search of the liveryman they'd been seeking to talk to, James was on his way back to the Dust Cutter. As he was coming up the street, he saw Chico exiting to meet him. Suddenly Chico stopped, shouted a

warning, and grabbed for his gun. James heard a shot from somewhere behind him and he saw Chico struck down before he could clear his holster. Turning, James then saw Earl Drake with a smoking gun in his hand. James realized Drake had been about to shoot him but had had to take care of Chico first in self-defense.

James darted down an alley as Drake fired again, only managing to hit him in the shoulder. In desperation, James ducked into the doorway of an abandoned building, hoping to elude further pursuit. He succeeded, but only because Drake had to take flight himself due to men pouring out of the saloons in response to hearing the shots fired. Unfortunately, someone had caught sight of James going into the alley and he heard himself being blamed for the killing of Chico. In a panic, he ran.

Under cover of darkness, he went to the livery stable where he and Chico had boarded their horses and rode off with his own mount and the pack animal. He went about a mile out of town and hid in a deep, rock-walled gully. There, he built a campfire and tended to his wound. Luckily, the bullet had passed clean through, damaging only meat and muscle, not any bones. He stanched the bleeding, treated to counter infection, bandaged it securely.

Then, before daybreak, he walked back to town and hid up in the loft of the livery barn where he and Chico had spotted Rosemary's horse. His intent was to spy on Rosemary and Drake when they returned for their mounts in hopes of finding out where they were headed next so he could follow. What he saw and overheard instead was only Drake returning to make arrangements for selling the animals, explaining that he and his "lady friend" had decided to make the next leg of their journey by stagecoach. Fortunately, from a loft window James had a view of the stage station and was watching when Drake and Rosemary boarded a coach for Laramie.

James stole back to where he'd left his horses and, doggedly, pushed on to Laramie. There, with the aid of some tongues willing to be loosened by money, he learned that the passengers he described as having arrived from Laramie took a subsequent coach to Promise City.

There, after a night of unobtrusively watching and listening in the different saloons, he picked enough bits and pieces to put together the story of the recent kidnapping and safe return of a "Rosemary Crawford." This was accomplished thanks to a ransom demand being arranged by the Crawfords' lawyer, a man named Lavin, and executed by Earl Drake, the private detective Lavin kept on permanent retainer.

It made James sick to his stomach to hear Drake praised in such a manner and he could barely hold his tongue. But he managed to. In the morning, he rode out into the valley and found the Crawford ranch.

From a hill overlooking the buildings of the ranch headquarters, hidden in some trees and using a powerful telescope, James spent hours watching/hoping for some sign of Rosemary. And then, as if a miracle in answer to a prayer, he saw her! Astride a beautiful Palomino gelding, she emerged from the complex out for an afternoon ride—one of the long-standing great joys of her life. The only trouble, from James's standpoint, was that two men rode out a short ways behind her—two men recently assigned as bodyguards in the wake of her recent alleged kidnapping. (Though, as Rosemary would later explain, they in truth functioned more as "keepers" to prevent her from fleeing.)

Stubbornly, though maintaining a safe distance and continuing to use the telescope, James kept pace with the riders. Until they arrived at a small, tree-lined lake up in a stretch of higher terrain. Seeing this, James's heart had quickened with the suspicion of what was coming next. Another of Rosemary's favorite things was to go for a brisk swim whenever she got the chance. Sure enough, signaling for the bodyguards to remain a discreet distance downslope, she made her way up through the screen of trees to the water's edge.

James wasted no time circling high around and coming to the lake at an angle well hidden from the bodyguards. But not from Rosemary. He stepped to the shore where she could see him plainly and awaited her response. Would she cry out to the men downslope . . . or would she be welcoming to him the way he'd insisted in believing from the start of his grueling journey to find her again?

It was the latter.

Immediately upon full recognition of him, Rosemary had raced toward the shore and James waded part way out to meet her. She came out of the water glisteningly, gloriously nude and threw herself into his arms. They embraced and kissed and Rosemary instantly began telling him, in frantic, hushed whispers, how sorry she was and how Drake had forced her to return with him under threat of horrible pain and disfigurement to her and gruesome death to James and Sue.

James tried to get her to come away with him that very moment, to flee with him to somewhere where he would keep her safe from Drake and find a way to ensure the villain never bothered her or anyone else ever again. She wanted to leave with all her heart but was too fearful of Drake's threats—to herself and more—and the reach and viciousness he possessed to carry them out thanks to being backed by the money and power of Niles Lavin. Try as he might, James couldn't convince her to go with him. Not that first day, which had been day before yesterday. But she agreed to meet with him again the following day, same place and approximate time, and had given him directions to the line shack as a place where he could find shelter in the interim.

They met again as planned. This time, in addition to bringing James some food as well as salve and fresh bandages for his wound, Rosemary had gone on to explain her dire situation at greater length. How she first met Drake on a Missouri River paddle wheeler during the period of her original abandonment of James. How she'd been charmed and seduced by him and had ended up working with him in his seedy investigations, often serving as a decoy or lure to entice information out of men. Then the scheme with Lavin had been put together and she was assigned to portray the previously unknown daughter-in-law to Ezra and Irene Crawford. She hadn't minded in the beginning, but before long she found herself growing very fond of the old couple, especially Irene, and her conscience began torturing her about the cruel ruse she was a key part of. It was through her—somehow, Rosemary wasn't exactly clear on what "legal" shenanigans would also be employed—that the overall scheme's end goal of Lavin acquiring full control of the Crawford holdings would be reached. As soon as he had that, he planned on starting mining operations in the front range of the Estelle Mountains, which were part of Crawford property. Though Ezra had forbade any exploring to be done there,

Lavin had commissioned some secret testing that determined the presence of both lead and silver. Once those were being brought out, he would force finally bringing a railroad (something else Ezra had blocked) into the valley to haul the ore. And Lavin would rake in the lion's share of the profits from it all.

The final straw where Rosemary was concerned, what caused her to break away and flee back to James (who she swore she had never really stopped loving but was previously too ashamed to ask for a second chance), had to do with Irene. In the beginning, when Lavin and Drake began to implement their scheme, her health had been very frail and fading fast. She hadn't been expected to last much longer and it was generally anticipated that a broken-hearted Ezra, though still in decent health for his age, would deteriorate soon after.

To everyone's surprise, however, the appearance of Rosemary in the guise of a daughter-in-law—the wonderful surprise of a living connection to at least one of their beloved lost sons—was so joyous to Irene that it rejuvenated her and her health took a sudden turn for the better. This so annoyed Lavin, seeing it as a setback that could delay the progress of his scheme for who knew how long, that he ordered Drake to supply Rosemary with some undetectable poison she was to slip into Irene's tea and get her failing health back on track. Presented with this, Rosemary had refused to be any part of it and had instead taken flight in an attempt to escape.

So all of that and what had ensued in relationship to it was what the four people now gathered in the line shack were recapping, sifting, and blending with the latest news from Lone on his experiences the previous day in Promise City.

Bringing Sue to declare with a sigh of equal parts despair and determination, "My. What we set out to do has certainly grown from the rather basic goal of chasing down what I believed to be a stubborn, foolish man refusing to let go of what I unfairly labeled his runaway wife. Now look at us. Within our ranks we have two murder suspects, an accused kidnapper, and three others who probably are considered horse thieves because of the spare mounts we took from Remson and his men. Yet, for all that, we're still the ones truly on the right side of things."

Lone grinned wryly. "Uh-huh. We just need to convince a whole bunch of other people that that's the case."

"Speaking as one of the murder suspects and certainly understanding the seriousness of that and the rest," said James, "I hope all of you realize that, for me, I still count rescuing Rosemary as a high priority too."

"That's all well and good," Lone told him. "But in order for that to work she's gonna have to make up her mind and be *willin'* to be rescued."

"That means overcoming her fear of Drake and how he'll retaliate against not only her, but me and Sue and who knows who else." James wagged his head sadly. "And that's not going to be easy to do. The cruel bastard has planted the seed of menace so deeply in her."

"Then it's time to convince her that there are other menacin' hombres around," Lone grated, "who are ready and able—and even a little bit eager, speakin' for myself—to take away any threat Drake poses."

"Consider me eager for a piece of that, too," said Johnny.

"What's more," added Sue, "if Rosemary is willing to believe that, then she also needs to see how—just like she's a key to Lavin's and Drake's takeover scheme—she can be key, as a witness against them, to their undoing. With Lone and Johnny keeping her safe and the involvement of law officials we can trust, not more who've been bought off by Lavin, *she* can be the menace—to them and their whole fabric of lies."

James replied, "I like what I'm hearing, and I believe and trust in all of you. I've certainly seen how formidable McGantry can be. And Johnny, too. But even if Rosemary were to accept all of that, I fear there would still be one more hurdle to overcome."

"What else?" Sue asked, unable to hide a touch of irritation in her tone.

"Irene Crawford," James answered. "Ezra also, but him to a lesser degree. Rosemary has become so fond of Irene that I know she would find it difficult, perhaps impossible, to make any admission that would break Irene's heart by ripping away the joy she's gotten from believing in the discovery of her late son's wife."

"That's ridiculous," snapped Sue. "Could she possibly think it's better to let the scheme of Lavin and Drake go ahead and succeed after the death of the old couple—maybe hurried along, if those rats can find a way—all for the sake of sparing their feelings while they're alive?"

"Not only that," growled Lone, "but her way of thinkin' is doggone insultin' to folks like the Crawfords. You're talkin' tough pioneer stock. Folks who came to this valley when it was nothing. They cleared it, settled it, fought bad weather and probably Indians. Put in the back-breakin' labor and endured who knows how many hardships, includin' losin' their only two sons to war . . . and somebody thinks they ain't got the grit to hold up under findin' out they been tricked and near whipsawed by a nest of snakes lookin' to snatch away all they spent their lives buildin'? I never laid eyes on Ezra Crawford in my life, but I bet I know his type. Instead of worryin' he might fall to pieces, the worry would be tryin' to hold him back from takin' a shotgun and settin' out to settle with Lavin and Drake all on his own!"

By the time he finished, the other three were regarding him closely.

"I wish Rosemary could hear those words, spoken just like that," James said.

"Why can't she?" Lone wanted to know. "Are you meetin' her again this afternoon?"

"Why, yes. About two o'clock."

"Well . . . ? Ain't the shoreline of that lake big enough to hold more than just you?"

Chapter Twenty-Eight

Lone McGantry had been uncharacteristically careless. Something his past years of surviving in the wilderness, often deep in hostile Indian territory, had honed him never to be. But the early arrival of Johnny carrying the news about him and Sue having found James had caused the former scout to anxiously, hurriedly saddle up Ironsides in order to get on the trail and follow Johnny to where Sue awaited . . . all in too big a rush to take time for properly extinguishing his breakfast campfire. This left the flames to die slowly down until the last remaining chunks of charred wood began giving off tendrils of smoke to drift up and hang as a slight haze in the still air.

And though the maneuvers Lone had employed to mask his trail the previous day had succeeded in puzzling Gus Teaford riding at the head of his morning posse, what the old marshal didn't miss spotting were the faint curls of smoke above the crest of the overlook. He didn't know exactly what it meant, but he reckoned it was worth checking out. And when he and his men reached the hastily abandoned campsite, he was glad he did.

"These ashes ain't more than a couple hours

old. Three at the most," judged Will Erby, a former cavalry trooper who'd fought in some Indian engagements and was the second-best tracker in the bunch, next to Gus.

"I agree," said Gus. "I make it one man camped here last night."

"Then it had to be him. Had to be McGantry, the kidnapper and the bushwhacking snake who gunned down Hoyt and Tevis," Drake was quick to say, looking to further pound home his efforts to paint McGantry as loathsome as possible.

"But if only one man was here, then who are those horses staked over yonder for?" somebody asked.

"I've been telling everybody there was a whole gang of kidnappers," said Drake. "I saw three at the ransom transfer when I got Miss Crawford back, but there could have been more lurking in the shadow. Those horses over there must be fresh mounts for more of his gang McGantry is expecting to show up."

"Could mean that, could mean something else," grumbled Gus, continuing to scowl down at the ground as he walked out a ways from the campfire ashes. "What I'm more interested in right now is the hombre we know about for sure, not who *might* be showin' up."

Walking beside him, Erby pointed and said, "A second rider came up out of the valley. Palavered pretty short with the fella who was here. Then

324

they rode off together, back down into the valley."

Gus nodded. "Uh-huh. I see that. Those are the scoundrels I mean to be stickin' with."

"But what about these other horses, Marshal—in case somebody does show up for them?" asked Ben.

Gus rubbed his jaw and considered. Apart from him and Ben, five other men made up his posse. Excluding Drake and Erby, the remainder were townsmen of limited past experience who saw it their duty to volunteer. And while this made their intentions brave and noble, it didn't erase the fact that none of the three were trail hardened or knew much about handling a gun. The last thing Gus wanted was to see one of his citizens get hurt; the second to the last thing he wanted was to see a culprit or culprits get away if there was a chance they could be nabbed.

"Alright, here's what we're gonna do," the marshal announced. "Just in case somebody does come around showin' interest in those nags, we'll leave a couple men to stand watch over 'em. Art and Gerald"—he pointed to the two oldest men in the group—"I'm askin' that of you two. Now I don't want no heroics that get you shot full of holes. Remember, these are some dangerous characters. Just hang back and keep a lookout. Get descriptions and listen for anything worth reportin' if any owlhoots show their mangy heads.

If they swap out horses and ride off again, especially if it's down into the valley the way we're gonna be headed, wait until it's safe then get off a couple warnin' shots and skedaddle outta here. Got it?"

The two men he'd selected nodded their heads obligingly. In truth, they'd already spent enough time in the saddle that morning to be grateful for the break.

"Okay then," said Gus, starting back to his horse. "Let's the rest of us get after this fresh trail and see where it leads us."

Lyle Basteen finished building a cigarette, hung it from the corner of his mouth, snapped the flame of a match to it. Inhaling deep and then releasing a cloud of smoke, he said, "I tell you she's sending a signal and we're a couple of chuckleheads if we don't wise up to it."

His brother Frank, who sat on the grass a short distance away, leaning back against the trunk of a cottonwood tree with his hat tipped down over his eyes, replied lazily, "The only signal being sent is that the girl wants to get out of that house once in a while, away from the musty smell of old age and medicine and looming death, and breath some fresh air. And to enjoy a private swim before the weather turns too cold."

"See? Right there's the thing," said Lyle, pointing a finger. "The swimming part. If she was to just go galloping around on that Palomino, I wouldn't pay it so much mind. But the swimming . . . three days in a row now . . . that fine, firm young body stripped nekkid up there just behind those trees. Oh, man, I get to picturing it and I get a down deep ache that causes me to need a cold plunge myself."

"Then *don't* picture it," Frank advised tersely. "And if you need a cold plunge so bad, throw yourself in a watering tank when we get back to the ranch."

"Very funny. Don't pretend you ain't thinking some of the same thoughts as me."

Frank was the older of the two brothers by three years, putting him about half that much over thirty and Lyle that much under. Both of the Basteens were tall, well-built individuals, with dark hair and even features. As befitting his elder status, Frank was (and always had been) the calmer and more sensible of the two. Lyle was bulkier, more thickly muscled, and had a vaguely wild glint in his eyes that he sometimes worked too hard to live up to. Frank was some better with a gun, Lyle had the edge in a brawl, though the difference in either case was minor. They had a reputation of sorts in the territory, and both Niles Lavin and Earl Drake had hired them in the past as backups for certain dealings. This current assignment as bodyguards for Rosemary Crawford, however, was the best assignment handed to them yet . . . if Lyle's near constant horniness didn't mess it up.

In response to Lyle's remark about Frank's feelings along those same lines, the older brother said, "Having thoughts and acting on them are two different things. It's called willpower. And I suggest you keep a tight hold on yours, little brother. This is a sweet deal we got going here and it could lead to more work for us, maybe something steady, in the future. And Lavin sure as hell ain't making no bones about how he's got big plans going forward."

"Yeah, yeah. But none of that would make any difference," Lyle argued, "if little sweetie over yonder is sending signals like I think. What if I'm right? That could make this sweet deal even sweeter."

"And if you're wrong," Frank snapped, "it could queer the whole thing and we'd be back to bouncing in beer halls for shit wages and whatever we're able to pluck out of the pockets of the drunks we toss into the back alley. So unless or until I see Miss Rosemary step through that tree line in her birthday suit and sing out 'Come and get it, boys!', you need to keep your mind off her and your pecker in your pants when she's around. Got it?"

Lyle squared his shoulders and gave a mock salute. "Yes sir, Captain Dull Pencil, sir. I read you loud and clear."

Frank shook his head and was unable to suppress a faint grin. He never could stay mad at his little brother for very long. "You horse's ass," he said. "I'm gonna lean back here and snooze some until Rosemary finishes her swim . . . in case you *are* right and she does call down for somebody to do the belly-to-belly stroke with her, I'd appreciate getting woke up for a turn."

Chapter Twenty-Nine

Having heard so much about Rosemary Risen (going as Rosemary Crawford these days), Lone still wasn't quite prepared upon seeing her for the first time. The main thing that struck him was how small and young looking she was. Petite, he supposed, was the proper word; almost doll-like. The womanly curves were all there, just in borderline miniature and capped by an angelic, button-nosed face framed by a thick mane of chestnut hair. It took a minute for Lone to see the rest of it. Yes, she could look angelic and innocent—but those smoky, lynx-like dark eyes and those full lips—he had a hunch that here was a gal who could also, at her whim, turn those same features very sultry, maybe even what could be termed exotic. He was willing to give her the benefit of the doubt, for James's sake, but at the same time it was easy to understand Sue's reservations. This little lady could be a diminutive package of dynamite if she ever decided to employ all her wiles.

But, in fairness, as Lone was making his assessment of her, Rosemary was faced with making a pretty big assessment of her own after James sprung on her the surprise of bringing Lone, Sue, and Johnny to their assignation. She at least had met Sue and Johnny in the past, but this former scout, so big and rugged in appearance, was most unsettling.

And the things he and the others were proposing, talking in hushed whispers so their voices would not carry from the lakeside through the trees and down to her "keepers" at the base of the slope. Stand up to Drake and Lavin, go to the law and testify against them, she was being urged, for her own sake and for the good of the Crawfords too. All things she badly wanted to do, had tried to bolster herself over and over into doing . . . but no one else knew the depth of her terror. None of them had witnessed, as she had, the vicious things Drake was capable of. Nor heard the punishment he promised if she ever crossed him again, describing it in skin-crawling detail with his lips held a fraction of an inch from her ear as he rasped the words while crushing one of her breasts in his grip. No matter how much she *wanted* to do the right thing, how could she make her mind move past that in order to do so?

"Please, honey. Please just listen," James begged her.

"If you don't help us stop Lavin and Drake," said Sue, "then they will turn Promise Valley into Ruthless Valley, and everything the Crawfords spent their lives building and what so many other good people are benefiting from . . . will be destroyed forever."

"Look, I know you're scared," Lone said firmly yet with a strange gentleness. "Vermin like Drake are masters at crowdin' the weak and vulnerable into feelin' that way, into feelin' helpless and thinkin' they got no way out from under a grindin' boot heel. But there are others who have the will and the ability to dig out the vulnerabilities in the Drakes of the world.

"Consider this: I'm only here because I have strong feelings for this woman"—a nod toward Sue—"and she asked for my help. You say Drake threatened her too if you crossed him? If I didn't have confidence that I can protect Sue *and* you, then I would never allow any of this to continue. But, backed by Johnny and James, I have that confidence and I swear to you that you'll be protected if you take a stand with us and do what you know is right."

Rosemary felt her pulse quickening and her heart beating faster. There was strength in the big man's words. She could feel that too, feel it wrapping around her. Yes. Yes, at last, maybe there was another way besides being pushed in directions she didn't want to go and always driven down lower . . .

"Frank! Frank, wake up! There's something going on over there at the lake—you'd better come with me and have a look."

Frank Basteen jerked upright and pushed his

hat up away from his eyes. Damn, he hadn't meant to slip into such a deep slumber. And now his brother was shaking him, all excited, and babbling something about a lake? No, wait . . . *the* lake—the lake where Rosemary Crawford, the girl they were in charge of watching, had gone!

Frank shoved to his feet. "What the hell are you talking about? What's going on over there?"

"I don't know exactly. I just know there's a bunch of people over there with her. A woman and three men who I never saw before—nobody I recognize."

"What are they doing with her?"

"Nothing. Just talking. Ain't looking like they mean her no harm or anything, else I'd be making a lot bigger whoop than this. She ain't even wet. Like she never got in to swim at all."

Frank shot his brother a sudden glare. "How'd you happen to be in a position for seeing all of this?"

Lyle thrust his chin out defiantly. " 'Cause I went to have me a peek, okay? Just a peek is all. My pecker was safe in my pants and I wasn't gonna do nothing wrong. But hey, it's a good thing I done what I did else we wouldn't know anything about what's going on over there. And it's something fishy 'cause they're talking all in whispers, meanin' for us not to hear."

"Yeah, I guess it is a good thing you went sneak

333

peeking," Lyle allowed grudgingly. "Grab our rifles. We'd better Injun up through those trees and try to figure out what those strangers are up to."

Lone went tense on the inside but showed nothing outwardly. Nobody else had seen it, but he'd caught the faintest flicker of movement back in the crescent-shaped growth of trees that curled around the northwest end of the small lake. Not animal. Human. The Crawford ranch was off in that direction and, in between, beyond the trees and down at the bottom of a slope, Rosemary's bodyguards were supposedly holding off at a discreet distance. Lone had checked earlier to make sure they were there, before he would allow himself and the others to expose themselves on the shoreline. Yeah, they'd been where they were supposed to be then . . . but it seemed something had now stirred them up and brought them closer.

Lone saw another flicker of movement about a dozen yards off to one side of the first one. So the pair had enough savvy to fan out on their approach, but they were damn clumsy about moving through trees and underbrush.

In the same whisper he'd been using, but with an unmistakable edge to it, Lone said, "Sue . . . Rosemary . . . keep smilin' and talkin' like you have been but slowly move around in a line directly behind me . . . Johnny and James, stay sharp and gradually spread apart some."

Johnny threw back his head and gave a little laugh like Lone had said something funny. Then, still smiling, he asked, "What's up?"

"Don't look around, but we got visitors movin' in through the trees."

"Right. See 'em."

"Good. Keep seein' 'em, but don't let on," Lone said. "If they're Rosemary's bodyguards, they ain't apt to do nothing too drastic with her right here in our midst . . . let's give it a minute, see what they got in mind."

"That's Rosemary's Palomino, I'm sure of it," stated Ben Langford. Like many young men in the valley, Ben had made a point of learning as much as he could about the fetching Miss Crawford.

"Boy's right. No doubt that's Rosemary's horse," agreed Earl Drake.

The posse was reined up a couple hundred yards back from where a flat, grassy stretch of C-Slash range rose to some tree-stippled higher ground. Frowning, Marshal Gus said, "What about them other two horses?"

"They must belong to the Basteen brothers, the bodyguards we hired to keep an eye on Rosemary after that kidnapping incident," explained Drake.

"Then where is everybody?" Gus wanted to know.

335

Drake scowled. "I'm wondering that myself."

"Maybe they went picnicking," suggested Steve Arnold, the remaining townsman still riding with them. He was a transplant from the east, not very far into his twenties, currently working as a store clerk but trying hard to build a more rugged version of himself to better fit the frontier.

Drake gave him a look. "Trust me, the Basteen brothers are hardly the *picnicking* types."

"Well whatever them and the girl are doing," drawled Will Erby, "these tracks we been following since that line shack—four riders now—swing out and head up into that higher ground on the opposite side. We gonna stick with them, or go check on that girl?"

"I don't like the way this is shaping up. I don't like it at all," said Drake. "We know that kidnapping murderer McGantry is one of the riders we've been following. And now it looks like he's converging once again on Rosemary. We need to warn her!"

"Ain't those bodyguards supposed to be protectin' her?"

"They could be caught by surprise. Anybody can," Drake insisted.

"We're only a handful of minutes behind these riders," Erby pointed out. "We veer off now and tip our hand by messin' in some other business, it might not be so easy to catch up again."

Drake glared at him. "Damn it, man, that 'other

business' might mean an innocent girl's life!"

"Why don't we split up?" said Ben. "Somebody go to warn Miss Rosemary, the rest continue on with these riders we been following."

"I like the sound of that," declared Gus. "That way, if these riders are circlin' to close in on Rosemary and the Basteens, then we can close in too, and have 'em in a pincer."

Drake's eyes flashed. "I'm all for it! I'll go warn Rosemary and the Basteens."

"Okay," Gus agreed. "Take young Arnold with you. Me, Ben, and Erby will stick on the trail of the riders."

Drake looked ready to balk, but then held off. "All right," he growled reluctantly. Then to Arnold: "Come on. Maybe there'll be some picnic lunch left for us."

Before the two men wheeled away, Gus halted them. "One more thing . . . don't you get trigger-happy again, Drake. Nobody starts throwin' lead until or unless I say so!"

337

Chapter Thirty

When the men in the trees stalled, perhaps sensing their presence had been detected, Lone grew impatient. Over his shoulder, he said to Rosemary, "Looks like your friends have turned a little shy about comin' out the rest of the way to play. How about you encourage them a bit so we can find out what their intent is?"

"Not sure I'm in such a big hurry to know," murmured Rosemary. But then, regardless, she leaned out a little ways from behind Lone and called, "Frank? Lyle? Is that you in the trees?"

After a pause, Frank's voice answered, "Yeah, it's us."

"Aren't you supposed to be waiting down the hill? Isn't that our arrangement?"

"It is as long as you stick to what *you* are supposed to be doing—which is taking a swim. Alone," Frank replied. "What's with all those other people?"

"They're friends of mine. We're having a private visit."

"Uh-uh. That ain't part of the deal and you know it," came a different voice this time; Lyle's. "You ain't supposed to meet with nobody when you go out like this. Not unless you clear it first with Drake and he lets us know."

"What is she, a slave?" snarled Lone. "Maybe you boys been livin' in the trees and bushes so long you ain't heard. But that kind of stuff don't go no more."

"Oh, you're a real funny man," sneered Lyle. "Who the hell *are* you, funny man?"

"Somebody who don't make a habit of talkin' to voices hidin' behind tree trunks," Lone said. "You want to know more, how about havin' the onions to step out here and ask me to my face?"

"All of a sudden you ain't so goddamn funny no more, mister," Lyle responded. "And maybe it's time somebody taught you about being careful what you wish for."

The bushes where Lyle's voice was coming from began swaying and rustling with aggressive movement.

"Goddammit, Lyle, hold on!" Frank hollered. "Just take it easy, don't do nothing stupid."

"That takin' it easy thing is real good advice— *for everybody!*" These words were spoken by a whole new voice. That of Marshal Gus, coming out of some brush-choked boulders crowding the shoreline at a forty-five degree angle off behind where Lone and his group stood. The former scout silently cursed himself for being too focused on the Basteens and not keeping more alert to the rest of his surroundings.

"I'm the marshal outta Promise City. I got a posse of armed men backin' me," Gus continued, "and a gutful of questions I need some answers to. If everybody keeps a cool head, we can take care of the last part without havin' to bring into play the first part . . . how about it?"

Lone slowly turned his head far enough to see the marshal—the same elderly, pot-bellied man he'd got only a glimpse of back on the street of Promise City—step out into plain sight with his gun hand held empty and wide out away from the six-gun holstered on his hip.

Their eyes met and held and Lone felt a guarded sense of reassurance. He said, "I got me some questions of my own. Had 'em the last time we briefly met, as a matter of fact, but it was kinda hard to get 'em out on account of how fast the lead started flyin'."

"That should've never happened like it did," Gus said solemnly. "If we play this right, it won't again."

"For starters then, how about havin' these hombres off in the trees on this other side step out where they can be seen? I'd sooner play a couple hands without them bein' hole cards."

Gus nodded. "Fair enough. You Basteen boys . . . step on out where everybody can see you."

But nothing happened. No response of any kind. Gus scowled.

Lone felt an icy trickle run down his spine. Something was wrong. Something outside the control of the marshal.

Lone said over his shoulder to Sue and Rosemary, "You gals move clear—quick!"

Giving that order damn near signed his own death warrant. No sooner had the women moved back away from him than yet another new voice—that of Earl Drake, though Lone had no way of recognizing who it was at that point—rang out from the same trees that held the Basteen brothers. "Cut loose, boys! Kill that sonofabitch!"

Gunfire erupted from the trees. Muzzle flashes, boiling blue powder smoke, and sizzling lead. Lone spun away, feeling his shirt collar tugged by a bullet and a fiery slash of pain rip the outside of his left thigh. He hit the ground, rolling, clawing for his Colt. Rosemary screamed and Johnny Case spat a curse as his own Colt began to bark in response.

"Goddamn you, Drake!" Lone heard the marshal holler.

Lone shoved to his feet long enough to make a low, scrambling, lunge-like dive into the bushes and rocks that ran behind the shoreline where he and the others had stood talking. Slugs tore into the ground all around him, kicking up mini geysers of dirt and spanging off the rocks he was headed for. He thrust his arm out behind and blindly triggered rounds in the direction of the shooters as he continued to dig for cover. Johnny was still shooting and James had joined in too.

Lone could hear the marshal roaring out more curses.

Over the jumble of low, gouging rocks Lone clambered, finally dropping in behind them. He sensed the others also tumbling in on either side. But the bullets kept hammering in too, splattering on the rocks and tearing through the bushes. Then, abruptly, after a couple sporadic final reports, the shooting stopped.

But what didn't stop was Gus's furious ranting. "Drake, you crazy bastard, what's wrong with you? Didn't you hear me order you not to get trigger happy?"

"I was just trying to save the county the expense of hang ropes," Drake hollered back. "If you would have joined in too, you gutless old fool, we could have had them wiped out. Can't you see they're the same kidnap gang who took Rosemary before and now are trying again to gouge more ransom pay out of the Crawfords? There's only one way to deal with snakes like them and that's to—"

He was cut short by a fiercely shrieking Rosemary. "That's a dirty lie, Marshal! He's the snake—the lowest, slimiest one that ever crawled! Him and that piece of filth Niles Lavin too. They forced me to crawl with them for a while, but I'm through. I'm not the Crawfords' daughter-in-law at all. Drake and Lavin made me pretend to be as part of their scheme to swindle the Crawfords out of all their property!"

"Don't listen to her, Marshal," Drake protested. "Those kidnappers have her scared half to death, talking out of her head! You can't possibly believe anything that lying little witch just said— Niles Lavin is one of the most respected and prominent men in the valley."

"Yeah," sneered Gus, "and he's the first one to tell that to anybody who'll listen, ain't he? That is, if he can beat you to crowin' his praises for him."

"You'd better be careful what comes out of that pie hole of yours, Teaford," Drake warned. "Lavin throws a lot of weight when your tired old ass comes up for election."

"If you're threatening the marshal," Ben Langford said, stepping up beside Gus, "then you're the one who'd better be careful what comes out of your pie hole, buster."

Now Drake edged into view. "What the hell is this? Has everybody gone loco? You two badge toters have got a pack of kidnappers standing right in front of you, and it's *me* you're giving a hard time?"

"You seem to be forgettin' there's also the matter of a young lady who just spewed some mighty interestin' things—things this old badge toter wants to hear more about," Gus told him. "And if there's truth in what she says, then you're just beginnin' to see me give you a hard time."

"You've got to be kidding! They've threatened her, scared her into saying those things. Surely you—"

This time it was Gus who cut him short. "Shut up! I've listened to enough out of you, I said it's the girl I want to hear more out of."

"And you'll hear plenty, Marshal," Rosemary stated boldly. "I'll swear to everything I just said and more. And part of what I'll testify to is how I know firsthand about being threatened and terrified into saying and doing what somebody else wants—because that's what that bastard did to me on a regular basis!"

"You bitch!" Drake hissed.

Lone could see it coming. Could see the changes flood over Drake's face. From anger to panic to rage. And then he could see the rifle start to rise. The cold-blooded bastard no longer cared about using Rosemary for his and Lavin's scheme, his only thought in this instant was to silence her testimony. Lone pushed up from behind the rocks and hurled himself crossways in front of Rosemary, firing his Colt as he did so. No time to aim, just thrust his gun hand in Drake's direction and pull the trigger. Freakish luck guided his bullet to strike at an upward angle just ahead of the rifle's trigger guard, knocking the muzzle up and sending Drake's shot harmlessly skyward. As Lone landed on Rosemary, driving her to the ground, he heard more shots crashing

into the trees around Drake and the Basteens—
shots fired by Gus and Ben, and also Johnny and
James.

As a result, he heard Drake's fading voice
calling, "Beat it, boys! Rattle our hocks the hell
outta here!"

Chapter Thirty-One

Gus held off giving immediate chase. There were wounded who needed tending first.

Lone had received a deep bullet gash to the outside of his thigh. Luckily it only tore through meat and muscle, missed hitting any bone. In a stroke of bitter irony, James took a bullet to his shoulder on almost the exact spot where he'd been hit before in Cheyenne. It ripped open the previous, partially healed wound, again passing all the way through and fortunately once more not doing any bone damage. "I don't know if I should consider myself lucky, getting shot in the same place twice with minimal damage," James quipped, "or if I should worry that this shoulder is some kind of magnet that might attract more bullets in the future."

To which his sister remarked as she was patching him up, "Just in case, warn anybody walking next to you to stay on the opposite side."

A third injury was to Steve Arnold, who had accompanied Drake when the posse split up. He was found at the bottom of the slope with a split skull from Drake clubbing him unconscious before going up to join the Basteens. It left Arnold with a cut to his scalp and a pounding headache, but nothing more serious.

A fourth and final injury was to Rosemary, who

got the wind knocked out of her and suffered a couple marginally cracked ribs from Lone throwing himself on her. "The next time you save me, Mr. McGantry," she said, "please try to not do it so hard."

"Not to mention near crushin' our star witness," added Gus.

Right about when the wounded were announced to be cared for as good as the circumstances would allow, Will Erby returned with a scouting report on Drake and the Basteens. "Don't know what it means," he told Gus, "but they headed straight for the Crawford ranch. I got close enough to where I could hear shooting coming from there."

"How much shootin'?" Gus asked.

"Quite a bit."

The old marshal ground his teeth. "Shit, that don't sound good. Not for the Crawfords, not for nobody." He swept his eyes over Ben and Erby. "Sounds like we got some more possein' to do, pronto-like."

"I'll get our horses," Ben said, starting toward where he and Gus had left their mounts.

"Count me in," Johnny was quick to say.

Gus nodded. "Consider yourself counted."

Then the old lawman set his eyes on Arnold, saying, "Steve, I need you to take that achin' head of yours and ride fast as you can back to town. Bring more men hell-apoppin' to the C-Slash. Can you do that?"

347

"Yessir. Want me to fetch Art and Gerald too?"

"No, that'd be out of your way. Straight to town!"

As Arnold hurried off, Gus turned and started to say, "Now you two wounded men stay here with the women and I'll be sure to send—"

Before he could finish, Lone was up on his feet.

"Where do you think you're goin'?" the marshal demanded.

"With you," Lone told him. "The only way you're gonna stop me is to shoot me in the other leg and do a better job of it than those polecats. And you got neither the time nor bullets to waste. So come on!"

The C-Slash ranch headquarters lay in the heart of a grassy, frying pan flat expanse that made an unseen approach by daylight nearly impossible. So Gus didn't even try. Him and his re-formed posse rode five abreast straight for it—Ben, Johnny, Gus, Lone, and Erby, left to right in that order. All flinty-eyed with mouths set grim and tight.

At the start, Lone and Johnny had given quick, concise accounts of their backgrounds and what had pulled them into this whole thing. Gus listened, had no comments or questions. Not right then anyway.

They drew rein about a quarter mile back. There was no longer any sound of gunfire. Lone appraised the layout. The main house was a two-story wood frame structure, impressive without being showy. Lone could make out what had been the original core if it, then where it had been expanded with rooms added to make it wider and higher. The former scout smiled faintly. This told him something about Ezra Crawford, the man. Something not surprising but rather meshing almost exactly with the image Lone had already formed. Ezra had left the original humble beginnings of his home as a point of pride, not tearing down and replacing but instead increasing and improving to show the progress and success of his dream.

Producing the field glasses from his saddlebags, Lone handed them to Gus. While the lawman put them to his eyes and had a closer look at things, Lone resumed his naked eye scan. The house was built facing southeast, putting its back to the north/northwest where the worst of bad weather usually came from. Behind the main house was the bunkhouse, corrals and holding pens, various sheds and outbuildings. The placement of these other structures seemed rather haphazard but they nevertheless all appeared sturdy and well maintained.

Gus lowered the glasses and said, "There's three rode-hard horses—Drake's and the other two belonging to the Basteens no doubt—tied at the hitch rail in front of the house. I take it that means our boys are inside, and I further take it that can't be good news for the Crawfords."

"Where's everybody else?" Johnny wanted to know. "Place looks dang near deserted."

"Expect most of the hands are out moving cattle to winter grass," said Ben.

"There's at least two who ain't," muttered Gus. "I saw a couple dead bodies sprawled over by the bunkhouse. Got a hunch there's probably a few more scattered about."

"Aw, damn," groaned Erby. "That really ain't good news for the Crawfords."

"No, and us just sitting our saddles jawing about it ain't doing 'em any good either," said Ben.

"Nor would bein' in a hurry to join the dead men already layin' down there," Gus told him.

Ben scowled. "So what are we supposed to do?"

"They'll let us know when we get in closer," Lone drawled.

Four sets of eyes cut questioning looks his way. "What do you mean?" said Gus.

"I mean I got a hunch they're waitin' down there, knowin' somebody'd be bound to show up soon, lookin' to palaver and try to strike a deal with whoever came. If they was meanin' to make a fightin' run for it, they'd've blasted their way in just long enough to grab some supplies and fresh horses, then kicked dust high and hard outta here for parts unknown."

"By gar, I think he might be onto something," said Erby. "I've seen crafty Injuns act that way. Figuring they have something to trade that'll buy 'em time to fight another day."

"What have these polecats got to trade?" asked Johnny.

Gus saw the answer all too plain. Setting his jaw, he bit out the words. "Ezra and Irene Crawford."

Chapter Thirty-Two

A rifle muzzle smashed away window glass and then poked out threateningly between two curtains. Unseen on the inside of the house, Earl Drake called out, "That's far enough, Marshal. Hold it right there!"

Gus Teaford halted and eased his creaky legs into a slight crouch next to the corral railings he'd been working his way up alongside. His posse, trailing behind him, also stopped. They were on foot now, spaced out at about five-foot intervals. Lone was next in line behind the marshal, Ben after him. Johnny and Erby were on the other side of the railings, inside the corral. As a group they were about fifty yards out from the main house.

"If you're supposed to be sneaking up, you're doing a piss-poor job of it," Drake observed tauntingly.

"Ain't tryin' to sneak," Gus told him. "Not much doubt you been eyeballin' us the whole while. More like we're easin' closer and keepin' tight to the corral in case you and your pet mongrels decide to open fire."

"And why shouldn't we? I don't see none of you bringing fresh-baked pies to welcome us to the neighborhood. All I see is each of you heeled with unfriendly-looking hardware."

352

"And I suppose you ain't packin' the same in there?"

"You damn betcha we are." Drake laughed nastily. "And can you guess where my 'mongrels' are pointing a whole bunch of it right this minute while you and me are having this friendly chat?"

"If you hurt the Crawfords," Gus growled, "you got to know you'll have a whole valleyful of people bent on hunting your sorry asses to the ends of the earth."

That got another snotty laugh out of Drake. "An army of Promise Valley inbreds out to get me . . . stop, I can't hardly stand such a terrible thought."

"Alright, knock off the cute shit! You obviously got in mind to offer a trade, try and make some kind of deal. Let's hear what you're after," Gus demanded.

Drake's tone changed, grew harsh and bitter. "You damn right. I'm after plenty. And don't even think about stalling and trying to buy time. I won't be tricked! You'll give us what we want and do it post haste, or these precious old relics we have in here with us will start dying—*in pieces*—faster and far more painfully than they already are."

"Goddammit, just say what you want. Get to it!"

"Okay, it's real simple. Listen and get it straight the first time. To start with, we want a team of strong horses and a buckboard loaded with supplies. Plenty of food, cartridges, blankets and warm clothes, a tent, and two or three extra tarps. Also three fresh saddle horses. And, last but not least, fifty thousand dollars in paper money. For that," Drake concluded, "you get Ezra Crawford dropped off safely and all in one piece after he travels with us for forty-eight hours, during which we'd better not see even a hint of anybody on our tail. Oh, and we want the buckboard, supplies, horses, and money by sundown."

"That's impossible!" Gus exploded. "Ain't nobody can pull all that stuff together so quick."

"Tsk, tsk. I'm real sorry to hear you say that . . . but not as sorry as Ezra and Irene are gonna be when we start taking out our disappointment and frustration on them."

"You're a sadistic, evil bastard!" blurted Ben.

Drake gave a kind of cackling laugh. "My, my. Listen to those great big words coming out of the dummy! Somebody better reach back and grab hold of some simpler ones like 'hurry the hell up' if any of you really care about these old goats."

"Okay, okay. Give us a minute to make some plans," Gus said. "But first I want to make sure we're startin' out square. Bring Ezra to that window. I want a good look at him and I want to hear him tell me him and Irene are all right so far."

"You're wasting time you can't afford to lose."

354

"Then get him to the window and be quick about it."

The rifle muzzle disappeared and there was some muffled cursing from the other side of the curtain. Half a minute later, the curtain jerked open and the head and shoulders of an elderly man with thick, iron gray hair was shoved out through the busted-away glass. "Talk to 'em, goddammit," growled a voice behind him.

The man, Ezra Crawford, lifted a deeply lined but still handsome face and showed a set of strong-looking teeth, baring them in a snarl. "Don't you make no deals with this scum, Gus! You hear me? Let 'em do their worst then hunt 'em down and blow out their liver and lights. Send 'em to Hell!"

He was jerked back out of sight before he could say more.

Unfortunately, that didn't mean Drake was done spouting off. "I hope you enjoyed the show, 'cause that's all you're gonna get. Now you'd better set to meeting our demands else I guarantee the next time you see that old man he will *not* be so full of piss and vinegar."

A weathered, sun-bleached old toolshed stood just outside one corner of the corral. Gus motioned the others to follow him in behind it, telling Drake, "We need to pow-wow and I'm damned if we'll do it with that rifle pointed at us the whole while."

"You go ahead and pow-wow. But no tricks. You'd better talk fast and start *doing* even faster," Drake called back.

As soon as the others were gathered in close around him, Gus locked his eyes on Ben. "This is puttin' a big weight on you, boy, but you're gonna have to hightail it back to Promise City and be my voice. You can ride way faster and harder than these old bones of mine can, and ain't no chance the town-folk will listen to anybody but one of us. If that. But you gotta try, for the sake of Ezra and Irene. Do everything you can to get that bundle put together—the buckboard, the supplies, the money—and churn dust to make it back here in time."

His expression tormented, Ben replied, "You know the last thing I want to do is go off and leave you here."

"I know."

"But I've always tried my best to do what you asked."

"I know that too. That's why I'm countin' on you. The rest of us will stay here and buy as much time as we can, do everything else we can if anything comes to mind."

"Okay. I'll burn up the trail between here and there," Ben promised.

"One more thing," Gus said. "Whatever else you do, whatever success you have or don't have gatherin' that stuff—before you leave town, throw that slimeball Niles Lavin in a jail cell and leave him to squeal and squirm until one of us gets back."

Gus then twisted around and leaned out, calling to the house, "Okay, my deputy is headin' out to fetch what you want, as quick as he can. The rest of us will wait here."

"You damn betcha you will. And I mean *right* there. I don't want to see none of your ugly mugs poking out no more and, if you know what's good for you, none of you had better try sneaking about or you'll catch a bullet. Now," Drake ordered, "tell that dummy of a deputy to get cracking! And all I want to see coming back is him on that buckboard. Remember, we can see a long way in every direction and if we spot any formation of riders forming anywhere on the horizon, all bets are off. Dummy there might be able to drum up enough of an army to flush us and cut us down, but before we check out we'll fire this whole musty pile of sticks and leave the Crawfords to burn alive!"

With those maniacal words ringing in his ears, Ben ran back to where they'd left their horses and could soon be heard galloping away.

Gus leaned back against the side of the shed and heaved a weary, ragged sigh. "Jesus God, what an awful mess . . . almost impossible to believe something like this could be happenin' in quiet, peaceful Promise Valley."

"Ruthless Valley," Lone countered.

"Eh? What's that?"

Lone shook his head. "Nothing. Never mind. Just a remark I heard."

Gus frowned. "Can't say I care for it much. Though, the way things stand right now, I guess it's kinda hard to argue against."

"Marshal . . ."

Gus looked around at the soft, raspy whisper. "What?" His gaze searched the faces of Johnny and Erby but got only blank stares in return.

The whisper came again. *"Marshal . . ."*

Everybody looked at each other until, suddenly, Johnny pointed and exclaimed in his own hushed whisper, "Holy shit! Look there."

What he was pointing at was an animal watering trough located just inside the corral at an angle about eight feet out from the back of the toolshed. On the muddy ground beside and partly behind the trough lay the body of a man, unnoticed by the posse members until now. He'd been shot and lay very still, but was alive, barely, and it was from him the whisper had come.

Gus leaned forward in a jerky motion. "Hec? Hec Haney . . . is that you?"

Unmoving, the side of his face pressed into the mud, Haney whispered again. "Don't come no closer. Don't make a fuss . . . they can see me . . . they'll put another bullet in me if they know I'm still alive."

358

The four men huddled behind the shed stared at him with agonized expressions.

He whispered some more. "I'm a goner anyway . . . Mud's got my wound plugged some, holdin' in my guts. But I'm still bleedin'."

"Don't try to talk," Gus urged him.

"No. Got to tell you while I can . . . inside the shed . . . an Injun tunnel . . . I was tryin' to make it when they nailed me . . . comes out in the old pantry . . . somebody needs to use it . . . try to get in and help Ezra . . . and I-Ireee . . ." His voice trailed off. Forever. He didn't have any more whispers left in him. Nor any more life.

Chapter Thirty-Three

"What's an Injun tunnel?" asked Johnny.

"Basically an escape route," Lone explained. "Back when the old pioneers and homesteaders first started settlin' in untamed areas, before all the Army posts were established and Indian raids on isolated ranch houses and farms weren't uncommon, folks had to build their homes with an eye for survivin' such attacks. Gun ports in the walls, hideout basements and the like. Some built long underground tunnels that gave family members the means to get out unseen and pop up somewhere a safe distance away. In fact, the sod house that's my home back on my Nebraska horse ranch—built by me, bein' a former scout and Indian fighter, and the old mountain man who was my partner for a while—has such a feature to it. I never had to use it on account of Indians, but it saved my bacon once against some hardcase hombres who showed up thinkin' they had me cornered."

"When Ezra first settled here, this valley was still untamed and seein' its share of Indian trouble. Would've made sense to put in such a tunnel back then," said Gus. "And Hec Haney started workin' for Ezra way back in those early

360

days. He might've been one of the few hands still ridin' for the C-Slash brand now who had any clue about the tunnel even existin'."

"And lived long enough to tell us," Lone added.

"So if it leads *out,* then that means it must lead back *in,*" said Johnny.

"That'd be the general idea," allowed Lone.

"But you think it's still clear after all this time? I mean, not all caved in and such?"

"My take on Ezra Crawford, without ever meetin' the man, is that if he went to the trouble of buildin' something, he'd go to the trouble of makin' it last."

"Yeah, that's Ezra right enough," Gus conceded.

Lone reached out and wrapped his fist around the handle of the toolshed door. "Reckon there's only one way to find out for sure."

"You thinking what I think you're thinking?" said Johnny.

"Expect I am. You up for joinin' me?"

"Now wait a minute," protested Gus. "If anybody sticks their neck out to give that idea a try, it oughta be—"

"It *can't* be you," Lone interrupted him. "You got to stay out here and be available in case Drake decides he wants to palaver some more. You wasn't here to answer him, he'd get suspicious as hell and do who knows what."

"But in case you didn't notice, your leg has

opened up and is bleedin' fresh. It's leakin' through your pants."

"I got plenty of blood," Lone countered. "If I feel myself runnin' low, I'll stop, wring out my pantleg, and drink some to top myself off again." He pulled open the door, paused to look over his shoulder at Johnny. "You decide whether or not you're comin' along?"

"Only if you let me go first. I don't favor crawling through the bloody mud you might leave in your wake."

The tunnel was dusty and musty and black as a carpetbagger's heart. But at the same time, it ran straight and level and, except for a couple minor pinch points, was wide enough for even Lone's broad shoulders. It no doubt helped (though Lone would be reluctant to admit it out loud) that the leaner Johnny went first, scouring out the passage some in advance. Lone also would never admit that his leg was burning like hell; that was for him to know.

Accessing the tunnel inside the toolshed had been a relatively easy matter of moving aside a keg of nails and some picks and shovels in order to lift the trapdoor, an assembly of 1 x 12 boards fastened with cross laths. Before going in, Lone and Johnny shed their hats and gun belts. They put extra cartridges in their pockets and stuffed their guns—handkerchief-wrapped to help protect them from dust and dirt—inside their shirts.

Once underway, the complete blackness that enveloped them blurred any sense of time or distance covered. They only knew that continuing to crawl forward meant progress.

Finally, Johnny halted his crawling and whispered back to Lone, "I see some little slivers of light up ahead. Like cracks between floorboards."

"Thank Christ. How much farther?"

"Only about half a dozen feet."

"Ease on up. Then hold and listen hard. See if you can make out anything."

Johnny did as instructed. After a few minutes he reported, "Yeah, I can hear talking. Real muffled. They ain't whispering so it must be two or three rooms away."

"Okay. Then it ought to be safe for us to wiggle out of this wormhole."

"It widens out up here where the tunnel ends. Those floorboard cracks are right above my head," said Johnny. "I think you can probably squeeze up beside me."

Lone moved up. The two of them rolled onto their backs and together pushed the palms of their hands up against the floorboards—or, they hoped, the bottom of a trapdoor such had been on the floor of the toolshed. There was some give when they pushed, a good sign.

When Hec Haney told them about the tunnel before he died, he'd said it *"Comes out in the old pantry.* " Lone reasoned this meant the original food storage space for the original kitchen. Since the house had been expanded and revised over the years, it seemed logical to further reason there likely was a newer, larger kitchen and the original pantry was probably (hopefully) a lesser used and more out of the way space.

He and Johnny held still again for a couple minutes, listening to the muffled, remote drone of voices from somewhere in the house.

Until Lone said, "We're gonna have to find out sooner or later."

"Yeah," Johnny agreed.

They took their guns out of their shirts, unwrapped them, laid them on their chests for quick access. Then they pushed again on the bottom of the trapdoor, this time with full determination to lift it. Up it went. There was a faint scraping sound of something sliding away off the top of it. Then it was all the way open—another assembly of 1 x 12s fastened with laths—and shoved to stand on one edge off to the side of the opening.

Lone and Johnny sat up, gripping their Colts. Their faces were covered with a film of dirt-caked sweat and both inhaled deeply of cleaner, fresher air.

The narrow, rectangular room they found themselves in was now a storage space. The old food shelves still lined the walls but now they held spare blankets and linens, a variety of no longer used plates, pots, and pans. There were also some containers of soap and other cleaning solutions and the item that had skidded off the lifting trapdoor was a large mop bucket with a handful of mops and brooms stuffed in it. A thin curtain was hung over the doorway of the windowless room, allowing in subdued light.

Lone and Johnny climbed the rest of the way out and rose quietly to their feet. They could hear the voices more clearly now, still muted though perhaps closer than first thought. After peeking cautiously through the curtain to make sure the next room was clear, they emerged out into it.

This had once been a kitchen. The old cookstove was still in one corner, its flat, cold surface now draped with a colorful tablecloth and set with a vase of flowers. The center of the room was open, covered by an oval carpet. Against one wall, in front of a tall window with a lacy white curtain, was a spinet harpsichord turned so that the light from the window shone down on the keyboard. Farther down the wall, situated diagonally at the corner, was a well-padded easy chair with a reading stand and lamp beside it. Lone could envision quiet evenings or maybe Sunday afternoons when a younger, more vibrant Mrs. Crawford sat playing the spinet while her husband sat nearby, listening and reading.

The exit from the room was a wide doorway

covered by a set of sliding double doors, rather ornately designed and highly polished. They were standing slightly ajar. Moving quietly to these, Lone and Johnny realized that the voices they could hear were coming from the next room.

Taking turns looking through the gap, they saw a large, well-appointed parlor. There was a stone fireplace on one wall, more tall, curtained windows on the opposite side of the room. Two couches, coffee tables, and upholstered easy chairs were carefully arranged in between. In the middle of all this, rather incongruously, two wooden chairs had been placed back-to-back. Ezra and Irene Crawford occupied these, also positioned rigidly back-to-back and bound in place. Lyle Basteen was slouched on one of the couches, his brother stood looking out the window. Drake was pacing restlessly back and forth.

Lone and Johnny backed away and returned to the opposite end of the old kitchen where they leaned their heads close together and began speaking in low whispers.

"That's damned hard to look at and not do something," said Johnny.

"Don't worry, we *are* gonna do something," Lone assured him. "We just need to keep cool heads and play it smart. We can't hardly go chargin' in and start blastin' away, not with those

366

two old folks plunked right there in the middle of everything."

"You got any ideas?"

"I'm thinkin', I'm thinkin' . . ." Lone's eyes raked the room. They moved past the spinet, then shifted back to it and lingered there for several beats. Until he asked Johnny: "How are you at playin' the piano?"

"Huh?"

Chapter Thirty-Four

When the realization hit him that he was pacing just like Niles Lavin had a habit of doing, Drake abruptly stopped. The last thing he wanted was to emulate that chickenshit weasel in any way. Damn him. Damn him and his blowhard *"We'll rule the whole valley!"* scheme. Yeah, *We.* Where was Lavin now when the bullets were flying and it was down dirty and dangerous time? Sitting on his fat ass shuffling and forging papers, that's where. Just like always. While Drake was the one out on the hard edge and down in the trenches. *Plus* coming up with the clever ideas and doing the arm twisting that, time and again, had kept their asses out of a sling.

Well that was over now. The lid was blown off, thanks to that double-crossing little bitch Rosemary and those meddling sons of bitches from South Dakota. He should have settled for getting a couple bedroom romps out of her—which were never that special anyway, not until he taught her a few tricks—then dumped her ass back in the Missouri and left her there. But her time would come, just like it always did for duplicitous little tramps like her. And for lazy connivers like Lavin, too, now that he didn't have Drake running interference and doing his dirty work for him.

Right now one of the things Drake was regretting most was not making Lavin part of what he'd demanded be brought to him from town. How sweet would that have been—to see the look on the simpering fool's face when he first thought he was being saved from the shit storm descending on him only to find himself stripped down and carved up and left for the buzzards and other scavengers to finish off out somewhere in the wild?

"That poker you got stuck in the fireplace is plumb cherry red, Drake," Lyle drawled from his couch. "You want to go ahead and use it on that old buzzard to try and get him to talk?"

Speaking of buzzards . . .

"Yeah, bring it over here," Drake said. He went to stand directly in front of Ezra Crawford and held out his hand for Lyle to place the poker in. Waving the smoldering, red-tipped rod under Ezra's nose, he asked, "How about it, you stubborn wretch? You held up pretty good to some slapping around. Are you really going to force me to use this?"

Ezra glared at him. "Yeah . . . how about you use it to shove straight up your ass?"

Drake used the unheated shaft of the rod and cracked it down across the old man's forehead. There was the sound of bone-crunching impact and a trickle of blood ran down into one eye. Try as he might, Ezra couldn't hold back a groan of pain.

"God *damn* you, you stubborn old fool!" Drake exclaimed. "I know your type. I know your kind don't trust banks all the way so you're bound to have a stash of holdout money somewhere here on your property. What good is it gonna do you if you're beaten to death."

"You ain't gonna beat me to death." Ezra chuckled harshly. "You need me alive for your trade . . . remember?"

Drake leaned his face down close. "The joke just might be on you . . . your wife will work for the trade just as good. How about that?"

"Tell them nothing, Ezra," spoke Irene, firmly but in a very weak voice.

Frank Basteen turned away from the window for a minute and said to his brother and to Drake, "How long is it gonna take you two geniuses to wise up? The old bastard ain't gonna talk from his own pain. But how long you figure he'll hold out if you start toasting the missus?"

"You swine!" spat Ezra.

Frank laughed. "That give you a clue as to the answer?"

Before Drake could respond, the soft tinkle of piano keys drifted into the room.

Everybody looked around. The Basteens appeared puzzled, Drake wore a fierce scowl.

"What the hell was that?"

Lyle said, "It sounded like . . . a piano?"

"How the hell can it be a piano?"

"There's one in the other room. I saw it when we was checking through the house."

"I don't give a shit if there's ten pianos in there," growled Drake. "Who'd be playing it?"

"How am I supposed to know!"

Drake threw down the poker and left it smoldering on the carpet. Drawing the gun from his shoulder holster, he marched toward where Frank still stood at the window. "Is that stinking marshal out there where he's supposed to be?"

"Behind the shed, just like you told him," said Frank. "Nobody's come out."

Lyle drew his Colt and started for the double doors. "Let me go look in here again." He shoved back one of the doors and went through. His gaze cut immediately to the spinet, never looking the other way at all to where Lone was pressed tight to the wall near the old cookstove.

Lyle quickly saw how one of the shutters on the window behind the piano was standing open and the curtains were streaming in and fluttering across the keyboard. "Well, hell," he declared. "The window blew open is all, and the curtains are slapping in and ticklin' the ivories."

"Then close the goddamn thing and get back in here," growled Drake.

"Unless you want to stop and play us a tune," laughed brother Frank.

Lyle started across the oval carpet to the spinet.

From that moment a sequence of events took place very rapidly.

First, Johnny popped up behind the spinet with a wolf's smile on his face and a Colt in his fist aimed level at Lyle. "Hi. Here for a piano lesson?"

While Lyle was freezing in reaction to that, Lone was in motion behind him, gliding along the wall and out through the open door with his own Colt thrust forward, cocked and ready. His narrowed eyes locked on Drake and Frank standing close together in front of the tall window. "Do anything but grab your ears," he grated, "I blow a hole in you."

For a fraction of a second it might have ended right there.

But Drake wouldn't allow it. He was too enraged, too hell bent on salvaging something out of the dream—Lavin's dream at the start, yes, but one that *he* had propelled along with *his* grit and sweat—to let it go now. Bellowing "No!" he twisted in a desperate half turn, knocking Frank Basteen out of his way, and threw himself headlong out the window.

Lone fired instantly. But the sweep of Drake's arm to shove away Frank doubled the older Basteen brother forward and caused him to lurch directly into the path of Lone's bullet. As Drake crashed through glass and ripping curtains, Frank was spun and jerked upright, driven back by the impact of the slug. With amazing fortitude and speed, he jerked the gun free from the holster on his hip and started to raise it. Lone fired again and sent a second bullet slamming into the center of Frank's chest, punching him back even harder than before and spilling him half out, half in the gaping, jagged-edged window opening. Lone raced forward, springing to plant one foot on Frank's chest and then launching himself on through to the outside.

In the old kitchen, Lyle, hearing the shots and smashing window glass from the next room, abandoned his temporary frozen pose and decided to try and make his own fight. With both men having their guns already drawn, they fired almost simultaneously. Johnny's trigger pull was a clock tick faster and considerably more accurate. His bullet tore into Lyle's throat half way between chin and Adam's apple, blowing a spray of gore and gristle out the back of his neck and immediately dropping the younger Basteen brother straight down into a lifeless bundle. Lyle's shot did not go entirely amiss however, ripping through Johnny's left side, tearing meat and muscle and shattering a rib. Johnny fell to his knees, cursing, then immediately grabbed at the piano—striking discordant notes off the keyboard—fighting to stand back up so he could go try to help Lone.

Outside, Lone was in a foot race to prevent Drake's escape. His burning leg wasn't doing him any favors but his determination offset it and proved equal to his quarry's desperation. Drake was trying for one of the horses he and the Basteens had left hitched out front of the house. He made it as far as grabbing the saddle horn of the nearest one and hoisting a foot into the stirrup when Lone caught up to him.

Lone grabbed a handful of shirt collar with his left hand and yanked Drake back toward him while at the same time swinging the Colt in his right fist clublike at the back of the man's head. Drake fell away with unexpected ease, pitching back hard against Lone and taking both of them to the ground. Lone landed on the bottom, getting a good deal of air driven out of him. He lost his grip on the shirt collar and as Drake rolled away, flailing, the .44 was jarred from Lone's grip.

Drake scrambled frantically to rise up but his feet were tangled with Lone's and, when he tripped and fell back, Lone was waiting with a now empty right fist that shot straight up and crashed against Drake's jaw. Drake was sent rolling across the grass.

Lone lunged after him. When Drake tried to get up again, Lone hit him again. A roundhouse right followed quickly by a left hook. Drake was knocked back into a loose, flopping backward somersault. This time when his face lifted,

Lone peppered it with two short, rapid left jabs.

Drake fell back and rolled over a couple times. When he stopped rolling and shoved up, his roguishly handsome face now battered and bloody, he came to rest on his right knee and left leg raised, the foot planted flat. His hand flashed down and across and, from the low-cut boot on his raised foot, he pulled a punch dagger—four inches of gleaming, needle sharp steel made for lightning quick in-and-out thrusts into a jugular or intestine.

Lone, leaning in to deliver another blow, held himself in check and could only glare, breathing heavily.

Drake smiled through bloody teeth. "Come on, big boy," he taunted. "Step in a little closer—I'll puncture that tree trunk throat of yours a half dozen times before you can blink."

Lone paused only a moment before reaching around to the small of his back and unsheathing the ten-inch Bowie knife he'd tucked in behind his belt there. When he and Johnny had shed their gun belts before going into the tunnel, Lone had made the decision to still hang on to the Bowie. He hadn't done so thinking he might need it for fighting, but rather in case he might have to do some digging and gouging should they encounter a narrow, partially collapsed spot in the passage. At the moment, motives didn't really matter; what counted was that he had it when needed.

Drake's eyes widened at the sight of the superior weapon.

Now it was Lone's turn to smile. "Figures," he sneered, "a tiny peckered little shit like you would bring a needle to a knife fight."

Once again, Drake's rage propelled him beyond sense or restraint. With a guttural sound coming out of his throat, he uncoiled from his crouch and hurled himself at Lone, thrusting ahead with the punch dagger. Lone blocked the thrusting arm with an upward sweep of his left forearm, knocking the dagger up and away. Twisting his torso inward as part of the same motion, he brought the Bowie around and in, burying it to the hilt just left and down from the tip of Drake's breastbone, splitting his black heart wide open.

Epilogue

An hour and a half after Lone violently dispatched Earl Drake, Irene Crawford died peacefully in her own bed inside the house. Her husband sat at her bedside, head bowed, fighting to hold back tears. On the other side of the bed, Rosemary stood holding one of Irene's hands. Irene passed without having ever been told the truth about Rosemary not being her daughter-in-law, the widow of her son Theron.

The events of the day had nevertheless taken their toll on the frail lady, and she'd at last succumbed to the illnesses she'd been fighting so bravely beyond expectations. As soon as they untied her from the chair she'd been bound to, she went into a swoon. Because James and Sue had been closer than a doctor from Promise City, they'd been hastened from the lake to the ranch. But all they could really do was make Irene comfortable in her final minutes.

Ezra had been given a rough breakdown, by Gus (who still had a lot to learn himself), of the details behind Drake and the Basteens making their bloody appearance at his ranch and all that subsequently transpired. Though somewhat numbed by what he was told, especially coming on top of his wife's passing and the news of how

Hec Haney and some of his other wranglers had been cut down, Ezra still went out of his way to sincerely thank everyone who'd kept it from being worse, especially Lone and Johnny for their efforts. Looking on and listening, Lone knew it was going to take weeks and months before all the legal shenanigans and preliminary inroads Lavin had set in motion would be sorted out. But Lone also knew that if anybody could hold up seeing it all through, the tough old rancher could.

Something else Lone perceived as he stood off to the side watching things unfold ahead of Ben's return from town, was how Rosemary and James seemed genuinely attached to one another. Maybe Sue was wrong about the girl. Maybe, as James clearly believed and was willing to accept, Rosemary had gotten her wild streak purged out and was ready to settle down and make a good wife.

Even more intriguing, by way of observations being made by the former scout in the midst of this ongoing aftermath, was the near fawning attention Sue was paying to Johnny and his wound. With a feeling bordering on jealousy (an emotion Lone thought totally foreign to him), it seemed like she was making a much bigger fuss over that than she had his thigh wound. Could it be, after the years of Johnny getting nothing but the cold shoulder, all that was needed to gain Sue's affection had been a quirky thing like getting shot while helping to chase down her brother?

Strange things sometimes have a way of happening.

But was it so strange . . . or was it all part of the promise to be found in Promise Valley?

About the Author

Wayne D. Dundee is an American author of popular genre fiction. His writing has primarily been detective mysteries—such as the Joe Hannibal PI series—and Western adventures. To date, he has written several dozen novels and forty-plus short stories, .ranging from horror, fantasy, erotica, and several "house name" books under bylines other than his own.

Dundee was born March 24, 1948, in Freeport, Illinois. He graduated from high school in Clinton, Wisconsin, in 1966. Later that same year, he married Pamela Daum and they had one daughter, Michelle. For the first fifty years of his life, Dundee worked his way up from factory laborer to various managerial positions. In his spare time, he was always writing. He sold his first short story in 1982.

In 1998, Dundee relocated to Ogallala, Nebraska, where he assumed the general manager position for a small Arnold facility there. The setting and rich history of the area inspired him to turn his efforts more toward the Western genre. In 2009, following the passing of his wife one year prior, he retired from Arnold and began to concentrate on his writing full time.

The founder and original editor of *Hardboiled*

Magazine, Dundee's work in the mystery field has been nominated for an Edgar, an Anthony, and six Shamus Awards from the Private Eye Writers of America.

Center Point Large Print
600 Brooks Road / PO Box 1
Thorndike, ME 04986-0001 USA

(207) 568-3717

US & Canada:
1 800 929-9108
www.centerpointlargeprint.com